Staged River
The Bluefield Beach Series
Heather Grey

Staged River is a work of fiction. Names, characters, places, and incidents are the product of the author's imagination or are used factiously. Any resemblance to actual events, locales, or persons, living or dead, is entirely coincidental.

ISBN: 978-1-0688737-1-3

Ebook ISBN: 978-1-0688737-2-0

Cover Design by KBG Designs

Edited by Tayler Bailey McLendon at Bailey & Bloom Ink.

Contents

To those of you with all the plans that never quite work out,
deep breath
Simon Cadwell is just waiting to call you his good girl.

Author's Note

Staged River contains mature content and is suited for those 18 and older. A list of content warnings can be found on my website, or at the back of this novel.
Bluefield is an imaginary town in Canada; the spelling in this book reflects Canadian English.

Chapter 1

Aspen

LILLIAN:

> Happy New Year! I'm so sad we couldn't celebrate together. Call me when you get home! Love you!!

ASPEN:

> Too hungover for that many exclamation marks

January is for new beginnings and fresh starts.

It's also for waking up hungover and bumbling your way home after drinking too much tequila and making poor decisions. At least that's how mine started. It's not that uncommon for most people. But I'm not like most people—I have a plan for this year. I have rules for this year.

I'm going to make this year my bitch.

So why can't I pick up the phone already?

1

It's not like accepting Jackson's offer to work at Mane Construction doesn't meet all my rules. Well, most of my rules.

Rule #1: Get rid of anything you don't want to be in your life ten years from now.

I'm not talking about material items. This isn't about me decluttering my apartment or throwing out my old clothing, although that is something I should probably do. I'm talking about people, places, and situations.

And the first one I'm getting rid of is my job.

Industrial Design Co. was the end-all, be-all for most of my life. It was *the* place to work if I wanted to be successful in Toronto. But you know what? I hate everything about it.

I'm overworked, overmanaged, overstimulated, and just plain over it.

I've worked there for a decade at this point, between interning during university and working full time since I graduated. I'm turning twenty-eight this year. Enough is enough. The red flags have been red-flagging for too long and I just can't anymore.

I can't.

If there was even one redeeming quality about that place, maybe I could make it work, but there isn't.

My clients are boring.

I'm sorry to say it, but having a white and beige home isn't a personality trait. When your five-year-old spills grape juice on your beige shag rug, do not come running to me. I warned you. I gave you so many options. And yet, you chose beige.

My boss is the worst.

You'd think I have never stepped foot in a design lab based on the amount of control Sharon holds over me. Every step I take, she's there—checking my work and having me make changes, only to then suggest I change them again until the design plan looks exactly how I had it initially. Somehow, she managed to tell me I was too independent and that I also needed to work on being more autonomous in the same sentence during my last performance review. You can't have it both ways, Sharon.

My colleagues suck.

Most of them are old enough to have birthed me, which wouldn't be a problem if they didn't treat me like a child throwing a fit every time I voiced my opinion. The ones that are my age act like we are competing against each other to the death to get assigned to the good jobs. Reality check: there are no good jobs.

So, I need to get out of there. And I'm going to.

I can't not have a job. I have some savings, but I've been paying off student loans for a while now and I'm uncomfortable not having a steady income. The truth is, I've been waiting for a safety net to catch me. And that safety net has appeared in the form of Jackson Mane, my best friend Lillian Shaw's swoony boyfriend.

Jackson works for his father's construction company, Mane Construction, as a project manager and architect. He had a falling out with the design firm they normally use and offered me a job as lead designer on his new project. At first, I was worried he was just offering it to me to be nice, but then I remembered who I am—a very talented interior designer with a portfolio to prove it. Mane Construction is lucky to have me.

Jackson and Lillian met last summer in Bluefield and have

been happily in love ever since. I could not be happier for my friend. Lillian is the sweetest and most kind-hearted person you will ever meet, and I can't believe she's put up with my bullshit for so long. Speaking of bullshit...

Rule # 2: No men and their bullshit

I'm what some would call a serial monogamist. Not intentionally, but my dating history shows a pattern. I've been dating the same guys in a rotation for years, and it's not healthy.

I met Liam at a dorm party at university, and we hit it off until I caught him cheating on me at a party six months in. Then there was the history major from my study group, Jason. We did a lot of studying together for about a year. Next was Lorenzo. The second I got my own place after university, he tried to move in with me and I said goodbye, only to say hello again a couple of months later. I also dated Jason again after running into him at the theatre one weekend. After we broke up for the third time, I met John, my most recent ex. He worked in finance and was kind of boring. His last name is Dudley, which should have been the red flag, but I dated him for a couple of months until he got transferred to Vancouver. Somehow, I managed to reconnect with Liam in that period, and got cheated on. Again. Lorenzo was back for a bit, and then I tried long-distance with John. When he transferred back to Toronto, we broke up. Again. Lorenzo came back, then Jason again, until I ultimately got back together with John again last year.

A part of me thought we would figure it out this time, but we didn't. After a lot of reflection, I can confidently say I was dating duds. And I think I was doing it on purpose. I haven't figured out why I was on a self-sabotage streak, but I knew none of the men were keepers, and yet I couldn't stop getting back together with them. They were all a little bit boring, passive, and douchey. I'm ashamed that is the only way to describe "my type."

But not anymore.

Rule number two will stop me from wasting my time and energy on men who are not on my level. I am not a charity centre, and I am not dating down anymore. Really, we are not dating at all. At least until I figure my shit out. Easy enough.

That is why what I did on New Year's Eve cannot and *will not* happen again. I may have had a tiny slip from the rules right at midnight, but that's fine. I'm on the East Coast, and it was still the night before in British Columbia, so it doesn't count.

Rule #3: Get a hobby

This one is very important for my sanity. I didn't know I needed hobbies until Lillian moved to Bluefield and suddenly, I had all this free time. I work and I exercise, but that's basically it. I need things that spark joy and keep my brain flowing. Even if I do plan to head to Bluefield, where I have Lillian and our other friends, I still need to fill the void. With the removal of men from my social life, I've gotten bored. And boredom leads to dumb decisions.

Rule #4: No breaking the rules

This should go without saying, but I think writing it down as a reminder might be beneficial. The only rule I'm worried about breaking is number two. I have needs and battery-powered "friends" aren't always the solution. For the time being, though, they will have to do it. That and my imagination; certainly not the blurred memories from the early hours of January

1st.

Rule #5: Don't get kidnapped

Weird rule. Shouldn't be necessary, but given what I've just heard through the grapevine, I'm going to add it, just in case. A girl around my age from Bluefield is missing. She went out on New Year's Eve and never went home. There are lots of theories floating around as to where she is, but most people assume she met a guy and is getting to know him. I don't know her personally, so I don't think I can form an opinion at this time. All I know is accepting this job offer puts me not only in Bluefield—with all its gossipy locals and kooky characters—but in a city with an open missing persons case. Maybe not the smartest move, but the move I'm going to make. *I think. No, I know.* I'm taking the job. Dramatics aside, it's time to bet on myself and make my dreams a reality.

So, I only have five rules right now, but I'm not opposed to adding to the list as the year goes on. This is all about growth, so I'm choosing to stay fluid with it.

To get the ball rolling, I have to let Jackson know I accept his offer. He is rarely more than ten feet away from Lillian at any given time, so I figure video calling her is an easy way to get to him.

It rings a couple of times before my beautiful best friend's face fills the screen. Lillian always tells me how jealous she is of my straight brown hair, but I think the grass must be greener because I would die for her hair. Lillian has naturally bright blonde, wild curly hair. It's beyond thick and what she describes as unmanageable, I would call luscious. Right now, those curls are on the top of her head, being held by a scrunchie that looks like it's hanging on for dear life. Her blue eyes light up when she sees me. Since we couldn't get together on New Year's Eve due to a snowstorm, I haven't seen her since Christmas.

Of course, we still text every day, but we were inseparable from age five to twenty-two, if not longer, so I miss her no matter how often I see her.

"Asp!" she greets me. "I miss you." I'm glad she feels the same way I do. If you aren't a little bit obsessed with your best friend, I can't relate.

"I miss you too, Billy."

She rolls her eyes at the use of her nickname, but I know she secretly loves it. She doesn't suit Lilly, and as a child, I wasn't the most creative, so I decided to combine the words beautiful and Lilly and I got Billy. She thinks it's silly. I think it's perfect.

"Is John still sending you flowers?" Lillian asks. I look over my shoulder at the god-awful bouquet on my kitchen island. I love flowers, and I can't bear to throw them out until they are wilted and shedding, but the arrangement is so bad. I didn't know they dyed daisies neon green, but there's proof sitting right behind me.

"Yes, unfortunately."

"You need to tell him to stop, or call the florist or something."

"I have his number blocked and it's staying that way." Rule number two insists on it. "Plus, there is never a florist's card attached. They just appear at my door every couple of weeks."

"He's so weird," she says. I have to agree. The guy could barely put in the effort while we were actually together, but then the second we broke up, the flower deliveries started. I texted him the first time to verify they were from him. His response was, "Would buying you flowers give me a second chance?" I immediately blocked him and moved on. It appears he hasn't.

Lillian and I catch up for a couple of minutes before I see Jackson's arm wrap around her shoulder as he joins her on the couch.

"What kind of trouble are you two planning?" he asks as he greets me.

"Wouldn't you like to know, Jackson Mane?" He shakes his head at my response. I don't want to delay the point of my call any further because, frankly, I am excited about working for him. "I'll take the job," I blurt out while Lillian is mid-sentence, talking about the mouthwatering meal she made yesterday.

Neither of them looks shocked by my outburst, or my answer to his job offer. I don't know if that is because it was an obvious decision, or because my personality tends to err on the side of dramatics.

"Wooo!" Lillian cheers, shimmying her shoulder as much as she can from under Jackson's arm.

"I am so glad—and relieved—to hear that, Asp," Jackson says.

"And you'll stay with us?" Lillian asks, or more like demands.

"I don't know. I don't want to be in your way," I say, though I would love to stay in their beautiful home that Jackson built and I helped Lillian decorate and furnish. It's right on Lake Huron with an entire wall of windows looking out on the water. Something I may never be able to afford for myself.

It's a literal dream home, though everything is a dream in Bluefield.

Lillian's family has owned a cottage on the shore of Lake

Huron for generations and because Lillian is my bestie, I would visit her there each summer. As we've gotten older, two-week vacations have turned into quick weekend trips, but I always prioritize getting to Bluefield a couple of times each summer. This will be my first time being there for an extended stay, and I feel like I'm ready to slow down and embrace the Bluefield way.

Bluefield, Ontario is a tourist town where most of the full-time residents are retirees, either hunkering down for the winter and counting down the days until spring, or they head to Florida to get away from the cold. From May to September, Bluefield's population quadruples. Vacationers flock from all the nearby cities to get a break and bask on the picturesque beaches that rival the Caribbean with their white sand and crystal blue water. Lake Huron is the fourth largest lake in the world, and from Bluefield, you can't see land on all three sides, giving it that ocean vacation feel.

This trip isn't a vacation though, it's a job relocation.

Staying with Lillian and Jackson might be a lot, especially while I'm also working with him. And I really don't want to be in their way. They are either still in the honeymoon phase of their relationship or are just very touchy people. Jackson requires maximum body contact with Lillian at all times. As he currently wraps one of Lillian's blonde locks around his finger and stares at her like she is his entire universe, my point is proven. If it wasn't so cute, it would be kind of gross.

"You won't be in our way," Lillian defends.

"Please stay with us, Aspen," Jackson adds. "You are saving my life by taking this job, so it's the least I can do." Considering the compensation package he offered me, it is, in fact, not the least he can do, but I appreciate the sentiment, nonetheless.

"What if you guys have other guests or visitors over the summer?" I don't use specific names, but they have to know I'm talking about Jackson's cousin, Simon. We do not get along, to say the least. I've never met someone who gets under my skin the way he does, so I try to steer clear of him when I can. Staying in the same house as him, even for a couple of nights, would be a setback to my rules.

Lillian and Jackson share a look that I can't quite read. Lillian shakes her head at Jackson and then looks to her lap, avoiding making eye contact with me.

Jackson clears his throat. "That won't be a problem. Everyone will have their own place to stay."

I have no idea what he means by that. Lillian's family cottage is just next door to their place, so I guess any overflow guests will be staying there. It isn't really up to me to determine that, but if my best friend is asking me to stay with her for the summer, it's not going to take much to convince me.

"Okay, fine," I drawl out, like this is an inconvenience. "I guess I could stay with you guys."

I tell myself the smiles on both of their faces are worth any uncomfortable situations I may find myself in this summer in Bluefield.

Chapter 2
Aspen

Who knew redesigning your life would be such hard work? And I don't mean like mentally and emotionally, although that has been tough. I mean physically. Something about swearing off men, switching jobs, and relocating to a beach town for the next couple of months is kicking my ass.

January was a blur.

February was more of the same.

Now it's already the third month of the year, and I need things to both slow down and hurry up.

I gave my notice at Industrial Design Co., and they had the audacity to insist I work a three-month notice period. Okay, that was actually part of my contract, and I knew I would have to, but it still wasn't fun. They asked me to wrap up as many projects as I could and pass anything I wouldn't be able to see to fruition to another designer. I am always a professional, so I did as I was told and got the job done with only a few more eye rolls than normal.

Thankfully, I only have one week left of working at the horror show. One week left of Brenda from accounting stealing my lunch out of the break room fridge. One week of Lionel giving me a dirty look every time I voice my opinion, even if I'm agreeing with him. One week of Sharon trying to break all the confidence I've built in myself, my talents, my career. One week and then I'm free.

I've given myself the month of April to get my ducks in order, pack, and settle in Bluefield. Jackson has asked that I be there before May 1st, so as long as we don't have any complications, I will be there mid-month, ready to hit the ground running. Figuratively running, of course. If you asked me to run even one hundred metres right now, I would probably throw up.

I'm not one of those people who take gym selfies or is constantly talking about hitting the gym and what pre-workout I use. No offence to those who do, it just isn't my style. But I am in good shape.

I typically take kickboxing classes a couple of times a week and then use yoga as a recovery. If I'm not active, my brain goes squirrelly. I'm in good shape, only because if I didn't exercise, I would be too stressed to function. And yet, I can't climb a flight of stairs, or even fold laundry without wanting to take a nap. I don't know if it's hormones or what, but I'm starting to be concerned.

I had a minor cold a couple of weeks ago. Typical winter sniffles, nothing out of the norm during the colder months, but I feel like I haven't completely recovered.

My late-night Google session a couple of weeks ago prompted the doctor's appointment I am currently waiting for. I don't want to be someone who self-diagnoses themselves, but I think I might have mono. The symptoms are there. During my cold, my lymph nodes were probably swollen, but I just thought it was my tonsils. I've been tired constantly and just feeling completely off. Everything has piled on top of each other, so I've been skipping workouts and eating like crap. I swear my jeans were a bit tighter than normal this morning.

The other option is it's a hormone issue. I haven't had regular periods since I went off birth control months ago, so I couldn't even tell you where in my cycle I should be right now.

A nurse comes from the back, and I anticipate she'll say my name when she calls on the small girl beside me instead. I settle back into my chair and lean into the space the girl left. The man next to me has been coughing continuously. I've tried to breathe into my jacket as much as possible, but I know his germs must have spread by now. I'm not sure what I want more—to be called next so I can get away from the white sterile walls and floors of the waiting room, or for the man next to me to be called so he can get the help he needs so I can pretend I'm breathing clean air.

The steady sound of a plastic chair squeaking draws my attention away from the man's coughing. It's a pretty annoying noise, and I look around to find the culprit, only to realize it's me. My leg is bouncing, causing the blue plastic chair to make an awful noise. I put my hand on my leg to stop the movement and hopefully stop me from starting up again.

Get it together, Aspen.

An older lady in a floral scrub top and pink pants comes through the waiting room doors. "Aspen Arthur," she calls. I bolt from my seat more aggressively than necessary, causing the nice nurse's eyes to widen as she gestures for me to follow her.

I guess I'm more nervous than I thought.

I'm not sure why. If it's mono, I'll deal with it. If it's hormones, I'll add more supplements to my pill routine. If it's something else entirely, I will figure it out. But I know it's something. That much I'm sure of.

It's something alright.

Holy Mother Mary, is it something.

New rules.

Rule #1: Breathe

Rule #2: Don't panic

I don't remember my drive home, which is concerning considering Toronto traffic is horrendous at all times of day. The second I get my apartment door unlocked, I beeline straight to the powder room off the kitchen. I almost don't get the toilet lid open in time before I empty the contents of my stomach into the bowl. Once I think I'm done for now, I lean against the wall behind me and take a deep breath. My doctor asked if I had been experiencing nausea or vomiting, and I told her only a small amount of nausea. That isn't true anymore. I try to stand up so I can at least rinse the horrid taste out of my mouth when another wave hits and I curl myself forward over the toilet again.

I'm not sure how long I sit on the cold tile floor before I hear Lillian shouting from my door as I flush the toilet again. God, I can't wait for this part to pass.

"Open up, Asp! You barely convinced me to go to this pilates class with you. If we don't leave in the next five minutes, I'm going to talk myself out of it!"

I know she isn't exaggerating. Lillian hates social settings and doesn't like to be sweaty in public. The only reason she agreed to go in the first place is she made a New Year's resolution to try one new experience a month and I have been personally ensuring she keeps to it.

I've been so focused on my appointment today that I completely forgot about our plans. Since Lillian lives in Bluefield more than Toronto now, I always make sure we get together when she is in the city, but there is no way I am going to that pilates class.

Lillian must have let herself into my apartment with the key I gave her when I moved in a couple of years ago. I hear footsteps wandering from the living room to the kitchen until she is outside the bathroom door.

"Asp? Are you in there?"

I can only muster up a groan in response as I let my cheek rest on the cold toilet seat. Normally I would be grossed out by my proximity to the porcelain, but it's my toilet that I know I cleaned yesterday, and the cold texture feels so good against my clammy skin.

"Asp?" she asks again. "Can I come in?"

She only takes a moment, not waiting for a real response, before she pushes the door open. We were roommates all through university, and we've both walked in on things we wish we didn't see, so there isn't a lot of privacy between us anymore.

"Are you okay?" she asks softly, taking a tentative step towards me. I flutter my eyes open for a moment before closing them again. Even basic body movements feel exhausting right now. "Aspen. Say something, please. You're scaring me."

I mumble, "Not okay," while keeping my eyes closed. If I look at her again, I know I'm going to cry, and I never cry.

"Not okay how? Not okay as in you ate something you shouldn't have? Or not okay as in you're dying?" She crouches down beside me and rubs my back. The gesture warms my heart and makes my stomach lurch simultaneously. The second I open my eyes to look at her, the tears start.

Fuck.

Lillian looks shocked. She starts to open her mouth, probably to ask if I really am dying, but I cut her off.

"I'm pregnant."

A laugh bubbles out of Lillian's mouth before she's able to stop it. She smacks her hand over her lips, choking the noise.

She composes herself before saying, "If this were anyone else, I would think you were joking, but it's you and you're crying. Aspen! You're crying! I haven't seen you cry more than five times in my life." She isn't wrong. I pride myself on controlling my emotions. Schooling my face, planting a smile on my lips, whatever I need to do to keep the mood light and positive.

I push away from the toilet, my stomach feeling momentarily settled, and fall against Lillian's chest. She wraps her arms around me and presses her cheek to the top of my head.

I'm having a baby.

My doctor went through a general physical exam and then took a urine and blood sample to check things over. I don't know if I was giving off very worried vibes, or if she was concerned, but she had my labs rushed and thirty minutes later, she was back in the room telling me I was pregnant. She reminded me of my options, but offered to get the referral to an obstetrician sent out regardless. I don't know what else she told me because I think my brain was frozen by the word pregnant.

I'm having a baby.

I *am* having a baby. This may not have been planned, or part of the rulebook I created for myself, but I am going to have this baby. I know not everyone would if they were in my shoes, and I'm lucky to live in a country where I do have choices on how I could proceed, but I want this baby. I know that to my very core.

I've always wanted to be a mother. Always. This is a blessing, regardless of the circumstances. I want to show a child the love I wasn't given growing up. I have parents and a sister, but none of those relationships give off the warm and fuzzies. I am going to give my baby the family I always wanted, but wasn't born into.

My tears slowly dry and I sniffle back the snot that is probably all over both of us. When I pull away from Lillian, she stands and offers me her hand.

"Do you think you're up for sitting on the couch? I want to get you some water and crackers for your stomach."

I nod and take her hand, letting her use her full strength to pull me to my feet. I don't have the energy. Once I've brushed my teeth, I settle on the couch and take the glass of water from Lillian's hand. I take a sip, not fully trusting my stomach, and then have some more when I think it will stay down. Lillian sits down beside me and fidgets a bit. I know she's dying to ask me a million questions, but she doesn't want to say the wrong thing since I'm clearly way more emotional than we are used to.

"So, I had a one-night stand," I begin. I may as well get straight into it. Lillian knows nothing about what happened on New Year's Eve since a snowstorm prevented us from being together. The guy I slept with that night is the father of my baby. He's the only person I've been with in months. It was a drunken mistake that I am going to have to deal with for the next eighteen years. Not that my baby is a mistake, more like an accident. But having a baby with this specific person is definitely a mistake. "I was drunk, he was drunk, and I know there was a condom involved, but it must have broken. So, yeah. I'm pregnant." I try to feign nonchalance while internally freaking out. If I freak out, Lillian will freak out, and I just can't even handle my emotions right now, let alone someone else's.

I can see Lillian processing the information. She has lived with anxiety for most of her life, so she defaults to overthinking her responses or just staying quiet when it spikes. This doesn't normally happen when we are together, just the two of us, but these are different times.

"When?"

"The beginning of the year," I answer. I'm being vague on purpose. Lillian knows where I was and who I was with on New Year's Eve. It wouldn't take much to connect the dots.

"With whom, Aspen. Who did you sleep with? Who?"

I'm not sure if she's too stunned to form a full sentence, but Lillian has an English Literature degree and is normally the more eloquent of the two of us. I would laugh, but honestly, I'm scared I might cry again if I let any strong emotions out.

"I want to tell him first," I say. Not only is that the truth, but I'm buying time. Lillian is going to be shocked when she finds out not only that I slept with him, but that I'm having a baby with him. This makes us more like family than I already feel with her. Before Lillian has a chance to ask any more questions, I jump in and explain all my symptoms that led me to my doctor's appointment, and then everything that happened up until she found me in the bathroom. She listens mostly in silence until I'm done.

"Wow, I'm...shocked. How do you feel? I know that's probably a stupid question, but really. How do you feel?" she finally says.

"I'm shocked too," I say. "And overwhelmed, a bit scared, nervous, worried." I pause to think for a moment. I haven't let myself do that yet, but I realize I am all the things I just listed. I think most women in my position would be. But deep down, there's a part of me that's excited. It seems crazy to be excited to be pregnant after a stupid, drunk hookup, but here I am. I know Lillian won't judge me, so I say, "I'm also excited."

"Okay, me too," she squeals. "I didn't want to say it in case it would freak you out, but I'm already mentally planning your baby shower. Ahhhhhh. My best friend is having a baby!" She grabs both my hands in hers and lifts them in celebration. "Jackson is going to freak! When can I tell him?" This is another reason why I love not only Lillian but also Jackson. Lillian would never tell Jackson a secret about someone else without their permission. She doesn't go running to him with gossip. And Jackson would never be mad at her for keeping something from him if it wasn't hers to tell. Lillian being in a happy relationship makes me happy. Lillian being in a healthy relationship makes me ecstatic.

"Can you wait a week or two? I need to wrap my head around everything. Also, Jackson is my boss now, so...yeah. A week?"

"I'll wait longer if you need," she assures me, and I know she means it. "I'll just need to pretend I'm not giddy about something when I get home. Take all the time you need. This is a big deal."

"What are the odds you can stay over tonight? I don't want to be alone," I admit. Even if I am excited about it, I'm also terrified.

"Done," Lillian says without any thought, further proving that she really is an amazing friend.

We spend the rest of the day and night watching movies and ordering takeout, which I can actually eat now that my stomach is settled. We don't talk much more about me being pregnant, which I am thankful for.

When my brain finally wraps itself around everything, I realize it's probably time to rewrite the rules.

Rule #1: Breathe
Rule #2: Don't panic

Rule #1: Get rid of anything you don't want to be in your life ten years from now.

Rule #3: Get rid of anything that does not contribute to you being the best person and mother

Rule # 2: No men and their bullshit

Rule # 4: No men and their bullshit, especially your baby daddy

Rule #5: Get a hobby

Rule #4: No breaking the rules

Rule #6: Be flexible

Now I need to break the news to my baby daddy.

Chapter 3
Aspen

Age 17

Be safe tonight! Text me if you need a ride!!

ASPEN:

Are you sure you don't want to join me???

LILLIAN:

HAHAHA YOU ARE SO FUNNY. No.

This party is way crazier than I was expecting. I'm not sure why I thought it would be anything different, though. This is one of Jackson Mane's legendary parties. Anything can happen. Jackson doesn't even go to the same school as me and I've heard of his wild parties and the rumours that the police never shut them down because he pays off his neighbours. Maybe he pays off the police too? The parties are always kept secret until hours before and you need to know someone to get in. I've never had a way in until tonight.

One of the girls on the dance team got an invitation and even though my best friend Lillian didn't want to come with me, I knew I couldn't let this opportunity pass.

Tonight is going to be one to remember.

I weave my way through the crowd of mostly drunk and very sweaty bodies to the kitchen, where there is a row of alcohol bottles, pop, beer, and a large cooler of jungle juice. The fact that a high school kid is throwing a party with what's essentially an open bar is kind of crazy but based on the size of houses in this neighbourhood, I don't think money is an issue. And the fact that there are girls dancing on what looks like a formal dining room table, I think it's safe to assume there are no parents here.

The girls and I immediately head to the living room, where it looks like a makeshift dance floor is set up. The couches, full of drunk teens making out with each other, have been pushed toward the walls and way more people than should fit into the space have their bodies pushed against each other while they grind to some song that's always playing on the radio.

This is exactly what I came here for—some dancing, maybe a little drinking, but mostly letting loose. My parents have been on my case all week about the B I got on my history test. If it isn't an A, they don't want it on my report card. I know I can get the grade up; I just don't really care to. I'm going to be an interior designer. I know it, they know it, and we should all stop pretending that the French Revolution is going to affect my ability to design beautiful spaces for the rich and famous of Toronto. I'm going to work at Industrial Design Co. one day and my high school grades won't matter.

After an hour of getting lost in the music and fending off sweaty boys, I head back to the kitchen to get something to drink. I lost most of my friends somewhere on the dance floor, but we have a plan to meet up out front just after midnight so we all make it home for our curfews. I'm fine being a lone wolf anyway. Those girls are my friends, but we aren't super close. I don't need them to have a good time.

There's a younger-looking guy sitting on the counter beside the cooler that hopefully is keeping jungle juice chilled. You never know what's in the juice, but as long as there's enough sugar to hide the taste of the cheap alcohol, I don't really care.

The kid is all but asleep when I ask, "Can I get a cup?"

"Oh, yeah, yeah. Sure." He grabs a red cup and liquid just as brightly coloured fills it.

"How did you get stuck with this job?" I ask to break the silence.

"Rookie on the hockey team." He shrugs and tosses his long hair out of his eyes. "Mane doesn't want anyone spiking any drinks. The rookies alternate each party."

I can't help but laugh. Not because people spike drinks at parties. Gross. But because Jackson has the power over this kid to say this is how he's spending his Friday night. I wonder what it's like to be a high school hockey god. At least he uses his powers for good.

"Keep up the good work," I say as he hands me my red cup. The blush covering his cheeks is adorable. If he's manning the jungle juice all night, he needs to get used to drunk girls chatting him up.

I take a sip of my drink and it tastes like a cavity waiting to happen, but that's exactly what I need to make the most of the night.

Since I'm mostly on my own here, this will be the only drink I have tonight. I'm already a disappointment to my parents, so no need to spend the night with my head in the toilet to help prove their point.

I don't really know anyone here, which normally doesn't bother me. I'm what some would call a social butterfly. I love meeting new people, having a good time, and getting into a bit of trouble. But for some reason, I can't find anyone to talk to. It feels like they are all in their own conversations and I don't want to seem like an annoying drunk girl interrupting them. Lillian always says she wishes she was as confident as me, but I don't think she understands how much of that is faking it until I feel it.

Do I feel confident in most social situations? I guess? But sometimes it all feels like an act. Everyone loves the fun party girl. That's the girl people want to be friends with. She's the one who gets invited to all the parties, who the boys like, who's always surrounded by people. She's the one who feels seen. She's the one who's not lonely. She also doesn't feel like she's completely who I am. But being here feels like the better option right now.

Maybe I'll go to the bathroom to freshen up and then see if

I can find any of the girls I came with. Or I'll head back to the dance floor and let some guy hit on me.

I head down a hallway with multiple doors, hoping one is a bathroom. Just as I turn the corner, I'm hit with a tall wall of a person and the entire contents of my drink dump down their white shirt.

Shit.

I look up and immediately regret everything that has brought me to this point. Simon Cadwell, Jackson's cousin, is staring down at me.

How is he so tall?

I'm 5'7" and until very recently, most of the guys my age were hardly taller than me. Not Simon. He's towering over me with his dark fluffy hair, sparkling eyes, and his soaked shirt is making the muscle hidden beneath it appear very defined. Simon Cadwell doesn't look like the boys at my school. He looks like a man. And even though I've very clearly ruined his white shirt, he looks very happy to see me.

"I'm so sorry," I sputter out when I realize we've been standing here in silence far longer than appropriate. He was probably waiting for me to apologize and instead, I stood there checking him out. He probably thinks I'm so weird.

He ignores my apology and offers me his hand instead. "Simon Cadwell. What's your name?"

I take his hand in mine and regret it. It's firm and warm and I don't know if it's what little alcohol I've had or if I've completely lost it, but it's so big that I want to curl up to him and take a nap. Oh yeah, I've lost it.

Instead of doing the local thing—letting go of his hand and

offering him my name—I say, "I know who you are!" I've been known to lack a filter, but it isn't normally this bad. Something about Simon has thoughts exiting my mouth before my brain can decide if they are inside thoughts or outside thoughts.

Simon raises his brows, so I continue. "I mean, I know your name is Simon. This is your cousin's party. I think everyone here knows who the two of you are..." I sound like a fan girl right now. I need him to say something so I can figure out how to stop the flow of words.

"I'm sure not everyone knows who I am, but I appreciate you thinking I have that kind of status here." He chuckles to himself and it puts me at ease.

"Sorry. I'm Aspen. And I'm sorry about your shirt. Sorry." We're still holding hands, so he shakes mine again and then laces our fingers together. The move shocks me, but I'm not going to pull away. Simon is easily the hottest guy I've ever met. If he wants to hold my hand, I'm not going to stop him. Lillian is going to lose it when I tell her about this!

"Aspen," he repeats, more to himself than to me. "I like it. And don't worry about my shirt. My mom is really good with bleach." I'm not sure if that's a joke or not, but I laugh anyway. Simon gives me a mischievous smirk and I can't help but blush. There is a whole crazy party happening a few feet away, but Simon's attention has never left me once. I don't know what it is that is keeping us in this bubble, but I hope it doesn't pop.

We stand there in silence for a couple more seconds before Simon shakes his head and pulls our joined hands towards his chest. "Do you want to go talk somewhere or something?"

I nod my head before I can even think about what that really means. There's a very real chance that Simon is just trying to hook up with me right now, but I don't think that's actually his intention. There's only one way to find out.

He leads me down the hallway to a bedroom but doesn't stop. We continue through the room and into the adjoining bathroom. "Sorry, this probably wasn't what you were imagining hanging out would look like when you came to the party," he says, dropping my hand and crouching down to look under the sink. "I just thought I might try to get a little less sticky." Simon makes a poor attempt at cleaning his shirt before he quickly gives up. He approaches me quickly and for a moment, I think he's going to kiss me. I would let him. Boy, would I let him kiss me. Instead, he grabs me by the hips and plops me on the counter, making space between my thighs for him to stand. I'm glad I decided to wear jeans instead of a skirt tonight, otherwise Simon would be seeing a lot more of me than he should be right now.

He leans forward so our faces are inches apart and laces our fingers together again.

"What's the craziest dream you've ever had?" he asks, his voice just above a whisper.

"Like an actual dream?" I ask, a bit confused by his topic of choice. "Why do you want to know about my dreams?" It feels like I'm yelling in the quiet bathroom, even though my voice is no louder than his.

"I want to know anything you're willing to tell me," he answers, like it's the simplest thing in the world. Meanwhile, the butterflies in my stomach are swarming and my heart feels like it's beating outside of my chest. I'm sure Simon can hear it too. I don't know what's going on, but I'll be kicking myself tomorrow if I don't embrace this moment.

"I once had a dream I was an alligator farmer..." I say the second the thought enters my mind.

"Tell me everything." And that's how we spend the next hour. Trading questions back and forth, laughing and telling stories. It's not how I envisioned spending the night, but I'd rather be alone with Simon than in a room full of strangers. This feels like enough. Like *I'm* enough.

Chapter 4
Simon

Age 18

JACKSON:

I swear to god if I find puke in my underwear drawer again, I'm never hosting another party

SIMON:

Chill out

And lock your door??

T he hottest girl I've ever seen has ruined my favourite shirt.

That's not entirely true. It's a plain white shirt, nothing special, but I know I look good in it. I have a slight tan from my family vacation this winter and it's just tight enough to show off my muscles without looking like I'm trying too hard. It's now covered in the mystery red liquid partygoers are downing, also known as jungle juice. The only way to describe it is red and sugary. In reality, it's a mixture of vodka, tequila, sugar, and Kool-Aid. Red food dye can hide even the worst alcohol flavours. I would dump the entire cooler of juice on myself if it got Aspen's attention.

I've been watching Aspen since she got here. Not in a creepy way. I haven't been lurking around the corner waiting to pop out. I've just been keeping an eye on her. Constantly.

It's honestly hard to look away. She's like a magnet. I'm pretty sure every guy in the room was hypnotized by her dance moves. And her smile. God, her smile. Her big brown eyes crinkle at the corners the smallest bit as her entire face lights up. I want—no, I need—that smile directed at me.

I'm not sure what possessed me to hold Aspen's hand like we know each other, but when she didn't pull away, I took that as a good enough sign that she's as interested in me as I am in her. Directing her to one of the guest bathrooms in Jackson's house may not have been my best idea, but I knew it would be quiet and I would be able to talk to Aspen without feeling like every guy in the room was ready to step in and snatch her from me. Convenience trumps romance right now.

I don't think she even sees how eyes linger on her as she walks past. She said she knew me like I was some sort of teenage royalty. People here may know who I am, but she's the one they want to know. She's certainly the only one I want to spend my night with.

31

I don't know why I asked her to tell me about a strange dream she had. My brain is not firing on all cylinders right now, clearly. I just wanted to get her talking. I love the sound of her voice. I love the look on her face when she's thinking a bit too hard. I love the twinkle in her eye when she's observing her surroundings, deciding her next move.

Her best friend Lillian comes up in almost every funny story she tells me. Aspen seems like the mastermind of plans that landed them in trouble. Apparently, they both ended up in detention last month because Aspen sprinkled birdseed all over the cars in the school parking lot during football practice. Lillian was the getaway car driver, but they were both caught on camera. It makes me want to meet Lillian; she seems like such a big part of Aspen's life and I'm missing knowing a part of her without seeing her and her best friend together.

Aspen goes to jokingly smack me on the chest after I finish telling her about something stupid Jackson and I did, but she grimaces when her hands hit my sticky shirt. I've been so distracted by our conversation that I didn't notice that not only is my shirt stuck to my body, but it's also starting to harden. This is beyond uncomfortable. I want to keep talking to Aspen, but maybe changing into a clean shirt is the move. I don't want her to be grossed out by the prospect of touching me. And I want Aspen touching me.

"I think I should probably change my shirt..."

"Yeah, that's probably a good idea. Maybe soak it in some water before that thing grows legs and tries to join the party," Aspen jokes. Her nose crinkles the smallest bit as she tries not to laugh too hard at her joke. God, she's cute.

"I'll be right back. Maybe you could get yourself a new drink. I'll meet you in the kitchen?"

Aspen nods, biting her bottom lip between her teeth. It takes everything in me not to pull her lip loose, preferably with my mouth on hers. I settle for squeezing her hand and pulling her with me out of the room. We separate in the hallway where I need to take the stairs.

"Meet me in the kitchen."

"In the kitchen," she repeats, not making a move to let go of my hand. We stand there staring at each other with goofy smiles on our faces for way longer than necessary. If I wasn't now aware of how gross my shirt felt, I would have stood there with her until morning.

"I'll be so quick. No more than a couple of minutes, okay?" I ask.

"Okay. I'll see you soon," she says, finally dropping my hand. I want to pull her into my arms and kiss her. I want to feel her hands all over my body. Something about this moment feels important. I know I'm going to see her again. Probably in five minutes, but I try to memorize as much about her now.

Aspen takes a couple of steps backwards before winking at me and then turning back towards the party. I trip several times as I sprint up the stairs to where the rest of the bedrooms are. This area is typically off-limits during parties, but sometimes people sneak up here.

Jackson and I mostly split our time between each of our houses, so one of the spare rooms upstairs is essentially my bedroom. I have a couple of spare sets of clothes and toiletries I keep in there for when I stay here, mostly for when Jackson's dad goes out of town with a new girlfriend.

It's not that my parents don't suspect that we are getting up to no good when my uncle isn't home. They know. But my mom's relationship with her brother is strained and if Jackson isn't going to get in trouble with his dad for making a mess of his house, she doesn't want to step in. I can't say I understand any of how their relationship works, but as long as no one gets hurt and the cops aren't called, these parties seem to be okay.

I need to make this quick so I can get back to Aspen.

My dad always talks about how it was love at first sight with my mom. My mom says he's crazy but doesn't deny that she fell for him quickly. I always brushed it off and figured my parents were just trying to make my sister and me feel uncomfortable with all their lovey-doveyness, but I liked it. It was nice seeing how in love they were and still are.

Maybe that's why I'm so enamoured with Aspen. She walked into the house and everything else became background noise. I'm sure in ten years I'll look back on this night and think I was such a silly kid for thinking such serious things about a girl I just met. But if I'm being foolish, then so be it. I think I'm in love. And if in ten years Aspen isn't standing next to me, shaking her head at the fact that I was in love with her after only seeing her from across the room, then I've done something very wrong with my life.

Chapter 5

Simon

You good? You seemed a little bit off?

I'm fine, nothing to worry about! Just need a nap probably

If you weren't at the gym at the crack of dawn you probably wouldn't need a midday nap, old man.

You are only a couple of months younger than me

I feel like I'm going to be sick. And that makes me hate myself a little. My cousin Jackson is so in love, and I couldn't be happier for him. I really try not to compare our lives, but I can't help it.

My life is good. Actually, my life is great.

I've got a nice condo that I own. I have a great group of friends. I'm killing it in my career. And yet, I would throw it all away to have what Jackson has. If jealousy is a green monster, then I'm a giant raging broccoli.

My cousin Jackson is my best friend and has always been more like a brother to me. We are the same age and have been basically inseparable our whole lives—we went to the same elementary and high school, were roommates all through university, and until recently, lived in the same building in Toronto.

He has the same great group of friends as I do and is also excelling in a career he loves.

The big difference between us is Jackson is happily and so madly in love with his girlfriend.

I am happy for him. I am. But I'm also jealous. And I hate feeling that way toward someone I care about. But as I end the video call with Jackson and Lillian, I can't help it. They are connected on a level I have never experienced but want so badly. I was shocked when my cousin fell hard and fast for a girl he met in Bluefield last summer. Even bigger shocker, she's the same Lillian I spent the night hearing about at that party back in high school.

Every time Jackson and I hang out and Lillian is there, or she even comes up in conversation, I feel the jealousy. Jackson and I were just catching up on our weeks, but I knew Jackson's mind was only half in the conversation and I don't even blame him for it. I could see his eyes tracking Lillian, who was behind his phone making them lunch. If the love of my life had been in the room making me a gourmet meal, as I know Lillian was, I would have hung up the phone instead of listening to me describe a very boring bank meeting I had earlier this week. I appreciate him giving me any attention when he's got his future right in front of him.

I've tried to find it—love. A connection like what Jackson and Lillian have, but I've never gotten close.

I date. A lot. Or it was a lot until recently. But none of my relationships have been very long term. They're serious; I haven't just been messing around. I see what my parents have, what my grandparents have, what Jackson now has, and I want it. I'm dating to marry. I'm dating with the intention of finding forever. And that's why I haven't had a relationship last for more than a couple of months. Maybe my expectations are too high, my standards too hard to meet. Whatever it is, it's not working, so I'm taking a break. I've been completely single since last summer, around the time Jackson met Lillian, actually. Maybe seeing them together prompted it, but I'm not sure. But at some point, during my time in Bluefield, something shifted, and I knew there was a big love out there. A woman to challenge me, love me, be a partner with me, and I need to find her. The next woman I date will be forever, and I'm determined to find her.

Maybe moving to Bluefield will help, or maybe it will hinder. The dating pool isn't very large in a town that small, but considering I've had very little luck living in the largest city in the country, any change to my dating situation is welcome.

I don't want to fall at the feet of the first girl who gives me an ounce of attention. But for the right woman, I would worship them on my knees, happily.

I'm not going to force anything; I'm going to let the universe or whatever higher power put me into the right situations and it will happen for me. And when it does, I will stop at nothing to make sure I get my happily ever after, my partner, my best friend, and my lover.

I want it all.

There's a woman out there for me. She just doesn't know it yet.

Chapter 6

Aspen

BEN:

> Are you alive? Noah has been asking about you...

ASPEN:

> I'M SORRY

M y stomach is in my throat as I park my car and make my way up the steps to the house in front of me. The house I've been to too many times to count over the last couple of years, and yet this time feels different. I guess it's because I feel different. I *am* different. I have a secret that I need to share. But I'm not ready yet.

I gave myself a week to cry into my pillow. The week is over and now my big girl panties are firmly in place.

I lightly knock at the door, almost hoping no one hears it to answer. My wish is not granted as footsteps approach, and

I see a familiar face peek through the window at the top of the craftsman door before the lock is clicked and the door opens.

"Hey, Asp." Ben gives me a hug and a quick peck on the cheek, then gestures for me to enter his house. "How are you doing?"

I haven't seen Ben as much as I normally would. Benjamin Shaw is Lillian's older brother and I've known him for practically all my life. I was just as much, if not more, of an annoying little sister to him growing up as Lillian was. When Ben had his son Noah almost six years ago, I was given the privilege of being an honorary aunty to the little guy.

I try to make a point of either hanging out with Noah once a week, or at least making time to video call him. I've been so exhausted the last month that I dropped the ball. I knew I wouldn't be much fun, so I've limited our interactions to video calls only. I feel like a shitty aunt. It's like my body knew I screwed up and decided I should feel like I've failed in every aspect of my life.

"I've been busy. There is so much going on, and I haven't been around like I should have been. I'm sorry."

"Is that the only reason? That you've been busy?" he asks. I try to school my features to not give away how I'm truly feeling, but I can feel the tears starting to form behind my eyes. Dammit. Lately this has been my reaction to everything, and I'm still not used it. Ben knows me, probably too well, and if I start crying now, he won't let me leave until I spill all my secrets, but I'm not ready for that yet.

"Is Noah here?" I purposely change the subject, willing Ben to give me this out. I deliberately came on a Saturday when

Noah should be around to act as a buffer if I needed it.

Ben takes that bait. "Hey, Noah," he calls loudly. "There's someone here to see you!" I hear him coming before I see him.

A door slams against the wall upstairs, and Ben and I both wince before the sound of a herd of elephants stomping down the stairs follows. I don't know how such a small boy came to make such loud noises. When Noah sees me, he stops in his tracks like he's seen a ghost, and my stomach drops. I've been such a nonexistent aunty to him that the sight of me has him shocked. I know I'm not technically his real aunt, but it never felt like my role was any different from Lillian's.

I crouch to the ground, putting myself at Noah's height, and open my arms for a hug that I pray he will want. Thankfully, he takes off at a sprint and throws his little body into my arms. It feels like he's grown since the last time I saw him. Ben is probably 6'2" and I would say Noah is tracking to match that height one day. I squeeze his body against me as tight as I can without hurting him and breathe in that little boy smell that's always changing. Today it's the smell of Play-Doh. "I missed you, Aspy," Noah mumbles into my hair. I close my eyes to fight the tears. This little boy has owned my heart since the moment he was born. Probably before that, if I'm being honest. As soon as Billy and I found out Ben was going to be a dad, even as shocking as it was, we were both all in on being fun aunts and helping in any way we could.

"I missed you too, Noah. We won't go so long without seeing each other again. I promise." A promise I hope I can keep. Luckily, I'm not sure if Noah fully understands the concept of time completely. He's only six now, and even though he's very smart and thoughtful for his age, this might be over his head. He pulls out of my arms, and it feels too soon. I wish I could hug away all the torment happening in my brain right now.

"Can I show you my new toy?"

"Of course. Is it in your room?" I ask, taking his small hand in mine. He nods his head and then pulls me towards the stairs. I don't bother looking over my shoulder at Ben as I create space between us. I know I'll find a concerned look on his face, and I can't stomach that right now.

With excitement, Noah shows me the new superhero toy he got from his grandparents last week. It was a just-because gift. They are both retired and have chosen to fill their days by spoiling their only grandchild and travelling.

The thought of grandparents makes me sad. I'm not positive about how my parents are going to react, but I would be shocked if it was anything but disappointment or indifference. My relationship with them was never the best. They were very strict when I was growing up and I always tried to push their boundaries. Once I was out of the house and at school, we kept things civil since they figured their parental role was done. It was a blow-up with my younger sister, Sidney, that did our relationship in. Sidney did something really terrible. I stop the shutter from working through my body as I think about it. It was unforgivable, in my opinion. My parents said that I was being dramatic, and they had hoped I would have grown out of that by now. So, I cut ties. I don't need to surround myself with people like that. But that's okay, I have the Shaws. I can't help but think they will welcome my baby with open arms.

After about an hour, Noah gets bored of the superhero game

and declares he is going to read his book for school in the nook in his dad's office. With Lillian being a children's book author, it's not surprising that not only does Noah love to read, but that he also has a designated spot in the house. This was a project that Lillian and I worked on together as his Christmas gift last year.

Noah and I part ways as I roam through the house, looking for Ben. I find him in the kitchen with a mug of coffee in his hand as he scrolls on his laptop. He's wearing wire-framed glasses, giving him the stern but dreamy professor look. If my stomach wasn't in knots, I would make a comment about how he looks like he's ready for his calling as a porn star professor. Completely inappropriate, but most definitely my sense of humour. I lean on the opposite side of the counter from Ben and wait for him to finish what he's typing before I speak. The speedy clicking of his fingers against the keys matches my accelerated heartbeat.

Why am I so nervous? This shouldn't be so hard. This isn't actually the hard part. Everything that comes after this is. I mean, I'm going to be giving birth in like six months. Surely that will be the hardest part of all of this.

Ben finally looks up at me and removes his glasses. I track his movement and then stutter on my words. I knew I couldn't just come out and ask him this over the phone after I've been so MIA lately. I need information from him before I make my next steps, but he can't know why I'm asking. I don't want to answer any more questions than I need to. I might chicken out if that's the case, and I pride myself on dealing with my shit and being brave about it. If I'm going to be a good mom, I can't let this pregnancy make me too soft.

Ben knows that I'm planning on heading to Bluefield soon. As soon as I signed on the dotted line, Lillian was on the phone with him, trying to bait him into spending the summer there too. I know he can't because of his work, and he already has Noah signed up for summer programming here in the city, but hopefully with Jackson, Lillian, and I all in Bluefield, he'll make more of an effort than last summer.

When Lillian thought she was having a quarter-life crisis last year, she decided to move herself to her grandparent's cottage for the summer. She was hoping to get herself out of writer's block, which she succeeded in, but she also succeeded in catching the eye of a fellow city slicker who was spending the summer renovating cottages there. Ever since, Jackson and Lillian basically live in Bluefield, only spending one week a month in Toronto at Lillian's condo. Otherwise, they work from the beautiful cottage next door to Lillian's grandparent's place, which Jackson now owns. I had planned to stay there with them in one of the many bedrooms, but now that my situation has changed, I should probably look for a place of my own. There's no way they'll want a hormonal pregnant lady intruding on their alone time all summer, especially after all the drama from last year.

A disgruntled employee and ex-cottage owner were targeting both of them in a vandalism and attempted arson case. Only when Lillian was kidnapped on Jackson's boat but was able to free herself and subdue her captor did the torment finally end. I'm sure they are looking forward to a drama-free summer this time around, and I can almost guarantee that when everyone finds out what I did and with who, it will be anything but drama-free.

Ben cocks an eyebrow at me and clears his throat. I know he's waiting for me to speak first, but for some reason, my mouth doesn't seem to remember how to form words. I'm sure if I tried right now, it would come out garbled.

Come on, Aspen, you can do this. You're a bad bitch. You're a boss bitch. Do it.

"You know how you play poker with Jackson, Dylan, and Simon?" I ask. It definitely seems like it's out of nowhere, and Ben's expression is a mix of humour and confusion.

Dylan is a police officer in Bluefield whom Jackson befriended last summer during all the trouble he was having. He is a total hunk. Muscles for days and a panty-dropping smile. Simon, on the other hand, is typically public enemy number one. I don't even want to think about him right now.

"Aspen," Ben starts, shaking his head, "I thought you were about to tell me you were dying. Then you come out and ask about poker night?"

Okay, I feel a bit bad about that. I guess my behaviour is even more squirrelly than I thought if Ben's mind went to that extreme.

"I'm not dying. Don't worry. With work and everything else, my mind is just all over the place. I keep getting lost in thought." I hope that eases his nerves and provides a good enough explanation. It's almost the truth, too. My mind has been all over the place, sometimes with work, but mostly with other things. "So, poker night? What night is it?"

"Um, Thursday typically. Simon comes over here and we play

next to each other while Jackson and Dylan do the same in Bluefield. Noah is normally in bed, so I don't need a sitter if that's where this is going..."

It's not where this is going, but that is a smart cover.

"Yeah, that's exactly what I was thinking. I'm only in town for a couple more weeks, so I thought if I could help out more, I would. But if you don't need the help, never mind." I turn away from him and grab my purse that I left on the table by the door. Ben follows close behind me and I can tell he's suspicious. That he thinks I'm up to something.

Probably because I am.

"Aspen..." he starts.

"Sorry, I have to get going. I have a final meeting with a client this afternoon that I need to prepare for, but I'll call you tomorrow." I give him a peck on the cheek before I quickly open the door and all but run through it. I won't stop until I'm securely inside my car parked on the street in front of Ben's house. He waves to me from his spot on the front stoop, and I can tell he's confused by my actions. Yeah, that makes two of us, buddy. I wave back at him and then pull out onto the road, making my way back to my place.

Chapter 7

Aspen

LILLIAN:

Why is your location turned off??

ASPEN:

Shhhh

LILLIAN:

Aspen...

This has got to be one of the weirder things I have done in my life, and that's saying something. I've always marched to the beat of my drum and forced Lillian to follow me wherever I take us. One time in grade nine, I forced her to ditch school because our favourite TV actor was rumoured to be in town filming at the mall downtown. We wandered around the mall for an hour until we thought we saw the back of his head and then proceeded to follow him out of the mall and around the city for the next hour. When he finally turned around to ask why we were stalking him, we discovered it was not the person we thought we were following at all, and we were so embarrassed. I ran in the opposite direction and pulled Lillian along with me until we couldn't see him anymore. We had to use a pay phone to get Ben to come pick us up because we were so lost and our phones were dead. Thankfully, he could track Lillian's phone to our last location and save the day. He told on us and honestly, I don't blame him. It was reckless and stupid. But it was also a lot of fun. I felt like I had a little taste of freedom, wandering the city with my best friend, no one knowing us or where we were. That feeling became a bit addictive and has led me into other weird and awkward situations.

My current one is certainly weird and honestly not my best. I've been sitting outside of Ben's house for a couple of hours. I parked far enough away that if he were to look outside, he wouldn't immediately recognize my car, but close enough that I can see who is coming and going through his front door.

Simon arrived soon after I got here. He walked up to Ben's door in jeans and a three-quarter zip sweater with a collar peeking out, somehow looking sophisticated and casual at the same time. He's so annoying. He had a paper bag in his hand with what looked like a bottle of whiskey inside and his laptop case. I have to say, the fact that there are two grown men inside playing poker online, but beside each other, makes me laugh a little. They are such dorks. And knowing that Jackson and Dylan are doing the same thing in Bluefield right now makes it that much funnier.

I'm glad he brought whiskey. I was hoping they would be

drinking. Alcohol will make what I'm about to do easier to swallow.

Around 10 pm, I see the outside light turn on before Simon exits Ben's house. He has his laptop bag, but no bottle of alcohol. This is a good sign. Either he's leaving it behind, or it's empty. Based on the goofy-looking smile on Ben's face as he waves goodbye to Simon, I would say it's the latter.

I know this is my perfect opportunity, and with the alcohol warming his system, I have to make my move. I quickly and quietly exit my car, locking it from the inside so I don't have to beep the lock and make my presence known. I slip onto the sidewalk and stay lightly in the shadows.

This seemed like such a great plan in my head, but after walking ten blocks to stand in front of his door about to knock, I'm not so sure. I'm ambushing him. I made sure to pick a night when I figured he would be drinking and now I'm going to drop a bomb on him. A big bomb. An *I'm pregnant with your baby* bomb. Maybe I should have run all of this by someone first. I'm not always the best voice of reason. But the one thing I know I'm doing right is telling him first. Well, mostly first. Lillian doesn't count.

I have to do this. It's the right thing. If the roles were reserved, I would hope I heard it straight from the source. I press my ear against the door and listen for a moment. I hope he hasn't already gone to bed. If he doesn't answer the door and I have to come back again another time, I don't know what I'll do.

I take a deep breath and muster up all the courage in my body while raising my hand to the door. Before I have the chance to chicken out, I hit my fist against the wooden door, making three solid thuds ring out around me.

It feels like both hours and seconds pass before I hear the lock click and see the door handle move in front of me. I feel like I'm going to puke and pee my pants all at once. His tall frame fills the doorway, and his face looks shocked to see me here.

"What are you doing here?"

Chapter 8

Aspen

Four Months Prior (New Year's Eve)

ASPEN:

I HATE MOTHER NATURE

LILLIAN:

We'll celebrate soon

E verything is ruined.

Well, not really, but it sure feels that way. How am I supposed to start being a brand-new version of myself if my New Year's Eve plans suck? I had great plans. Low key, but great, and now Mother Nature has ruined them. *That bitch.*

I was supposed to be spending the night with Lillian, Jackson, and all our Bluefield friends at their brand-new cottage. Now I'm spending it alone.

A huge snowstorm hit just after I got here and now everyone from Toronto, including Lillian and Jackson, is stuck there because of the road closures. Dylan had to put on his constable pants and head into work because there is a chance for increased calls tonight, and my friend Julia, who works and lives above the bookstore in Bluefield, is worried about the pipes freezing when the power inevitably goes out. She's staying in and keeping a fire going instead.

So here I am, trying to climb onto the garbage bin outside Lillian's grandparent's cottage to get the spare key. Her and Jackson's place next door looks very cozy and weatherproof, but I have no way of getting in. If it weren't for her family always keeping a spare key in the same spot, I would be sleeping in my car tonight.

Just as I get my fingers around the teeth of the key, the bin below me shakes and I lose my footing. I probably should have had both feet on it for support, but it's a bit too high up for me. Lillian is at least four inches shorter than me. There's no way she could ever reach this thing. We need a new hiding spot.

I know most people say your life flashes before your eyes before you fall to your death, but mine doesn't. Right before I'm sure I'm about to crack my skull open on the icy cement landing, I see Simon's face.

Maybe I've skipped a few steps and found myself in hell.

My body connects with his. I yelp out a shocked noise at the same time I hear him grunt at the impact. I may look to be on the wiry side, but I've got hard-earned muscles hiding underneath my clothes.

"What are you doing?" he says, while I yell, "Let me go!"

I push my way out of his arms as he tries to steady me on the slippery ground around us. Bluefield is like a winter wonderland right now. In Toronto, most of the snow is already brown, slushy, and depressing. Here it still has that fresh snow globe look.

"What were you doing up there?" Simon asks as I adjust my coat back into place. We're standing almost toe to toe, and I don't like it. I prefer to be nowhere near him, so this is very uncomfortable.

Taking a step back, I reply, "I was getting the spare key. What are you doing here?"

"The New Year's Eve party? I'm assuming the same as you."

Ugh, no one told me he was invited. I should have expected it. Jackson is rarely anywhere without Simon, and since most of my friends are Simon's friends, he typically shows up at most of the events I'm at. Just because that's my reality, doesn't mean I have to like it.

There was a point in my life when I was young and stupid where I had the smallest of small crushes on Simon. I got over it about 20 minutes after it started and have loathed him ever since. I try not to think about it too much because it makes me angry, and rude, two things I try not to be if I can help it.

Before I can say something that would sound angry and most definitely be rude, Simon asks, "Why are you trying to get in here? I thought we were meeting at Jackson and Wildflower's place?"

Jackson and Simon have both called Lillian Wildflower since last summer. I don't know the story behind it because I've never asked. I would find it endearing and a bit cute if I was able to feel any of those things when Simon is involved.

"Didn't Jackson call you?" I ask, my annoyance very present in my tone.

"He did, but the roads are rough, so I didn't want to answer and be distracted. What's going on?"

I sigh as I begin to climb the garbage can again. It's getting cold out here, and I want to get inside and away from Simon as soon as possible. I can feel his hands on the back of my thighs to keep me stable. I want to scold him and tell him not to touch me, but I guess this is better than me falling into his arms again. There is a small tingling sensation right where his gloved hands meet my jean-clad legs. I'm sure it's because his hands are warm and my legs are cold. There wouldn't be any other reason.

I'm able to successfully grab the key this time and jump down as quickly as possible to break the contact between our bodies. I turn to face Simon and his annoying bright smile. He smiles a lot around me. I think he knows it annoys me, so he does it more than a normal person would.

Finally answering his question, I say, "No one else is coming. They are all stuck because of the weather. I don't have a key for next door, so I figured this is a better option than my car."

I turn away from him and jiggle the key in the lock a couple of times before it opens. Taking a step inside, this cottage is marginally warmer than outside, mostly just blocking the wind. I know the Shaws close the place up for the winter completely since they don't have a furnace. This means the water and hydro are turned off until spring. My only saving grace from the cold is the wood stove in the corner of the living room and the pile of wood I know is stacked outside of Lillian and Jackson's place. I take a couple more steps inside and drop my purse at the table by the door. I am all too aware that there could be furry creatures that have made this place their home for the winter, so as I step into the kitchen to the left, I do so cautiously. I stop to grab my phone from the pocket of my wool coat when I feel body heat behind me. I look over my shoulder to see Simon has followed me inside.

"What are you doing?" I ask, annoyed that he's still here.

"You said we can't get in next door."

"And?"

"And I'm not sleeping in my car. We can both stay here."

Over my dead body.

"No."

"What do you mean, no? Aspen, it's freezing out there and the roads are closed now. What else am I supposed to do?" He huffs out, seemingly just as annoyed as I am.

"That sounds like a 'you' problem, buddy." I shine my light over the kitchen and see that the coast is clear. Then do the same in the dining room beside me, before making my way to the living room in the front of the cottage.

The entire front wall is glass and windows, but thankfully they have been equipped with storm windows for the winter. I can't see out of them, but at least they are trying to protect the place from the elements. The wood stove is in the corner and now that I'm looking at it, I'm a bit worried it may be harder to use than I thought. It's not that they are overly complicated, but I've never used one before. If I burnt this cottage to the ground, my life would be over. Whatever, this is a problem that Google will solve for me.

When I turn around, I expect to see Simon scowling at me, but instead, he's gone.

Good, he does know how to listen after all.

I make a quick trip upstairs to grab blankets. I don't even want to know if there are things living in the bedroom closets. As long as they stay up there and away from me, I'm not going to be the one serving an eviction notice. I grab a couple of garbage bags out of the bathroom cabinet. I know all the pillows and linens are bagged to keep them semi-safe over the winter, so I hope I at least find a pillow and blanket in my stash.

As I make my way downstairs, I feel the heat instantly.

When I look towards the stove, I see Simon slowly feeding the fire more logs from the stack he has beside him.

"What are you doing?" I ask. I know what he is physically doing. I just don't understand why he's doing it, or why he's still here, for that matter.

"This place is freezing; I'm trying to warm it up." His face gives off a look that none of this is fazing him, but I can hear the annoyance in his voice.

"What are you doing here? Like inside? I thought you were leaving?"

"Aspen, can you just not for once?" His stern tone takes me aback. Simon is almost always happy-go-lucky. He makes friends everywhere he goes and is always the life of the party. I can admit we are a bit similar in that sense. But where I exist in a bubble of sass, he is way happy-go-lucky.

When I don't say anything, he continues, "It's freezing outside, and I am not staying in my car. You and I know if I call Lillian right now, she would say it's fine for me to stay here. But

I'm not going to do that. Frankly, it would be embarrassing for you, because I would have to explain to our friend that you are acting immature and fighting me on this. You don't like me. I get it. This wasn't how I planned to spend my night either. But can you act like a grown-up for once in your life?"

Wow.

What an asshole.

I mean, he's not wrong, but he could work on the delivery.

I stomp my way over to him, leaning into the fact that I'm acting immature, and drop the garbage bags I'm holding at his feet.

"I get the couch," I state, and then turn around and head to the kitchen to look for food.

Simon and I have existed in silence for over an hour now. Normally that wouldn't be a problem, but the tension is getting to me. Simon is sitting in the corner with his laptop working on something while his phone is plugged into his computer charging. I am all too aware that my phone battery is dwindling and there's nothing I can do about it. I am certainly not going to ask if I can charge my phone too. That would only give him a chance to turn me down. The easiest way to avoid being in situations where you are at someone else's mercy is to never give them the opportunity for power over you. I think I read that some European dictator said something similar in a history book once, probably my asshole ex, Jason.

So far, I found some jam and stale crackers left over from summer. It isn't the most nutritious meal I've ever had, but certainly better than nothing. I'm so glad I ate dinner before I left my apartment this evening. I left the food on the counter in the kitchen. I've considered that neutral territory. Simon is staying warm by the stove in the living room, so I'm playing solitaire with a deck of cards on the dining room table. I found some candles and am using them as a light for now, since the batteries were dead in the flashlight I found.

I just can't help thinking about how I imagined this night would go. I planned to gossip with Lillian and Julia, probably flirt a little bit with Dylan, and then kiss a bottle of tequila at midnight. I have a lot of plans for next year, and none of them involve men.

I'm tired of dating.

I have been dating the same six guys for most of my 20s. I turn 28 this year and I've finally admitted to myself that none of them are my future. Finance bro, be gone! I have personal and professional goals that I plan to achieve before 30, and I am tired of silly men who are only concerned with their plans for the weekend.

Jackson has offered me a position as the design lead for the second phase of the Bluefield project, and I plan to take it. The company I work, Industrial Design Co., will send me to an early grave if I let them. It had been my dream to work at Industrial Design Co. for most of my school-age years. I interned there during school and was hired on after finishing my degree. I've been trying to hold on to that dream, but it's time to give it up. If I join Mane Construction, I get creative freedom on all new builds. Everyone has been screened for projects with in-house clients, and the expectations for both sides are agreed upon.

It's my dream job and step one in achieving my goals.

Tonight doesn't have to ruin that. And it won't if I don't let it. I can pivot and start fresh tomorrow.

The sound of Simon closing this laptop catches my attention, and I can't help but eye the charging cable dangling off the side of the table as he unplugs his phone and puts it in his pants pocket. He walks past me, not making eye contact, and heads outside. I think we have enough wood stacked beside the stove to last us all night, but what do I know?

He returns only a couple of minutes later, empty-handed.

"Where did you go?" I ask before my brain has a chance to stop itself from engaging with him.

"I had to go to the bathroom."

"Do you typically avoid modern plumbing?" What a weirdo. Who pees outside in the middle of a snowstorm?

"Aspen." He says my name as if I exhaust him. "We can't use the toilets without power and running water."

Oh no.

"What do you mean?" Even I can hear the fear in my voice. I am not a roughing-it kind of person. I am a cottage or hotel vacationer. You will not catch me in a tent, ever.

"The water is off; the pipes are empty and there is no power to correct either of those things. If you use the toilet, it will be sitting there all night."

He says it all like this is common knowledge and maybe it is, but none of that crossed my mind.

This night is ruined.

Chapter 9

Simon

Four Months Prior (New Year's Eve)

JACKSON:

Be nice

SIMON:

I'm always nice

JACKSON:

Be less you, or something

SIMON:

I'm trying not to be offended by that

A spen has been quiet since I dropped the bomb on her that she wouldn't be able to use indoor plumbing for the remainder of our stay. I probably could have been a bit nicer on the delivery, but my nerves are shot.

I didn't expect to be spending the night alone with Aspen, but if I'm being honest, I'm not upset about it. Aspen intrigues me. She's gorgeous, feisty, brilliant, talented, funny, honest, and so much more. She also hates me.

Why does she hate me?

Well, isn't that the million-dollar question? I have no idea.

The first time we met was in high school. I remember the interaction being civil, flirty even. I had known of her and seen her around at parties. When we finally got a chance to talk to each other, it was great. Every other time after that, she avoided me. At the time, I racked my brain for what I could have done wrong, but I couldn't figure it out. When I graduated, I put all of that behind me and didn't see her again for years. Imagine my surprise when my best friend and cousin began dating her best friend. Now Aspen is everywhere, including haunting my thoughts. This would be great if she did not avoid me every chance she got, and then when I'm unavoidable, she is nothing but hostile.

I've tried to play nice, and I am successful most of the time, but no one knows how to push my buttons the way Aspen does. She was pushing my buttons earlier.

I don't know what delusional world she was living in, thinking I wasn't going to be staying in this cottage with her. I understand she is very close with Lillian's family and has more of a claim over this place than I do, but human decency? Did she really think I was going to freeze to death in my car just because we weren't friends? Delusional.

There's only about an hour until midnight and I can't stand the silence anymore. Aspen hasn't moved from her spot in the dining room, and I feel a bit bad about it. It is a lot warmer in the living room near the stove, but that's where I'm sitting, so of course she won't come near me.

"Aspen?" I look over at her, hoping I get an acknowledgment. When she looks up at me, I continue. "Can we have a truce for tonight? You need to stay warm, it's warmer over here, and we can play cards. Try to make the most of this?" I sit there and wait for her to respond. We sit in a stand-off for a couple of moments before she stands and collects the deck of cards from the table. Before she heads towards me in the living room, she stops in the kitchen and grabs a bottle from the cabinet above the fridge. I scoot off the couch and sit in front of the coffee table with my back resting on the couch behind me while Aspen takes a seat on the other side of the table, closest to the stove. She plants a large bottle of tequila on the table in the middle of us and starts shuffling the cards.

"If we're doing this, I'm going to need a lot of tequila," she says. Aspen flings the lid off the bottle and takes a large pull of the liquor, swallowing without wincing.

I should probably be offended that Aspen thinks she needs to be drunk to be around me, but honestly, something about the way she just chugged the tequila with such confidence has me a bit turned on. I take the bottle from her hand before she can put it down and take a couple of large gulps of the potent liquid. "Game on."

I'm not sure if it's the empty bottle of tequila or how bad Aspen is at Go Fish, but we can't stop laughing. I'll probably skip the gym because my stomach muscles are going to be feeling this tomorrow. The truce is working well and I'm actually enjoying myself. I mean, I'm not that surprised. I've always known Aspen was a fun person to be around. She hasn't shown me that side of her since that night.

I glance at my phone and see that there are only a couple of minutes until midnight. All things considered, there are worse ways to spend New Year's Eve. Sure, it's a bit chilly here, there isn't much to eat, and of course the whole bathroom situation is not ideal, but I've got one of the most beautiful women I've ever met, sitting across from me with a soft smile on her face as our laughter dies off. We already made a trip outside so Aspen could go to the bathroom. She didn't really want me out there with her, but she also didn't want to go alone. I stayed a respectable distance and faced away from her while shining the flashlight on my phone over my shoulder so she could see where she was going. She then instructed me to talk really loudly to myself so I couldn't hear anything. If we aren't bonded after that, there is no hope for us.

"The countdown is almost on," I say, as we finish up our game.

"Oh, is it? My phone died a while ago." She shrugs her shoulders like it's no big deal, but I know Aspen likes being connected to the world. Being without her phone is probably killing her. I grab my laptop that's sitting on the side table with my charging cable dangling from it. I'm very thankful it had a full charge when I got here. I was able to hotspot my phone earlier to check weather reports. Looks like we'll be able to get out of here in the morning.

"Here. Charge your phone." My tone holds more authority than I meant it to. Aspen is so stubborn that she wouldn't even ask to charge her phone and would have just let it stay dead all night. If it was anyone else, I know she would have asked already.

Her cheeks turn the lightest shade of pink as she connects her phone to the charger. "Thanks."

I don't know if I've ever seen Aspen blush before. It's so subtle that if you aren't staring right at her, you would miss it. I'm not sure if the alcohol has enhanced it, or if she's embarrassed for not asking, but it's a cute look on her.

I search my phone for the live stream of Times Square so we can watch the ball drop. I prop it up so it's leaning on the empty bottle of tequila and beckon for Aspen to come and sit beside me. She makes a show of grumbling something I can't hear and very slowly crawling over to me. She can act like being stuck here with me is torture, but I know she's having fun too. As they begin the countdown, I notice Aspen rubbing her hands up and down her arms. Aspen dug through her suitcase earlier but didn't have anything thicker than a plain long-sleeved workout shirt with her and she, of course, refused any of my sweaters. I grab a blanket out of one of the garbage bags sitting near my feet and wrap it around her. As I'm making sure it's secure on her shoulders, I notice how close I am to her. We are practically nose to nose and I can't help but stare into her green eyes.

Just as I'm about to pull away, figuring I've probably creeped her out, she grabs hold of my wrist and keeps me in place. She looks from my eyes to my lips and then back to my eyes again.

"Happy New Year, Simon," she whispers before leaning towards me.

I don't know if it's being trapped here, the tequila, or the tradition of kissing someone at midnight, but I am not taking this chance for granted. I meet her in the middle with the lightest of kisses. Before she can pull away, I take one hand from where it is still holding the blanket and weave my fingers through Aspen's hair on the back of her head. My other hand moves to cup her cheek so I can deepen the kiss. Aspen doesn't put up any sort of fight and leans her body into me, running her hands over my shoulders, down my torso, and back up again. Somewhere behind me, I can hear the cheering coming from my phone as people in New York celebrate, but my brain can only focus on what's happening in front of me, Aspen.

Aspen, Aspen, Aspen. Maybe they're cheering for us?

Suddenly it doesn't feel so cold in here. The heat between our bodies could burn this whole place down. I'm not sure how far we are going to let this go, but the one word that keeps repeating in my brain is more. I need more of her, more of her skin, more of the little noises she makes when I bite down on her lips. More, more, more, more.

I pull away from her lips to see them swollen and red. If the kissing wasn't enough to wake up my cock, it is now rock hard and fighting against the material of my boxers. I grab the hem of her shirt and wait for the nod she gives me, before rolling it up for her stomach and over her head. Her nipples are hard under her sheer bra, and they are begging for my attention. I lower us down so Aspen is lying on her back on the floor while I loom over her. I drop my mouth to her breasts, soaking her nipples through the fabric of her bra. She moans my name and grips the hair on the back of my head, keeping me exactly where I am. No argument from me on this position. I pull the cup down for more access and lap my tongue against her perky pink nipple before pulling her whole breast into my mouth and biting down. That may leave a mark, but based on the noises Aspen is making, I don't think she cares right now. I move my head to her other breast, giving it the same attention, before slowly kissing down her stomach. When I reach the button on her jeans, I start to undo it, but Aspen stops me.

"You don't have to..." she begins.

I stop her before she can continue. "Aspen. I don't have to do anything. I want to do this. No. I need to do this. Is that okay?" She's nodding her head before I've even finished my sentence, so I shove her jeans and panties down in one go.

Fuck.

Her pussy is gorgeous. A tiny strip of hair, pointing towards my prize. Pink swollen lips that are absolutely drenched for me. I know I said there wasn't much food in the cottage. But I'm about to make a meal out of Aspen Arthur.

I drop my face and begin circling her clit with my tongue. I alternate between nibbling, swirling, and sucking, watching her face to see what she likes. The harder I push, the more she quivers. Noted. I add one finger and then another, pumping them in and out as I continue to devour her clit. She's so tight that I have to stretch her to fit a third finger, but I want her full and ready for what comes next.

She grips my hair and starts grinding it against my face.

"That's it. Fuck yourself on my face. Get yourself off." I can feel her walls squeezing around my fingers and I know she's about to come. I pull her clit into my mouth and give it a couple of pulls before I hear Aspen cry out as she comes undone. I ease off the smallest bit, continuing to pump my fingers and lap up her come, as she rides out her orgasm.

I gently kiss back up her body, trying not to miss even an inch of her. When I kiss her neck and behind her ear, Aspen practically purrs. Her orgasm has turned her from a fierce tigress to a cuddly kitten.

When I reach her lips, I hesitate a moment. I know some girls don't like being kissed after a guy has gone down on them, but Aspen doesn't let me hesitate too long. She grabs me by the neck and pulls our lips together. I know she can taste herself on my tongue, but it seems to be turning her on even more. Her hips start to grind against my jean-clad waist as our tongues duel.

Aspen pulls away slightly. "You are wearing far too much clothing." I look down at her. Aspen is completely naked, aside from her bra, which isn't even covering anything.

"Let's fix that," I respond. As I make work of taking off my sweater and undershirt, Aspen undoes my belt and jeans. I lift to slide them off my legs and shuffle my socks off. We may be lost in the moment, but there is no way I'm fucking Aspen with my socks on.

We stare into each other's eyes for a moment, and I think we're both coming to terms with what we are about to do. We've both drunk a fair bit tonight, but neither of us is black-out drunk right now. I would love to say I'm going to take this slow and savour this, but I know once we start, I won't be able to hold back.

Thankfully, my brain has enough blood flowing to it that I think to move us onto the couch. If this is about to be rough, I don't want to be fucking her into the hardwood floor.

Once I have Aspen situated on the couch, with a cushion under her head, I quickly grab a condom out of my wallet. Aspen takes the packet from me, opens it, and rolls the condom onto my stiff cock. She slowly strokes it up and down a couple of times before guiding it between her legs. It's cute that she thinks she's in control right now.

I grab both of her hands and hold them over her head.

"You move these, and you don't get to come."

Aspen's eyes widen a fraction in mock anger, but her cheeks heat, giving her away.

Aspen likes being told what to do.

I dip the tip of my cock into her dripping pussy, sliding it around and then massaging her clit with it. I repeat this a couple of times as Aspen squirms underneath me but keeps her hands above her head.

Good girl.

Aspen whines, "Simon, don't tease me." I chuckle to myself and continue to tease her for another minute. Her face is getting red, and I think she may be able to come from this alone. That's not going to happen though. The next time Aspen comes; it will be around my cock. I don't give her much of a warning before I slam myself into her all the way.

Shit. She's tight, but with how turned on she is, she adjusts quickly.

"Oh my god," Aspen moans.

"Not god, Simon. The only name I want to hear out of your

mouth is mine," I demand.

She nods her head, so I continue.

I grip both of her hips and thrust into her with all my might. Aspen can only grab the armrest of the couch to stop her head from hitting it. A part of me wishes we were in a bed so I could hear the headboard slam against the wall with every thrust.

Aspen hooks her legs around my waist and meets me thrust for thrust. Her boobs are bouncing up and down with our pace and I can't help but drop my head to her chest and feast on them. I'm not sure if Aspen knows it, but she's chanting nonsense between her moans, and it's making me impossibly harder. I grab one of her legs and hook it over my shoulder, allowing me to go even deeper.

"Fuck, it's too much," she cries.

"You can take it. Be a good girl for me and take my cock deep."

"Ahhhh, fuck," she whines, but doesn't stop or slow down our pace. I can tell she's close by how tight she's gripping me all over.

"Good girl," I praise again as I swipe my thumb over her clit only once before she screams and comes all over my cock.

"Oh my, Simon. Fuck." she continues to mumble nonsense as I fuck her through her orgasm.

Her body relaxes slightly, but I'm not done yet. I flip her over so she's on her hands and knees on the couch. I place one foot on the floor to get a better angle and then drive into her. Aspen drops her head but turns her face so she can watch me over her shoulder.

"Fuck, you feel so good."

She moans in response as I drill into her. Her brown hair is splayed all over her back and face, so I can't help but gather it up into my fist and pull her head towards me. Her pussy contracts around me more aggressively, so I know she likes this.

I pull her all the way up to me so her back is against my front and then pull her face to mine. I want to touch her everywhere, but I really want to kiss her too. She meets my level of need, kissing me ferociously as my strokes start to get sloppy. I'm so close, but Aspen is too. I find her clit with my free hand and drum my finger on it until she's crying out again. As soon as she starts to come, it triggers my orgasm, and I feel like I'm coming forever. This has to be the most intense feeling I've ever felt.

"Fuck," I murmur into her neck before pulling out and tying off the condom. Aspen giggles. Giggles! I don't think I've ever heard such a dainty noise come out of her mouth while in my presence. I throw a blanket over Aspen's naked body and then quickly run to dispose of the condom. It's so dark in here now that I trip no less than five times before I'm back in the living room. Aspen opens the blanket for me, so I position myself between her and the couch. I wrap my legs and arms around her, pulling her back as close to my front as I can get her. I nuzzle my face into her hair and neck, dropping light kisses as I hear her breathing even out. It doesn't take long before we are both drifting off into our post-sex haze of dreams.

I wake in the morning to the sound of a snowplow outside. I turn over to pull Aspen into my arms but come up empty.

Not only is Aspen no longer lying beside me. Her spot is cold. I wrap the blanket around my waist. I'll find my sweatpants in a minute. First, I have to find Aspen. I call her name a couple of times but get no answers. When I take a quick look outside, I see that her car is gone, and fresh snow has already covered her tire tracks.

Looks like we've got a runner.

Chapter 10
Simon

SIMON:

Dude

JACKSON:

What??

What???

Answer your phone!

"I'm pregnant."

Aspen is standing in front of me, and I swear she just said she was pregnant.

"Pardon?" There's no way I heard her right. I must be in shock. I didn't even think Aspen knew where I lived and yet she's standing in front of me right now. *Pregnant?*

"I'm pregnant," she repeats. I choke on the air I was about to inhale and cough a little.

Holy shit. Aspen is pregnant.

I need to call my mom.

She takes my momentary lapse in brain function as an opportunity to push past me, through the door, and into my condo. That's probably a smart move. I don't know what's going on, but it's not something my neighbours should have the opportunity to witness.

Aspen is pregnant. I don't know if I want to cry, scream, or puke. My stomach feels like it's made of cement. Remembering to breathe is suddenly something I feel like I should be conscious of. Passing out right now would do me zero favours and probably freak Aspen out. I need to be thinking about her. This is probably way more terrifying for Aspen. It's her body, after all.

I've always wanted to have children, but in my mind, this is something you plan, and the mother of your children doesn't hate you. *What am I going to do?* I'm going to step up and be the best dad there ever was, aside from my dad. Okay. I can handle this. I just need to ask Aspen a million questions first.

"How?"

"Uhh...I'm assuming the condom broke? I'm pretty certain there was a condom involved."

"Yeah, there was," I say. "I always have one in my wallet, and it was gone the next day... I'm clean, anyway. But yeah, we used a condom. I remember throwing it out."

"Me too," she offers awkwardly. "Clean, I mean. I'm not on birth control so, the condom must have broken." I feel like we're both just saying the same thing. The condom broke.

The condom broke. The condom broke. Pregnant. I'm going to be a dad.

"I'm going to be a dad."

"I mean, if you want to?" she says quietly, but I take a step back like I've been slapped.

"What do you mean, if I want to? The condom broke. You're pregnant. I'm going to be a dad." It took both of us to make this kid. I'm going to do my part in raising it.

"Well, we didn't plan this. Obviously. If you don't want to be involved, you don't have to be..." Aspen is so hard to read, she's always been hard to read. I can't tell if she's being polite and giving me the out, which I don't want. Or if she doesn't want me to be a part of this. It's always her way or the highway and that is not happening here.

"I want this baby. My baby. Our Baby. I AM going to be a dad." My voice comes out with more force than I intend, but I don't want her to doubt my position on any of this.

"OK," she says back matching my volume level. "Okay, you're going to be a dad." There's a small smile on her face now, but she turns away from me to hide it. It gives me a small amount of comfort that maybe she does want me involved.

"So what's next?" I only have an older sister; I have no idea how pregnancy or any of this works. I've never been around someone who is pregnant.

"I'm already in my second trimester. I didn't have many symptoms during the first, that's why I didn't realize I was pregnant. I should have already had a couple of appointments with the obstetrician, but I've only seen my family doctor so far for a blood test to confirm... I actually have an appointment next week for an ultrasound...we could find out its gender."

"Don't call it an it," I say without thinking. I just called it an it. I think I'm losing it. Aspen rolls her eyes but doesn't give my demands a response. I deserve that.

Wow. The second trimester seems like a big deal. I am going to have a lot of googling to do tonight. I feel like I'm already behind, or like I missed part of the parent course and am expected to take a quiz tomorrow. I don't really know what I'm supposed to do here, but I think the best thing to start with is just showing up. For this baby. For Aspen.

"I'll be there. Tell me the time and place. I'll be there."

"Are you sure?" Aspen blinks her eyes a couple of times and I think she's fighting off tears. One sneaks past her defences, and it takes everything in me not to teach to her and wipe it off her cheek. Aspen does not seem like the type of person who cries very often. We haven't spent a whole lot of time together, but I've never seen her show any emotion like this. I don't know if it's the hormones, or that she stuck with me for the next 18+ years, but I can tell her emotions are getting to her.

"I'll be there," I tell her again. And then I do something I know she will hate. I pull her into a hug.

Aspen and I are having a baby together, and we are just now sharing our first hug. We're doing this all backwards.

She softens against me for only a moment before pulling away and wiping below her eyes. She clears her throat and makes her way towards my kitchen, ending the moment.

"You can tell Jackson," she blurts out suddenly. "Lillian knows I'm pregnant, but I didn't tell her who the dad was because I wanted you to be the one to tell Jackson. Since he's your cousin and all."

"I really appreciate that, Aspen. Thank you."

I have no idea how that conversation is going to go down or how our friends are going to react. Jackson will probably laugh, think I'm joking, and then laugh some more. Lillian will be excited, I think. Dylan will be right along with Jackson, laughing. And Ben will probably try to fight me. I've basically knocked up his sister. We are friends and all, but I think this might be against some sort of bro code.

"Can I tell my family, too? Is it safe to at this point? That's a thing, right?"

"Um, technically yes. But can you wait until after the appointment? I want to hear the heartbeat before anyone starts freaking out. I think that's normal."

"If that's normal, then sure. I'm good with that."

"Don't quote me on that! I don't know nearly as much as I probably should about this. I'm hoping the doctor sends us home with reading material or something."

"Okay, yeah." The second Aspen leaves, I'm ordering every book ever written about pregnancy, parenting, and babies. If Aspen needs me to be an expert on things, I will be.

"So, this is your place?" She asks while shuffling through my cabinets and finding herself a glass.

Seeing Aspen in my space is wild. Something I never thought would happen, but I don' hate it. My hardly decorated apartment suddenly seems brighter. There's more life here now, and I know it's all Aspen. No wonder Jackson wanted her at Mane Construction; all she has to do is walk into a room and it looks award winning. Although right now I don't even know what colour my walls are. I can describe in perfect detail the caramel flecks in Aspen's brown eyes though.

I take the glass from her hand before she can make her next move and fill it with filtered water from the fridge. "Thanks," she mumbles when I hand it back to her.

"Yeah, I just moved here a couple of weeks ago. Since Jackson sold his unit in the building, I bought one closer to Wildflower's place."

Jackson used to have a condo a couple of floors below me. It was like having a roommate without actually having one. We would meet up at least a couple of times a week to watch sports or have dinner together. Since we bought a place in Bluefield, he is hardly in the city anymore. When he is, they stay at Lillian's condo, which is in a quieter neighbourhood than we were. Even though they aren't there that often, I wanted the option of being close to them when they are. The place is on the neutral side. This building is brand new, so I have all the high-end appliances that I don't use. Light grey wood floors, white cabinets, and countertops, and grey and blue accents in my furniture and decor. It's kind of depressing now that I look at it. Aspen is the only thing exuding warmth in the whole place with her thick cobalt blue knit sweater and puffy coat. I haven't done much to make the place feel like home. I haven't even had anyone over yet.

"So, how was poker night?" she asks.

"Are we really making small talk right now? Are you going to comment on the weather next?"

"I don't know Simon. This is uncharted territory. What do

you want from me?" she seethes. Looks like we've moved on from tears to anger. Noted.

I can tell she's freaking out. I'm freaking out. If small talk is what she wants, she just unknowingly asked a loaded question and isn't going to get a light and fluffy answer.

"Poker night was pretty heavy, actually. We didn't play any poker."

Just as expected, Aspen wasn't prepared for my answer. She probably assumes we just bro out all night and talk about sports and women. I'm not going to lie that happens sometimes, but poker night is more of an excuse to talk about what's going on in our lives and support each other. That may sound soft, but I don't care. I grew up with an older sister. I know how to talk about my feelings.

Aspen doesn't say anything, so I continue. "Dylan is dealing with another missing persons case in Bluefield." Something he hasn't had to do much of, aside from the incident with Lillian last summer and one earlier this year. "They aren't sure how long she's been missing for, but her friends thought she was going on a trip to Europe to find herself. Apparently, no one has seen her for over a month. When they searched her house, her suitcases were by the door, packed and ready to go. It looks as though she never left the country." I get a chill just thinking about it. It could be something non-sinister that happened, but Dylan is very concerned and stressed. Normally he tries to keep us out of police business, but it is all weighing too heavy on him and he needed to let it out.

"Oh my god," Aspen gasps. "Why haven't we heard anything about this? Billy hasn't mentioned anything!"

"The news will break tomorrow. It will be on every news station in the country by the time we wake up. Since this is the second missing person in a couple of months, they don't think the New Year's Eve case was a one off. There's talk of this being a serial situation." That's also why Dylan wanted to tell us. With Lillian and Jackson living in Bluefield, practically full time, this is very close to home for them. He wanted to make sure he could give Jackson the facts before the gossip mill in town went wild with the story.

"Wow..." Aspen starts, seemingly at a loss for words. She looks away, blinking rapidly, and I'm suddenly terrified she might start crying when she adds, "That is crazy. That's something I would expect to hear about happening here in Toronto, not our precious Bluefield."

"Agreed," is all I can manage as I mentally wrestle with the urge to comfort her. How, I'm not sure, but it's clear she needs it. We both do.

We are both quiet for a moment, letting the heaviness of the conversation settle on us. I'm trying to figure out how to lighten the mood when a thought pops into my head.

"How do you know where I live?"

She diverts her eyes to the ground and mumbles something.

"What was that?" I ask.

She mumbles again, so I take a couple of steps towards her.

"Okay, okay, personal space buddy." She raises her hands to her chest, gesturing to me to keep back. "I followed you."

"What do you mean by that? Followed me how?"

"I knew you would be at Ben's tonight. I followed you here." She looks away, seemingly embarrassed by her admission. I'm not sure why. That sounds like exactly something she would do instead of just asking Jackson, Lillian, or Ben where I live. Hell, even Dylan and Julia know my new address.

"You followed me all the way here?" I ask, just to make sure I understand this exactly.

"Yes, okay. You walk pretty slow."

"I don't think I do, but that's beside the point. It's dark and late. You should have said something. I don't like the idea of you walking alone at night."

Aspen's face drops and she glares at me. I said something wrong.

"Let's get a couple of things straight. Right now." She pokes her manicured finger into my chest. "You do not tell me what I can and can't do. You will never tell me what I can and can't do. When this baby is born, we will have a democracy. But until then, keep your opinions to yourself." She pokes my chest once more for good measure and then takes a step away from me.

I take one step towards her and bend so we are at eye level. "If we're voicing our opinions and demands right now, I have a couple too. You, Aspen, are growing my child inside of you right now, and I will be forever in debt to you for that. I care about you. I care about our baby. I will tell you when I have concerns because I care. I am not trying to take away your independence or tell you what you can and can't do. But I will do everything in my power to keep you as safe as possible for the rest of your life."

"For the rest of my pregnancy, you mean?" she whispers.

"No. For the rest of your life," I reiterate. I don't know if it's arguing or how vulnerable she looks right now, but I drop my head to hers and kiss her before I can stop myself. She kisses me back for a moment before planting her hands on my chest and pushing me away.

"What are you doing? We are not going to be doing any of that ever again. Okay?"

Um, not okay. I would like to do a lot more of that, among other things.

"Why? You're already pregnant. It's not like I can knock you up twice!"

"You're on my shit list, Simon." Her tone is cold and harsh. A mask of indifference covers her face, and I hate it.

"Was I not already on it?" I ask.

"No. I can be much colder to you if I want to." And with that, she storms past me and out my front door before I can even know what just happened.

If how she was acting toward me before wasn't because I was on her shit list, I have no idea what I'm in for. All I know is I need to get off that list, and fast. We're having a baby together and I won't let that child see anything but us having the utmost respect for each other. I guess I need to earn their mother's first.

I give Aspen a three-minute head start before grabbing my keys and running down eleven flights of stairs. I don't need a coat; I'm not leaving the building. By the time I get to the lobby, it feels like I'm breathing through a straw. I need to add more cardio to my exercise regime.

I stand behind a pillar with a view of the front door. The security guard gives me a strange look until he sees what I'm watching. Aspen stands just outside the front doors, looking from her phone to the street several times until a large SUV pulls up to the curb with a female driver behind the wheel.

Good girl, Aspen.

I wait in my hidden spot until I see the car door close and pull back onto the street before making my way to the elevator.

Aspen may not know it or agree with it, but she's mine now. Looks like I'm getting a second chance. It may not be how I envisioned my year going, but this is the best change of plans I could have asked for.

Chapter 11
Aspen

W as stalking my baby daddy and showing up at his house unannounced to drop the bomb that we are having a baby together the appropriate way to handle things?

Not likely.

But neither is getting knocked up by someone you can't stand. And yet, here I am. Aside from New Year's Eve, when our little problem was created, telling Simon I was pregnant was probably the longest conversation we have ever had. I'm having a baby with a man I've only been alone with three times. Great.

I can't lie and say I'm not relieved that he wants to be a part of our baby's life. I can confidently say I could raise this child on my own and do a very good job. I've always wanted to have kids and both men and women raise them on their own every day. With that being said, I would never want to keep my baby away from a willing father.

I may not be very close with Simon, but he is Jackson's best friend and cousin, and I know Jackson very well. There is no way they could be as close as they are without Simon being a good person, deep, deep down.

But it doesn't mean I have to like him. Tolerate? Yes. Be civil towards? I guess.

I just have to remind myself that this is all for my baby. Our baby.

Eighteen years isn't that long, right?

Maybe it's for the best if I don't think that long term for now. Right now, I need to focus on my first ultrasound next week, catching up on all the things I should have already been doing for this pregnancy, and moving to Bluefield.

Based on the conception date and my last period, my doctor said I am due at the end of September/early October. The ultrasound measurements should be able to give a more specific date. The timeline is not the most ideal, but it could be worse. Jackson expects me to be in Bluefield and settled by the end of the month and to stay there until around Thanksgiving in October. I may have to cut out a bit early. Thank god firing someone because they are pregnant is not only frowned upon but also against a bunch of labour and employment laws. Not that I think Jackson would try to fire me. Lillian would skin him alive if he tried.

Speaking of my best friend, I'm expecting a call from her any minute now. When I told Simon he could tell Jackson about me being pregnant and him being the father, it wasn't for purely unselfish reasons. I know the second Simon tells Jackson, Jackson will turn around and ask Lillian if she knew about it. Essentially, I'm letting Jackson break the news that Simon is the father of my baby.

It's not that I think she will react poorly. I just don't think I would be able to get the words out of my mouth. I'm hoping that this spreads like controlled gossip among our friends and I can avoid being present for any big reveals. Just something I planted and can watch spread from afar. Now, if anyone questions me on it, or tries to get juicy details, they will be stopped in their tracks. This isn't some nefarious scandal. It's two people having a child together and I won't allow anyone to make jokes or speak ill of my child, even if they haven't been born yet. I may be the life of the party, and a social butterfly at times, but I am a private person. So much is about to change, and I know I need to maintain my privacy more than ever.

I figured that Simon would wait until this morning to tell Jackson, so the fact that it's almost lunchtime and I haven't heard from Lillian is a bit worrisome. I've tried to keep busy by packing the clothes and any essentials I want to bring to Bluefield, but my mind won't quiet. Normally, I would get a quick kickboxing session in, but my energy level is almost nonexistent today. When I spoke with my doctor about my exercise routine, she said to listen to my body and not to push myself too hard.

Instead of staring at my phone for an hour while I binge-watch some show I don't care about and stuff my face with popcorn, I decide to practise yoga. I got my instructor certification in Peru a couple of years ago, but I rarely teach. I mostly did it to prove to myself that I could and so I could understand the principles at a higher level. I spent so many years of my life trying to make my parents proud. It's something that is for me and me alone. I remember standing on a mountain, looking out at the clear sky and feeling like truly myself. Just me doing something for me. The calm and introspectiveness clear all the outside noise and allow me to breathe.

Just as I roll my mat out in the middle of my living room, someone bangs at the front door with a heavy fist. I didn't buzz anyone up and there is only one other person with a fob to get into the building.

I guess I should have expected this.

I stand frozen on my mat as the sound of a key turning in the lock rings out throughout my apartment. The door flies open and a sweaty, red-faced Lillian Shaw storms towards me.

She didn't call or text when she found out. She drove two hours to me instead.

"IS IT TRUE? SIMON?" she yells as she reaches me in the living room. I shrug my shoulders and nod. It's not like I can lie and say they are pulling some prank on her.

"Simon?" she asks again, grabbing me by the shoulders and shaking.

Lillian is a couple of inches shorter than me, but she makes up for it with the height of her hair. Right now, I'm making eye contact with her wild blonde curls that are piled on top of her head in a very large, messy bun. If she didn't look like she was about to cry, I would laugh.

I grab her hand and drag her with me over to the section couch against the wall. I'm not doing yoga now and I would rather have this conversation sitting down. She stares at me expectantly and I realize I haven't said a single word since she stepped foot in my apartment.

"Simon is the father," I state in a calm tone. I may be the dramatic one in our friendship, but Lillian is more outwardly emotional than I am.

"Oh my god. How? When? Where?" she stands again and opens the nearest window for fresh air. "I think I'm having a hot flash."

"Hey, I'm the pregnant one, not you. Stop stealing my symptoms," I try to joke, but based on the look on Lillian's face, it falls flat. She comes back to the couch, sitting as close to me as she can, and grabs both of my hands.

"Are you 100% sure it's Simon's?"

If anyone else asked me that question, I would be offended. I may be a flirt, but I stay away from casual hookups. Lillian is probably concerned that I have been seeing one of my many loser ex-boyfriends again. I don't blame her. I was stuck in a cycle of recycling my boyfriends and hoping for better results. When I ended things with my most recent ex, John, last summer, I quit them cold turkey. I was abstinent for almost six months before my night with Simon and haven't been with anyone since.

"1000% sure," I answer.

"Okay. So, let's go back to my other questions. How? When? Where?"

I duck my head slightly before answering. I've avoided talking about what I did stuck in her cottage with Simon all night up to this point and I guess Simon kept his mouth shut too.

"New Year's Eve, your cottage. Too much tequila and a broken condom."

"You told me you two barely said anything to each other. How does that lead to unprotected sex?"

"Protected sex," I correct. "The condom broke, but it was too dark for either of us to notice."

"That is beside the point, Aspen. You had sex with Simon. Someone who you claim to hate and avoid any chance you get. How does that even happen?"

"I don't even know how to explain it. There was a truce and lots of tequila. We were laughing. It was midnight and then suddenly all our clothes were off. I honestly planned to put it in the back of my mind and never tell anyone about it. When I woke up the next morning, I left without a word and carried on with my life."

"Until you learned you were pregnant," she finishes for me.

"Yeah," I say, my voice full of emotions. I'm not sure why this is all making me so emotional, stupid hormones, but I can feel extra moisture forming around my eyes. I will not cry about this. I won't.

"Oh, Aspen." Lillian pulls me into her arms in a comforting hug. I'm not sure if it was the way she was raised or if it's some sort of genetic trait, but the entire Shaw family gives the best hugs. They pull you close and squeeze just the right amount.

"I'm okay," I say, as I wipe a single stray tear on her sweater-covered shoulder.

"This makes me a double aunty!" she exclaims. "Cause I'm an aunt on your side and his side."

It doesn't, but I get her logic. At least she's excited about it. A part of me was worried she was going to lecture me or something. About what? I don't know. Lillian has never lectured me in her life, but we are in uncharted territory now.

"What was Jackson's reaction when Simon told him?"

"First off, did you do that on purpose? You had to know Jackson would tell me." I can't help but laugh. She knows me well. "Okay, that tells me I'm right. You brat. Jackson was shocked. He was mad I didn't tell him you were pregnant for all of five seconds, and then he drilled Simon with a million questions. He had him on speakerphone while we packed up and got in the car. Jackson's with Simon now."

Shit. Simon seemed shocked last night, but relatively calm, all things considered. If Jackson's reaction was to pack up and drive all the way to the city, Simon must not be handling it as well as I thought he was. I try to remember that I've known about this longer than he has and have had more time to accept our fate. Everyone else is still catching up to me.

"Simon probably hates me even more now. I ruined his life."

"One, he doesn't hate you, he never has," Lillian says. "It's not like you were ready for this either."

"That's not entirely true," I confess. "I was actually starting to think about starting a family on my own. I went off birth control after I broke up with John and was going to see a fertility specialist next month to talk about freezing my eggs and what my options were. I didn't want to be waiting years for Mr. Right to come along and make my dreams come true. I was taking action. This is not how I planned on this going, but this is something I want."

I haven't told anyone this before. Aside from my doctor, I kept this close to my heart in case things didn't work out. I also didn't want the judgement that can come with choosing to be a single parent. Some people out there can be cruel, and with something as important to me as this, I wasn't ready for criticism.

"Well, if you're happy, then I'm happy. I mean, I would be happy no matter what because I love babies and you and Simon have excellent genetics, so this one is going to be smart and stunning. But I'm happy you are achieving your dream. Even if this isn't how you planned to get there."

God, Lillian really is the best. Even when I couldn't convince Lillian to take part in my hair brain schemes growing up, she always supported me. Did Lillian want to be part of the student council and run for president in high school? No. Did she stay up late every night for two weeks making handmade posters and driving me around the city filming videos for my campaign? Yes.

Everyone needs a Lillian Shaw in their corner.

I take a deep breath and then release it, trying to release all the built-up stress in my body. "Could you tell how Simon is handling it based on his phone call? I contemplated checking in with him, but I don't have his phone number."

"Aspen! You are in group messages with him! Save his phone number." Yeah, that was mostly a lie. I did think about checking in, but what would I even say? I don't technically have his number saved in my phone, so I allowed myself to use that as a lame excuse. "He's a good guy, Aspen. As far as unplanned baby daddies go, I think you ended up with a good one. You were meant to be an amazing mother, and he will be a great dad."

"I know. I just don't trust him." I made rules for a reason. This was supposed to be my year. It's still going to be my year, just a bit different. But that doesn't mean we are throwing caution to the wind. Simon can be my baby daddy and public enemy number one. If anyone can figure out how to accomplish that, it's me. New Year's Eve was a blip on the radar, that has turned into a bump on my body. That doesn't change my feelings toward Simon.

"Well, you better learn to. Raising a kid together definitely requires a lot of trust. Anyway, Simon seems a bit overwhelmed, but also excited. He said the words 'I'm going to be a dad,' no less than ten times and sounded more and more excited each time."

Is she trying to make me cry? I'm supposed to hate the guy. Right now, I want to cry because he's cute and excited about becoming a dad. These emotions don't feel like hate at all. Lillian breaks my train of thought. Thank god.

"You're stuck with me for the weekend now. This is pay back for you showing up at the cottage whenever you want."

"You love it when I do that," I argue.

"You better love that I'm here to support you in your time of need." Lillian just barely holds in her laughter as she says it. I grab a red throw cushion from behind me and throw it at her. She dodges it at the last minute and breaks out into the giggles. Jackson once accidentally told me that Lillian gets the giggles after they have sex. He made sure to reiterate that he loves that about her and thinks it's cute. If I wasn't such a good friend, I would bring that up right now just to make her stop laughing at me. Unfortunately, I am a good friend so I will save her the embarrassment, for now.

After snoozing through most of the movie Lillian put on, we decide we should probably just head to bed. Since I love to snuggle, Lillian knows not to even try sleeping on the couch. She's stuck with my flailing limbs all night.

Right before I'm about to drift off to sleep, Lillian gasps from beside me. "Did you see the news? I can't believe I forgot to ask you until now. Jackson came to bed after poker night so upset about everything, he's joined the volunteer search force and offering pay for any Mane Construction employees who want to help outside of working hours." Of course, Jackson is. That man is good to his core.

"Simon actually told me last night. I cancelled three Ubers until I got a woman driver on my way home last night because I got freaked out the second I stepped outside of Simon's building." Just thinking about the press conference I watched this morning prompts me to snuggle closer to Lillian. Dylan was standing beside an investigator who was speaking at the podium. His normally flush, but stoic face looked paler than normal, and I could see the depressions under his eyes from lack of sleep. I wanted to pull him through my screen and give him a hug. From the sounds of it, they don't have a lot of leads and are just asking people with any information to come forward.

So sad and scary.

"What was it like in Bluefield today?" I ask.

"We left first thing this morning, so we didn't get the full picture, but there seemed to be a lot of people milling about, gossiping on Main Street or hiding in their houses and peeking through the windows. We stopped by to see Julia this morning and see if she wanted to come into the city with us to avoid being alone, but she wanted to check over all the security footage she has for the store."

"So people are either scared or trying to help?" I ask.

"Mostly. It's all so surreal though. I know this happens far more often than we think, and I didn't know Stacy personally, but it's Bluefield. Bad things shouldn't happen there. And now there's two missing women?"

"I agree. Is it weird that I'm glad to be moving there soon?"

"You've always been a bit twisted, so not really."

I scoff in offense. Not that she's not entirely correct. I know for a fact that true crime drama is a lot more popular than people think. So what if I exclusively listen to unsolved murder podcasts regularly? If people didn't like it, they wouldn't make them. But that's not why I'm excited to be in Bluefield.

"I'm sure it's a one-off and they will find Stacy happily shacking up with some hot European man any day now, but if that isn't the case, I don't want to be all the way in Toronto while you and Julia are in Bluefield. I would be so paranoid."

"Aspen, my forever protector," Lillian mumbles as her eyes drift closed.

She's not wrong. I'm very protective of those I care about. As easy going as I seem on the outside, I'm not to be messed with.

Chapter 12

Simon

JACKSON:

I'm here for you. No matter what. Call anytime.

SIMON:

Love ya

JACKSON:

Right back atcha

Was I surprised that Jackson showed up at my door only two hours after I dropped the bomb on him that not only is Aspen pregnant, but it's my baby? Not even a little bit. If there's one person in my life that I know I can always count on, it's Jackson. I mean, my parents and older sister, Claire, are great. But the bond Jackson and I share is on another level. Being cousins and best friends, plus the same age, he's practically my fraternal twin at this point.

After Aspen left my apartment, I put my credit cards to good use and bought every book I could find on the internet about babies, parenting, and pregnancy. Those are set to arrive any day now and I can't wait to dig in. I fell asleep on my couch with my phone in my hand mid shopping spree and when I woke up, the first thing I did was call Jackson. He was shocked, for sure. I can't remember what I even said to him, or if I made any sense, but thankfully, when he showed up at my condo, I was able to explain everything properly.

Jackson offered me his complete support as my best friend, cousin and soon-to-be business associate. I don't even know what type of support I need right now. I could probably use some alcohol. Aspen doesn't know it yet, but I've decided I won't be drinking for the duration of her pregnancy for solidarity. I'm not sure if she will be charmed or annoyed by this, but it feels like the right thing to do. There was one thing I did get his help with though. There's a property in Bluefield I need him to scope out as soon as possible. I have a place to stay lined up, but I want something different given everything I know now.

"I guess it's a good thing we will both be in Bluefield this summer," I say to Jackson when there's a lull in conversation. Phase two of Jackson's Bluefield project involves a new subdivision in town. Last summer, he was in charge of phase one, which involved buying cottages in disarray, tearing them down, and then building much larger structures in their place. He had a waiting list a mile long for city slickers looking for a quiet place to get away to in the summer. After a series of terrible events, he somehow found himself the proud owner of one of those properties, next door to Lillian's family cottage. While there, he fell in love with not only Lillian but Bluefield and its residents. He was able to work with the town council to get approval for a new project, phase two, where he will build a variety of properties, from a small retirement home, to townhouses, condos and single-family homes. The hope is that this will provide housing for young families wanting to stay, or move to Bluefield, as well as potential income properties for locals.

As a Real Estate Agent, I will be in charge of the selling of the properties as well as management of the ones the two of us will be keeping as our own rental unit. For this to really help the community, we want to ensure they have housing available for longer-term lease or rental. The last thing Bluefield needs is a whole neighbourhood with only short-term rentals, while those who have lived there their whole lives struggle to find housing.

"Yeah, about that," Jackson begins. "I may have not mentioned to Aspen that you were coming on board the Bluefield project and would be there with us."

What?

When Jackson approached me about this opportunity, he told me upfront that he had a job offer out to Aspen. She's incredibly talented, so I thought it was a great idea. Clearly, my being involved may have been a deterrent for her, so no one told her.

"You didn't tell her?" I ask, to confirm my suspicion. Jackson drags his hand down the front of his face and then shakes his head.

"Honestly, I offered you both positions at the same time. You knew I was having issues with our designers, so mentioning

Aspen was hopefully a selling point to get you on board. I didn't not tell her on purpose. It didn't come up at first and I've been busy and sort of forgot." I can tell by his body language and tone that he's being honest. My relationship with Aspen isn't something I want our friends to worry about and as far as a working relationship, I know we can both be professional.

"Well, maybe this will be a good surprise now?" I offer. I don't know how she's going to react. She could be relieved. She also could be angry. This is between her and Jackson, and probably Lillian, so I will stay out of it.

"We'll see about that. I can't even buy her a nice bottle of wine to soften the blow. You and your super sperm had to ruin that," he jokes.

Aspen texted me the address for her doctor's appointment last night. I've been sitting in the waiting room on the sixth floor of the hospital for almost an hour at this point. The appointment isn't until 11:00 am, but I may have gotten here at 9:30am, just to be on the safe side.

I wasn't sure about parking, or if I would get lost once I was here. The last thing I would want to be is late, so early is fine with me. I brought my tablet with me so at least I can get some work done in the quiet of the waiting room.

I'm trying to close any open clients I have before I head to Bluefield. Being an independent contractor out of the broker-age I work for means that leaving wasn't that big of a deal. I simply need to hand off the clients I have to someone else. When we wrap up in Bluefield, I can return again, but I will be starting at zero. Not a problem for me. More like a challenge. And I love challenges.

Speaking of which, a body flops down next to me as I finish up an email to a listing agent I've been working on closing a deal with. I know it's Aspen without even looking at her.

Her scent sticks out to me in any room she's in. Aspen smells like citrus—grapefruit, I think. There's something floral too, but it's not a traditional feminine scent like rose or lily. No, it's more invigorating. Eucalyptus. That's it. The two scents are battling each other, each dominant in their own right, but together they are like a shot of espresso. It makes me feel alive. Or maybe that's just Aspen. I can't help but feel like I'm about to take off and conquer the world while in her presence. And as I sit here with her and wait to see my baby for the first time, I'm feeling on top of the world.

"Did you check in at the desk?" I ask after a moment of neither of us saying anything. I was too busy working to see her come in. Something I need to make sure I don't do around her from now on. I don't want Aspen to think our baby isn't my top priority.

"Yes," she snaps. I guess the excitement I'm feeling is not present for Aspen.

"Did you have any trouble finding parking?" I'm trying my best to make conversation so we don't sit here in silence for the next twenty minutes, but she isn't giving me much to work with.

"No."

Ooookay. I am not getting anywhere with these questions. "I've been here for over an hour. I didn't want to be late." The second the words are out of my mouth; I wish I could take them back. I was hoping for a laugh or something. I'm not sure why though. I sound like a bragging ass.

Aspen turns to me suddenly with fire in her green eyes. "Sorry, I was too busy vomiting up my breakfast to get here so early. It must be nice to not feel nauseous all hours of the day."

Shit.

I know I shouldn't try to wind Aspen up, but it's fun and normally the only way I can get for her to talk to me. This time it wasn't intentional though.

"Has that been happening a lot?" I ask, trying to keep my tone light and warm.

She nods her head but turns away from me. The slight hiccup of breath is the only thing that gives her true feelings away. Aspen is crying. Something I have never seen before in my life. I don't want to make a big deal out of it because she clearly doesn't want me to see her tears, but my body is humming with the need to hold her, as my brain screams "fix, fix, fix," at me. I try not to overthink it and instead grab her hands that she has clutched in her lap and bring them over to my leg closest to her. Holding them there as a form of comfort.

At first, Aspen's entire body is completely still and I'm sure she's going to pull away. Shockingly, after a moment, she relaxes back into the hard plastic chair and lets me hold her hand in silence while we wait to be called.

A nurse directs us to a small room with a desk and computer, an examination table and a chair. Aspen tries to pull her hands out of my hold multiple times while we wait for the doctor to come meet us. I gave up one of her hands so she could situate herself on the table, but I am not letting go of the other. I don't know the next time Aspen will let me touch her like this, and I want to make sure I'm close if her emotions get to her again.

Aspen has been silent, aside from answering the nurse's questions. I can't figure out how to break the silence because I'm scared I'll make her cry again. Just as I'm about to bring up all the baby and parenting books that have started to arrive at my place, the doctor walks in.

She has a cart behind her that holds what I am assuming is the ultrasound machine. After making introductions, Aspen lays down on the table and lifts her sweater.

"The gel is a little cold," the doctor warns before squeezing the bottle over Aspen's belly. I can see her stomach immediately break out in goosebumps and I try not to think about the last time I saw her skin like that.

Is it inappropriate to think about the conception of your child moments before hearing their heartbeat for the first time?

Probably, but here we are.

We sit in silence at first as the doctor clicks away at the computer. She said she would take measurements and check that everything was looking okay before moving the screen so we could see and hear the heartbeat. I'm trying to keep my focus on Aspen, holding her hand and mindlessly stroking her arm, which I'm surprised she's letting me do. But the look on the doctor's face has me on edge. She doesn't look worried, which I guess is good. She kind of looks amused. She clears her throat and then turns the ultrasound screen towards us. I have no idea what I'm looking at, but it resembles what I saw when I was looking at Google last night.

The doctor looks to us and says, "Well, Aspen, based on measurements you are at the 18-week mark, so your due date is tracking for September 29th. With that being said, we should expect an earlier delivery than that."

"Why?" Aspen asks immediately, reading my mind. An early delivery makes me think something is wrong.

"Is something wrong with our baby?" I ask before the doctor can answer Aspen.

"Sorry," she begins, and my stomach drops. I drop my head to Aspen's shoulder and try to school my emotions. "No, no, no, everything is okay!" she continues. Both Aspen and I whip our heads back in her direction.

"Our baby is okay?" Aspen asks, and I can tell by her voice she's fighting back tears again.

"Yes, sorry, I was apologizing for worrying you. Why don't I start again, and I will get all the information out in one go so you two don't worry further." She looks to each of us, waiting for our okay to continue. I squeeze Aspen's hand, and she squeezes back and then we both nod our heads. "Everything is healthy. I don't see any areas of concern, and in a moment, I will let you hear the heartbeat. Or heartbeats, I should say. You are pregnant with twins."

Chapter 13

Aspen

ASPEN:

> I need tequila

JULIA:

> I don't think that's recommended

LILLIAN:

> I think it's widely frowned upon

ASPEN:

> Drink tequila for me!!!!

"**Y**ou are pregnant with twins."

I must be dreaming.

Or having a nightmare.

I'm have not one, but two babies with Simon Cadwell. What sort of whack karma do I have? Should I have my aura read? Or my chakras aligned or something? Because I don't think I can take any more surprises this year. I've hit my quota. I am done.

You hear that mother nature? I'm done.

Twins.

Two babies.

Woah.

A voice pulls me out of my spiral. "Ms. Arthur? Are you okay?"

I look up to see both Simon and the doctor staring at me with concerned looks on their faces. I have no idea how long I was in my own head for or if I missed important information.

"What?" I ask.

"Are you okay?" Simon asks as he tucks a loose piece of hair behind my ear and cups my face. There's a part of my brain that's screaming "swat him away, make him stop touching you," but I can't seem to get my body to carry out the demands.

I wish I could because I have let Simon touch me a lot today. Way more than I should, for sure. I am a strong, independent woman who can have twins on her own. I don't need some man comforting me. I should make him stop.

But I can't.

"I'm okay," I finally reply. "Twins? As in two babies? Inside of me?"

"Yes," the doctor says with a smile. Maybe she's used to rocking people's entire worlds in these appointments, but I'm internally and externally freaking out right now and her being so even keeled is more annoying than calming right now. I look to Simon for his reaction. If you didn't know him, you would think he's calm, cool and collected, but as someone who takes great pleasure in cracking his whole facade, I can see more.

His left eye is trying to twitch, but he's fighting it. His skin, that somehow always looks like he has a light tan all year, now has a green undertone to it and the hand holding mine is clammy.

For some reason, Simon freaking out internally makes me calm. I should probably see a therapist considering I'm enjoying his distress, but I have bigger things to worry about right now.

Clearly, the doctor has no idea that the two of us are freaking out because she carries on with the appointment. Suddenly, a muffled heartbeat fills the room.

"That is Twin A."

A pause and then a mirrored heart rate begins.

"And Twin B."

"Oh. Oh, my," I mumble out. "Our babies." My voice cracks on the last word as a stream of tears slide down my cheeks and soak into my hair.

This is really happening. I'm going to be a mother. Those are my children's heartbeats. I'm growing humans inside me. Right now, there are tiny beings growing and one day they will join the world as very real people.

Woah.

This is a dream come true.

I'm about to ask if I can record their heart beats, because I would like to fall asleep to the sounds of them every night when suddenly my mouth is blocked by hair. Simon's hair.

Simon has his head wedged into my suddenly very wet neck.

Oh, my god.

Simon is crying into my neck.

I would love to say this has no effect on me, but that would be a lie. I'm going to blame the hormones on this one. As I wrap my arms around his neck and pull him even closer to me, I lose it. Snot and tears cover my face as we both cry together, while the sound of one of our baby's heartbeat fills the small room.

"We're going to be parents," Simon mumbles against my skin.

I can't even force words out at this point, so I only nod and hope he can feel my response.

After a couple more moments, Simon slowly pulls away. He grabs a pocket square out of his suit pocket and absorbs most of the snot off my face, before wiping the lingering tears off my cheeks with his thumbs. We hold eye contact for a moment before the doctor interrupts us.

"Do you want to know the genders?"

Do I?

Do we?

I always thought I would like to be surprised during labour, but I can't handle any more surprises.

Rule # 7: Avoid Surprises

I need to know.

Thankfully, I can see Simon nodding his head out of the corner of my eye. It seems as though we agree on something for the first time ever.

"Yes," Simon and I say at the same time.

The doctor clicks around a couple of times and then moves the wand back to the other side of my stomach. "Alright, Twin A is... a girl."

A girl. A little baby girl. A mini me. Queue the tears.

"And..." the doctor continues, moving the wand back to the other side. "Twin B is...a boy."

A boy. A little boy. One of each. The perfect pair. More tears.

I can hear Simon choking back tears from beside me, but I can't take my eyes off the monitor.

I'm really going to be a mother.

My dream come true.

The rest of the appointment goes by in a blur. I'm not sure how they expect me to retain any information after I found out I'm having two babies. I'm pretty sure Simon was recording the whole conversation on his phone, so maybe I can get a copy of that later.

When I don't make a follow up appointment at the reception desk, but instead ask them to forward my file to the doctor's office in Bluefield, I can just see the argument on Simon's tongue.

I have plans, rules and goal. And Bluefield is where I need to be.

I walk towards the elevator, Simon hot on my heels.

"I'm still going to Bluefield. Don't even try to talk me out of it," I say while we wait. If Simon thinks I'm about to lie down and let him dictate my life, he's got another thing coming. If he wants to be around during my pregnancy, he can figure out how to spend more time in Bluefield this summer. Not my problem.

"Aspen. I'm also moving to Bluefield. I'm working for Mane Construction on the new project. We will both be there until the fall. Jackson assured me he would tell you," Simon says.

Jackson did no such thing. Neither did Lillian, though I'm sure she knew all about this too. The excited phone call to my bestie is now going to be an interrogation, apparently.

"No, he must have forgotten to." Or he was putting off telling me because he assumed I would react poorly. A fair assumption to make, but I don't appreciate being blindsided. No more surprises. Isn't that what I said? Everything needs to get on board with this. "I'm supposed to be staying with them," I say, more to myself than him. Now that I know I'm having twins, I need to re-evaluate everything. The doctor said I will most likely deliver early and if I don't plan on being in Toronto, I need to have a doctor and a birth plan for Bluefield. That includes a nursery, even if temporary. If I give birth in Bluefield, I'm not lugging two newborns back to the city. We're staying for the Fall. I need to find a place to stay with room for a crib. No, cribs.

I'm having twins.

"I need to make some calls, find a new place to stay. Look up cribs and how to baby proof a rental." I'm rambling.

"Aspen, stay with me, please. I have a whole house in Bluefield."

"A whole house? You rented a whole house just for yourself?" Of course he did. Just another way to flash his success in everyone's face. A single man doesn't need to rent a whole house for a couple of months. He could have rented a room in The Inn in Bluefield. But no, that isn't Simon Cadwell's style.

"Yeah. I have a whole house. Lots of room for you, and a nursery. Room for cribs."

This should be an easy yes. But it isn't.

Do I want to live with Simon? No, not at all.

Do I need the space he is offering? Yes.

Does it make sense that we are living together before the babies come? Kind of.

Is there a chance I will kill him before my due date? Of course.

Am I going to agree to it? Unfortunately, yes.

There are so many changes going on right now, I need to give in and take what's being offered to me. Like I said, it should be an easy yes. I have enough challenges coming my way. I don't need to be making things even harder for myself.

Taking a deep breath, I say, "Fine. I'll move into your rental. Text me the address. I'll be there next week."

The smile that breaks out across Simon's face is too much for me. He takes a step forward like he might go in for a hug, or god forbid, a kiss, so I do the only reasonable thing I can think of. I turn around and jump into the open elevator behind me.

As the doors close, blocking Simon from following me, I see him shaking his head, a smile still firmly on his face.

Chapter 14
Simon

This is going to be entertaining

Should I bring popcorn??

....

What's going on? What are you guys talking about?

A spen declaring she would be moving into my place in Bluefield within a week really threw me for a loop. I hadn't planned on moving in until May 1st, so I practically had to promise my first-born child to get the timeline moved up. But of course, I didn't do that. How would I decide which twin to give away?

Twins.

I get to be a boy dad and a girl dad on the first try.

I don't think I've wrapped my head around it all yet. I know I haven't properly processed the emotions it has all caused.

I cried like a baby into Aspen's neck when I heard the heart-beats, and I am not ashamed of it. Those are my children. Aspen and I are going to be parents. We are having twins. What an absolutely wild life I get to live now.

I'm not going to pretend that the thought of bringing more than one baby into this world at a time isn't terrifying. It is utterly terrifying.

It will also be the best day of my entire life. Of that, I'm sure.

The second I got the Bluefield house situation set and ready for Aspen, I called my asshole cousin Jackson. He swore he would talk to Aspen about my working for Mane Construction. He did not do that. I'm glad she didn't react poorly to the news. Our doctor's appointment was so emotion filled I didn't want any negatives to sneak their way into the semi truce we seemed to have had. Aspen let me touch her, comfort her, as much as I felt like I needed to without complaint. That's a big step for us.

Aside from the night of the conception of our children, Aspen hardly tolerates being in the same room as me. So, hand holding? Big step forward. Her agreeing to live with me? Huge step forward. Her leaving me standing there like an idiot while she takes the elevator down? Small, but expected, step backwards.

I texted Aspen the address of the Bluefield house, but other than a thumbs up, I haven't heard anything all week. I had every intention of asking Aspen to stay here in Bluefield when I picked it out. This place will be perfect for both of us. It will also keep her close so I know what's going on.

I don't want to hover around her, but not knowing what she's been doing or how she's been feeling since I last saw her is driving me crazy.

I've been calling Lillian every night for updates since she's staying with Aspen while she packs up her apartment.

Lillian and Jackson have always stayed out of our feud, which I appreciate. They would never pick a side, and I wouldn't want them to. I know we are both very important people in their lives, and we always will be.

Jackson and I are cousins, but we feel more like brothers. Jackson's dad, my uncle Gord, is an asshole. I'm not being judgemental, or rude, it's a known fact. The man had a kid, got a divorce, demanded full custody and then prioritized his company over everything else. Jackson has made his peace with his childhood and is in the process of earning his right to take over Gord's company, but I still hate the guy. The only upside to the whole situation is that my mom, Caroline, Gord's sister, let Jackson be a part of our family as much as he wanted.

Jackson came on all our family vacations, both abroad and to the cottage my parents used to rent on Lake Muskoka. He slept over at our house every weekend, we played sports together, went to summer camp together, and were basically inseparable. We went to the same university, roomed together all four years, and then bought condos in the same building when our careers allowed it. Him moving to Bluefield was a bit of an adjustment for me. I was used to him always being just a couple floors away, and then suddenly, he's a couple of hours away instead. I'm not saying I have codependency issues, but when they decided they were keeping Lillian's apartment in Toronto as their place when they needed to stay in the city, I moved to a condo closer to hers so I could be near whenever they were around. I am a grown man, but I'm not too proud to admit that I have a lot of love for Jackson, and now Lillian.

My sister Claire used to make fun of us for how close we were when we were younger. I think she was mostly just annoyed that she somehow ended up with two younger brothers instead of one.

We were troublemakers, and she was our favourite target. After dumping her suitcase in the lake one too many times and hanging her underwear on the flagpole, my parents had to keep Jackson and me on a short leash. That just made coming up with our schemes that much more fun because the stakes for get caught were higher.

I didn't think Jackson's childhood affected him that much until he started dating Lillian. He has always been a friendly and outgoing guy, but it was all pretty surface level. Keeping everyone just at arm's length so they couldn't hurt him. Now that he's opened his heart to Lillian and essentially joined her family, the guy looks like he's floating on cloud nine. I couldn't be happier for him.

If only my relationship with Aspen wasn't a dark spot in the otherwise happy bubble they live in. The animosity between Aspen and me is probably annoying more than anything else. I would be fine if we all got along, but I have no idea how to get Aspen on the same page.

At exactly 10 am, just as Lillian said it would, a truck pulls into my driveway. I'm not sure why I expected a group of guys from a moving company to exit the truck. This is Aspen, after all. She never does what I expect of her. Instead, it's Lillian's brother Ben behind the wheel with Aspen. Jackson and Lillian pull in behind them in Jackson's truck, just as Dylan parks across the street in his police SUV. If Julia wasn't busy working at her family's bookstore in town, I'm sure she would be here too.

I meet Ben at the back of the truck, ready to help unload, when he grabs me by the collar and pushes me against the truck door. At six foot four, I have a couple of inches on him and could easily pull out of his hold. But whatever's got him upset with me, I'd rather deal with it now so we can move on.

"Ever heard of a condom, Asshole," he forces out between clenched teeth. I hear Lillian gasp from somewhere behind me and Aspen snicker. Clearly, no one is going to defend me.

If I was the asshole he's accusing me of being, I would point out that he is a single dad because of what I'm assuming was a one-night stand. No one talks about his son Noah's mother, and I'm not going to be the one to bring that up now.

"I used a condom," I state. I wondered if he would react poorly to the news. At one point last year, Jackson was convinced that there was something romantic going on between Aspen and Ben, even though Lillian told him he was delusional. I don't think this is a scorned lover's reaction though. This has protective big brother written all over it. "I used a condom," I repeat, since he still hasn't let me go.

Jackson finally steps between us, a shit-eating grin on his face.

He was terrified the first time he met Ben, but he had nothing to worry about, and they became fast friends. Since then, I have also developed a friendship with Lillian's brother. Ben, Dylan and Jackson are my closest friends.

"Alright, that's enough," Jackson says, gently removing Ben's hands from the collar of my shirt. "It takes two to tango, and I'm sure Aspen can handle punishing Simon for his part in this." He's right. I don't think Aspen needs anyone to fight her battles for her. I've never met someone so independent, confident and assertive in my life. If I wasn't so often the one on the receiving end of her verbal beatdowns, I would probably be turned on by it. Who am I kidding? Even when she's berating me, I'm insanely attracted to her.

Ben grumbles something under his breath, then slaps me on the shoulder like none of the last five minutes ever happened. I'm grateful he got that out of his system. He's the only friend I have that's a parent, and I plan on going to him and my dad for advice.

Everyone moves on and begins unloading the truck. I opt to walk over to Aspen, who's standing off to the side watching.

"Did you put him up to that?" I ask, gesturing towards Ben as he carries a box towards the front door.

"No, but I kind of wish I did. That was hilarious," she says with a chuckle. It seems as though she's in a good mood today. Or at least a good mood with me. She's typically a cheery person to everyone but me.

I hope that means she is feeling better than last week. The amount of relief I feel knowing I'll have access to her for the rest of the pregnancy is immeasurable. I told her I want to be there for her and our children, and I meant it. I didn't know living together would be so important to me, but it is, and this house will be perfect for our growing family.

"You going to stand around all day, or are you planning on helping?" Aspen asks full of sass.

"Why don't I give you a tour while everyone else works on unpacking?" I offer. Jackson has been here before since I had him tour the place while I was stuck in Toronto, but otherwise this is the first time everyone is seeing it.

"Probably for the best," Aspen concedes as she fans her face with her hands. "I'm sweating just standing here." It's not an overly warm day, pretty typical April weather. The sun is bright in the sky, offering some heat, but there is still a chill to the air. I read in one of the pregnancy books that an increase in body temperature is a normal symptom, so that must be why Aspen is unzipping her sweater and tying it around her waist... her round waist.

Aspen has a bump.

Last week I obviously saw her stomach, but she was lying down, so it didn't look very round, and she was wearing a large sweater over it otherwise. Now standing in front of me in just a tight, cropped exercise tank top and leggings, her round belly is on full display.

Holy shit.

Those are my kids in there.

Seeing the ultrasound and hearing the heartbeats was a surreal experience, but there's something about Aspen's visibly growing stomach that has me at a loss for words.

"I know. I'm already huge," Aspen says, breaking my rambling thoughts.

"No, you're beautiful," I respond before I can stop myself. It's not that I don't want her to know she's beautiful, it's just that complements don't typically go over well when they are coming from me and directed at Aspen. I once told her the dark green dress she was wearing made her eyes pop. She took that as everything else she had ever worn made her eyes look dull. That is not even remotely what I meant, but I didn't bother defending my comment. The damage was already done.

I look to Aspen's forest-green eyes, her gold surrounding her irises shimmering in the sun and ready myself for her angry response. Instead of a verbal smackdown, she blushes.

I called Aspen Arthur beautiful, and she blushed. This is a historic day.

She quickly schools her face and turns away from me and towards the house. I don't care that she's pretending whatever moment we just had didn't happen. I don't know if it's her pregnancy hormones driving her reaction, or some insecurity in her changing body, but a win is a win.

I cut Aspen off on her way to the front door and direct her towards the garage. I type the code into the keypad, one-two-three-one-two-three, making sure Aspen sees it so she can use it when she needs to, and wait for the large door to open. Instead of a space for our cars to park, I have a home gym set up inside.

I asked Dylan and Jackson where they had been working out since there isn't a gym in town. Dylan said they have a sad room in the basement of the station with a weight bench and punching bag that he uses most days, otherwise he drives forty-five minutes to the next town over, Saintrich, and uses the gym there. Jackson said he sneaks into the station with Dylan and does cardio with Lillian every day. I know for a fact that Lillian hates exercising, so I didn't ask him to elaborate what cardio they got up to.

A dingy basement gym is not up to my standards. I'm not a gym bro by any means, but I do like to work out most days. My life is busy; my job can be stressful, and exercising is the best way I've learned to cope with that. If I'm going to make small town life work for me, I need to make some adjustments.

A garage gym is the first one.

On the right side, I have a treadmill and a stationary bike. Along the back there is a door to the backyard with free-weights, medicine balls, ropes, bands and mats lining shelves on either side. In the middle, I have set up some thicker flooring I got from a farm supply store. It turns out the mats they use for horse stalls are also nice gym flooring. There's various other equipment around the space, all of which I got at an estate sale just outside of town. Jackson likes to make fun of me for spending my free weekends driving around and looking at dead people's belongings, but he'll be singing my praises now that he doesn't have to inhale mould while he works out.

I know Aspen likes to exercise. Lillian has warned me on more than one occasion that Aspen takes kickboxing classes and can kick my ass should she choose to. When I got everything in the gym set up last night, I thought this would be a space she would be impressed with.

She's not.

"What is that smell?" she asks. I sniff the air a couple of times to see what she's talking about. I guess it smells a bit like sweat in here; I did break the gym in this morning. I should maybe keep the door open when I'm in here from now on. Or buy a couple of fans. Maybe an air purifier. I can fix this.

I'm not sure if I should show her the backyard or inside first. Clearly, my plan to impress her isn't working. The decision is made for me when I hear a loud bang come from inside the house. If one of the guys broke something before Aspen's even had a chance to go inside, they're dead to me.

Chapter 15
Aspen

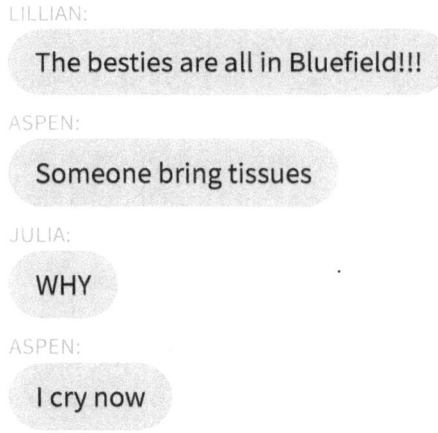

LILLIAN:

The besties are all in Bluefield!!!

ASPEN:

Someone bring tissues

JULIA:

WHY

ASPEN:

I cry now

T he house Simon rented for the summer is unfortunately beautiful.

I say unfortunately because I would normally be gushing over a place like this. I'm an interior designer, beautiful houses are my kryptonite, but I can't compliment this place. Anything positive would go straight to Simon's head, and I need to keep him in line now that we're going to be living together. I mean, I blushed when he called me beautiful earlier. What the fuck is wrong with me?

But the house is beautiful. It sits back off the road on a quiet street a couple of blocks from Main Street. The old Victorian home looks to have been completely restored on both the inside and outside. White siding and blue shutters are surrounded by the lush, mature maple and oak trees that are scattered around the property. I haven't caught a peek at the backyard yet, but based on the map we followed to get here, I think the house backs onto the river. Somehow, the inside is just as stunning as the outside.

We step inside the door coming from the garage into a large kitchen. I pretended to be unimpressed with the garage gym. It hardly smelled and I plan on spending as much time as my body will tolerate in there, only when Simon isn't, of course.

In the kitchen, everything is new and top of the line. Crisp white cabinets, creamy quartz countertops with just a hint of blue speckled throughout, an island that could seat six lined with wicker barstools. Yeah, I could live here. The kitchen is open to a living room where I'm sure I'll be spending most of my time. There is a large U-shaped couch facing a white brick fireplace that looks like it's open to outside. On either side of the fireplace are French doors that lead out to the patio in the backyard. I'm assuming the rental includes the furniture because the house seems to be fully furnished.

From the light oak floors to the crown moulding, this house has good bones. Of course, I would love to change out the furnishings for some items with more personality, but for a rental,

I'm impressed. On the main floor, there is a full bathroom, dining room, laundry room and office.

When we reach the office, I have to pause for a moment. The rest of the house, aside from the garage, looks to be untouched by Simon, but he must have messed with this room. There are bookshelves lining the walls on either side of the room and a large bay window looks out to the backyard. In the middle of the room, facing each other, are two matching desks. They look to be solid oak and antique. But there are two of them. Honestly, it looks like an ideal place to work except for the fact that I would be stuck staring at Simon all day. What was he thinking?

"Great, isn't it?" He asks.

"Not really," I respond truthfully. It's bad enough that we're working for the same company, but now he expects me to do that in the same room as him? Facing him? No, thank you.

"Why?" he asks, seeming genuinely confused.

"I like my space when I work. I listen to music, I talk to myself, I make a mess. We can't share an office." He obviously put some thought into this, and I don't want to offend him. I'm trying this thing where I'm nice to the future father of my children. I'm kind of dying inside holding my snarky comments in, but I'm making an effort. Living with him is a bigger benefit to me than it is to him, so he needs to know I'm grateful. I'm not going to openly compliment the house in front of him, but not shitting on his ideas is a good compromise in my mind.

"Why don't we talk about this later?" I ask. There is a whole upstairs to explore and I'm not sure this is the room in the house I want to fight about.

"Yeah, of course," Simon says. He seems relieved that this

room design didn't end in an argument, at least not right now. This only makes me worry even more about what I'm going to find on the upper floor of the house.

The staircase splits the main floor and is one of the first things you see when you come in the front door. At the top of the stairs, the hallway goes to the right and left. There are three rooms on the side of the hallway facing the front of the house, and three facing the back.

Simon points to the open doors at the front. "There are two spare rooms and a bathroom on this side. Across the hall is the primary suite and then two bedrooms that share a connecting bathroom." He points towards the farthest of the two bedrooms. "I thought you might want this one."

Well, he thought wrong.

"Can I have the primary?" I ask. I don't expect him to give it to me, but I have a lot of clothes. Odds are it has the biggest closet. I've learned in life that you don't get what you want if you never ask for it. This may not always be a positive thing, but my first instinct is to ask for an upgrade whenever I can. My parents used to do this every time we went on a family trip. You'd be surprised how many hotels will comp an upgraded room just because you asked nicely.

"I had planned on staying in the primary. You know, since this is my house," he argues.

"Your name may be on the rental agreement, but I never said I wouldn't pay my portion of the rent. I pay half, you get your smelly garage gym, and I get the primary. Sounds fair to me." Now I'm really glad I didn't argue over the strange office set up. Closet space is way more important to me.

"The closet is a decent size in that room." He points again to the room he thinks I'm staying in. "And the bathroom can only be accessed by the other room. It's not much smaller than the primary."

"Simon. Please. I'm about to become a whale. I need the extra space." I'm not actually worried about getting bigger yet, but anytime I think about my growing belly, I get emotional. Without much effort, the water works start. One lone tear makes its way down my cheek, and Simon looks horrified. I hate that I cry over everything now, but if it makes Simon agree with me, I'll deal with it.

"You can have it. The primary. It's yours," he stammers out. "Let's go back downstairs and see whatever one else is up to."

When we get back downstairs, Lillian, Jackson, and Ben are gathered in the living room.

"Hey, Peters, is the river clean enough to swim in?" Jackson asks.

When Jackson first met Dylan, he was the Constable working on Jackson's vandalism case. At the time, he called him Constable Peters. Even though Dylan's profession is no longer at the forefront of their relationship, Jackson still calls him by his last name. It's very jock bro of him.

"This time of year, it isn't bad," Dylan answers. "Once it gets warmer, you get a lot of bacteria in the stagnant areas. It's cold though."

Jackson shrugs in response.

"Yeah, I could go for a dip," Ben adds. "Aspen, those boxes were heavy. When you said there wasn't any furniture to move, I thought we would have an easy day."

"I have a lot of things I might need, okay? I'm probably nesting," I argue. I'm not nesting. I have never packed light in my entire life. The more the merrier when it comes to shoes, dresses, hair accessories. I can't help that I like pretty things, and I want to surround myself with them. So, no, I didn't bring any furniture to Bluefield with me, but once I started packing my clothing, I couldn't stop. I found someone to sublet my apartment for the summer, so I needed to get everything out of there anyway. That's why I brought everything I own with me. Probably.

"I hate to agree with your dramatization, Benjamin. But moving is exhausting." Just to further prove my point, I flop down on top of Lillian, where she sits on the couch. Lillian is beyond used to my theatrics, so she just giggles and cuddles into me, wrapping her arms around my belly and rubbing my growing bump.

I wasn't sure how I would feel about people wanting to touch my belly, but the rhythm Lillian is moving at, I could be asleep in minutes.

Suddenly, Simon is right beside us. "Do you need water, something to eat? Ginger ale? Crackers? A foot rub?"

"I ordered lunch from Ron's. Julia is bringing it over on her break," Lillian chimes in. Bless her heart, always remembering to feed us.

"Thank you, Billy," I mumble into the pillow. Yeah, I think a nap right here will do.

I wake to the smell of fried food. I don't think there is any better way to end a nap.

Everyone is standing around the counter grabbing food from the grease covered takeout bags. When Julia sees that I'm awake, she squeals and comes running over.

"Look at you hot mama," she exclaims, pulling me up from the couch and hugging me to her. Being five foot eight, I know I'm not very tall, but Lillian is at least five inches shorter than me, so sometimes it feels that way. Julia is only a couple of inches shorter than I am. Being at eye level when we hug means I can see the tears forming in her eyes. This is the first time I've been face to face with her since I found out I was pregnant. Once Lillian learned Simon was the father, all secrets went out the door and I let her and Jackson tell all our friends the surprising news.

Julia's family owns the bookstore in town. Lillian met her when she was browsing for books one day last summer. As soon as I met her, I knew she belonged to us. Julia is like a cute goth Barbie. I've never seen her in less than a full face of makeup, winged eyeliner and all. She has long, straight black hair that I'm too scared to ask if it's natural. It's either cascading down her back or in a high ponytail, always with a bow made of pearls as an accessory. She is so cool, and some days I want to be her. The three of us make an interesting bunch. If only my hair was red, we would practically be the Powerpuff Girls.

"Is there anything I can get for you? Any way I can help? Do you want me to take breathing classes with you? Let me help you, please," she says while holding my face in her hands.

I'm not sure what I was expecting as her reaction, but I'm a bit surprised this is it. Any time we've talked about children or having families in the past, because let's face it, any girl that wants to be a mother has a list of baby names in her phone that she compares with her friends, Julia has been firmly in the never wants children camp. Not only do I respect her decision, but I also applaud her for being so sure of her decision and not taking shit from anyone who disagrees with her.

Girl Power!

Just as I'm about to calmly tell Julia I will let her know if I need anything, Simon cuts in.

"Julia, we appreciate the support, but you are currently standing between my baby mama and her food, so let's table this discussion for later."

I can't help it when a growl slips through my teeth.

"Don't call me that. And don't butt into other people's conversations. And don't dismiss her. And, and don't speak for me," I spit out.

Julia takes a step away from us as I stand toe to toe with Simon.

"You haven't eaten in a couple of hours, Aspen. I am trying to look out for you," Simon grits out. I hear someone groan from somewhere in the room, probably Jackson, because Simon and I are about to have a showdown and boy, am I excited to unleash my hormonal fury on him.

"I have been feeding myself fine for the last twenty-eight years. I don't need your help now."

"I'm not saying you need my help. I'm just trying to be conscious of your new situation—our new situation."

I huff out a laugh. "Did you just refer to our children as a situation? Is that what you see them as?"

Simon's tough bravado withers before my eyes as he takes both of my hands in his much larger ones. "Of course not. I should have worded that differently. Aspen, I'm trying to take care of you, support you. If you'll let me?"

I know he's being genuine, but my brain is too much of a mess to deal with all the feelings I'm feeling towards him right now. I feel a tickle behind my eyes. There is no way I am allowing Simon to make me cry right now. I jerk my hands out of his hold.

"You call me baby mama again and I will only refer to you as a sperm donor moving forward."

Dylan chokes out a laugh from the kitchen, but covers it with a cough.

"Okay, you two are done," Ben cuts in, using his older brother tone. Ben is annoying right about this conversation needing to be over. I am very hungry and super annoyed that Simon was right about me needing to eat.

"They're going to kill each other before we make it to the due date," I hear Julia mumble under her breath to Jackson. He nods his head slowly before making his way to the kitchen to divide up our food.

I mentally add a new rule to my list.

Rule # 8: Do not kill my sperm donor

Chapter 16
Simon

SIMON:

Are you hungry?

I know you're reading my messages

Please come to the kitchen...

ASPEN:

Only because you said please

Did Aspen convince me to give her the primary bedroom suite? Yes. Was that my plan all along? Also, yes.

She didn't even question the fact that all her boxes had been left in the primary and all my belongings were already in one of the other bedrooms because she was too focused on winning the bigger room. If she realizes I played her, she'll be pissed. But it's not my fault she made it easy. Aspen isn't overly materialistic, but I've seen her suitcase explode all over Lillian and Jackson's place too many times to not notice that she has a lot of clothes. I knew she would want the bigger closet, and that's fine with me. The bedroom on the other side of my room's adjoining bathroom is the perfect nursery. I just got myself clear access to my babies. If I move my bed to the far wall, I might even be able to see directly through the bathroom to where their cribs will eventually be.

I know Aspen will be the one feeding them and who they will need in the beginning, but this feels like a good way to make sure she lets me be involved. I'm ready for the 3 am diapers. Bring them on.

Did I expect a showdown in front of our friends on move-in day? One hundred percent.

Aspen would hate me saying this, but I know her. We've had many arguments over the last year and without fail, they happen when there is a shift or a change. A stressor. I'm never the initial stressor. There have been countless times where Aspen and I are in the same room for hours and she simply ignores me. No interactions, no fights.

She ridicules every piece of clothing I own; I find out she's struggling with a client at work.

She pushes me overboard when we're out on Jackson and my boat; I hear her tell Lillian she got an email from her parents.

She serves me a piss warm beer at a family barbeque; her ex-boyfriend is sending her ugly flowers.

Aspen gives off this go with the flow, cool girl vibe, but she has these feelings she needs to get out.

So, I bait her.

She gets this look in her eye right before she delivers the first blow, and I just know she needs to unleash her pent-up energy and frustration on me. I think if we could figure out a way to work these emotions out naked, we would both be happier for it, but that is a work in progress.

So, I fight with her.

I didn't know calling her my baby mama would be so offensive—lesson learned. I do not want to be called a sperm donor in public or private. I wouldn't be opposed to hearing the word daddy come out of that smart mouth of hers, but again, work in progress.

We have lived together for exactly a week and that progress I am working on, well let's just say it is not progressing. If Aspen didn't leave a trail of her things everywhere she went, I would seriously wonder if she was even living in this house with me. I'm pretty sure she's decided to work and eat most of her meals from Jackson and Lillian's house. I don't entirely blame her. Their house is gorgeous, and Lillian is a great cook, but you know who can also shine in the kitchen?

This guy.

That's right, I spent many days in the kitchen with my Nona growing up. I know what I'm doing.

So, that's my new plan. Bait Aspen into the kitchen with delicious smelling food and then never let her leave. I also may or may not have given Lillian and Jackson a couple massage at the spa a town over for tonight. If all goes according to my plan, they will want some alone time after and Aspen will be forced back home.

Foolproof.

And here comes my fool now. Aspen huffs as she shoves her way through the front door, dropping a bag of clothing by the coat closet before she lifts her head in my direction and sniffs.

Oh, yes, this was a great plan.

In the kitchen, I currently have roasted red pepper sauce simmering, fresh pasta boiling, garlic bread broiling and a garden salad tossed. Not to mention multiple flavours of sparkling water chilling in the fridge while the tiramisu sets.

Will I have time to put this much effort into every meal moving forward? Not a chance, but that's part of the allure. She'll keep coming back with the hope of a gourmet meal.

"Simon," Aspen practically moans. "Did you break into some poor Italian woman's kitchen and steal her dinner?"

"No," I laugh out. Sometimes I think I know what to expect with Aspen, and then she spews out a line like that. "I've been cooking."

"You can cook? Since when?"

"Since always?" I've never been in a position to cook in front of Aspen, outside of barbequing, so she probably thought I'm as lost as Jackson was without Lillian. One of his genius ideas to get Lillian to spend time with him while he was pursuing her was to get her to teach him how to cook. The man was hopeless before. His plan worked, seeing as he can now make a couple of decent dishes, *and* he got the girl. "I learned from my Nona."

"You're Italian? How? Jackson isn't Italian and I'm sorry, but Simon Cadwell? You sound like you're thirty-seventh in line for the British throne."

She's got me there. My name does scream white-privileged male.

"My father's family is Italian. Shortly after my father was born, his father died. My Nona was so heartbroken, she moved from her village in Italy to live with her cousin in Toronto. She then met my grandpa, fell in love, he adopted my dad, and they all took his last name as theirs." After they married, he took my Nona and father back to Italy to pay their respects to her late husband and they try to return every couple of years. Even though my grandpa is the only father my dad has ever known, my grandpa has always been conscious of honouring the man that came before him and encouraged my Nona to engulf their house in her heritage and traditions.

"Oh," Aspen says. "So, this is like a family recipe? A straight-from-your-Nona-to-hopefully my-belly meal?" She slowly inches her way into the kitchen until she's in front of the stove, breathing in the aromas of my childhood.

Before she starts to drool into the pot, I gesture for her to sit at the island while I serve our meal.

I never knew Aspen was such a vocal eater. The moans and groans coming from her mouth are borderline erotic and it's taking everything in me to not throw her on the counter and devour her instead of this delicious pasta.

"I could eat this for every meal and never tire from it," Aspen says after wiping her mouth with her serviette.

"You could eat it every day if you stopped avoiding me," I joke back, raising my eyebrows so she knows she's been caught.

"Yeah, I've been avoiding you," Aspen says as a slight blush creeps up her cheeks.

Nona's recipes are making Aspen sheepish and agreeable, interesting.

"Aspen," I begin, trying to use my most soothing voice. "We are going to be parenting together in a couple of months; I need you to stop avoiding me."

"I know."

She knows? "You know?"

"I told myself I had a week to avoid our new reality before I got out on my big girl panties and learned to adjust."

First the moaning and now she is talking about her panties. All the blood I was using in my brain to drive this conversation has now made its way south. Awesome.

I clear my throat three times before I'm able to respond. "So, you're done hiding from me?"

"Don't get too crazy. I'll probably still hide from you. It will just be inside this house from now on."

"Are we about to play the longest game of hide and seek until your due date?"

Aspen laughs in response.

A laugh.

She just laughed at something I said. And it wasn't in a you're an annoying idiot kind of way like normal. If I wasn't the one to make all this food, I would think she'd been drugged.

I'm going to kiss my Nona extra hard next time I see her, because this food? It's magic.

Aspen and I catch each other up on our week. Aside from the actual conception of our children, it's the most domestic thing we've ever done together. Not so surprisingly, we both had onboarding and workplace safety tutorials to get through since we both start our official duties at Mane Construction next week. I will be working with the marketing department mostly until we have finished houses and units to sell. Aspen will be working on finishing said product. Our roles overlap just enough that I plan on making sure we cross paths a little more often than necessary. I'm excited to see her in her element. Aspen is magnetic when she's doing the most mundane things. When she's working, I'm sure she is breathtaking.

We also have a company project Jackson is planning for this summer. He put in a bid for the new retirement home the municipality plans to build, but they aren't ready to fully fund it. He suggested a fundraising event and now every employee at Mane Construction that is living in Bluefield for the summer is required to help. Lillian and Aspen are planning the dance portion of the event, so of course I have signed up to man the bar for the night. I get to keep my eyes on Aspen all night, plus use my charming people skills to encourage large tips for service going straight to funding the much-needed retirement home.

For two people who are living together because we are having babies together, her pregnancy is surprisingly not a topic we cover often. I don't want to push her. She's the one dealing with the most change, so she gets to set the pace. With that being said, I am bursting at the seams for a grain of information.

Based on my own research and readings, if we were having a single baby, it would be the size of a red pepper. Where do you think I got the idea for the sauce? Because we are having two babies, due to my super sperm, they are less than an inch smaller. We also should be able to feel them move around soon, and their ears are developing, so I would like at least an hour per day where I get to talk to my children. I know if I hold all of this in much longer, I'll let something slip out that may not be phrased the right way.

"So," I begin. "How have you been feeling?"

Aspen drops her head to her hands and rests them on the counter. Not good, I guess.

"I'm still somewhat nauseous and my energy is low. It shouldn't last much longer based on what I read online, but I would love to ask a doctor to be sure."

"And you haven't asked your doctor because....?"

Aspen turns her face towards me and sends daggers the second the words leave my mouth.

This.

This is why I'm scared to ask her questions. I must have foot in mouth disease or something.

"You remember how the obstetrician we met with in Toronto said I needed a doctor here? Well, there is only one doctor in town and when I tried to make an appointment, they said no. NO! What kind of doctor's office turns away a pregnant woman? So, I called the one in Toronto and they said no! Apparently, they can't take responsibility for my care if I'm choosing to carry out my pregnancy two hours away from their office. Like I get it, but also, I need a doctor! It's bullshit!"

"I'll figure it out," I say quickly. Aspen looks like she seconds away from spiralling, and I don't know if that will end in tears, anger, or angry tears. I would like to avoid all of the above given how nice of an evening we have had so far.

"You'll deal with it?" she asks, already sounding relieved.

"Absolutely," I respond, even though I have no idea how I'm going to convince one of these doctors to change their clinic rules. That's a problem for tomorrow Simon. Today Simon just wants to see Aspen smile at him.

"Okay, thank you." I get the smallest glimpse of a smile before she clears her throat and stands up. "You cook and I clean?"

I take her plate from her. "Don't worry about it. You've had a long day. Why don't you rest?"

Aspen bites her lip to hold back her smile from growing and nods her head before heading for the stairs. I swear to god, I think I have butterflies. If a small smile from Aspen Arthur makes me feel this fluffy inside. Boy, am I in trouble.

Right before she disappears out of view, I remember something.

"Wait, there was a delivery for you today. I put it in the office."

Aspen looks confused, but makes her way back down the stairs and towards our office quickly. She disappears inside before returning with a vase full of the most hideous bouquet of flowers I have ever seen. There's one word I would use to describe this colour palette and that is electric. Who knew blue could be that neon? I wouldn't be surprised if they were radioactive at this point.

"I'm assuming these aren't from you?" Aspen asks, gripping the vase like she might smash it for just existing.

"Not a chance. If I bought you flowers, they would be classy, like you." Pink roses, probably.

Aspen ignores my compliment and puts the flowers on a small table near the entrance to the garage. They will get almost no natural light there and be dead in a day. I have a feeling that's Aspen's plan. Aspen tries not to make eye contact as she heads toward the stairs.

"Aspen," I call, my voice harsher than I intended. "Who sent you those flowers?"

Her shoulders drop before she turns towards me. "Probably my ex, John. He's been doing it for a couple of months now.

"Why does your ex know where you live?" As far as I know, Aspen is single and very pregnant with my babies. I don't want some loser ex-boyfriend sniffing around what's mine.

"I have no idea, actually. I have him blocked and haven't spoken with him since last summer. Maybe he stopped by my place in Toronto and my sublease tenant gave him my address? I left it with her to forward my mail."

I feel slightly at ease knowing Aspen isn't still in contact with this asshole, but I would feel much better if he wasn't sending her flowers and stalking her location.

"Is this guy dangerous? Should we talk to Dylan about what's going on?"

Aspen snorts out a laugh. "Sending me flowers now is more effort than he put in the entire time we dated. He's harmless. Now if that's all, mister macho protector guy, I'm taking a bath and going to bed."

The mental image of Aspen naked in the bath completely erases the jealousy and worry from my mind. While she bathes, I'll be having a cold shower. Just like I have been since Aspen moved in.

Every day for the next week Aspen works from the back patio, coming in when I have dinner ready. We discuss our day while we eat and then she hides in her room for the rest of the night.

Would I say this is a normal relationship? No.

Would I even consider this a friendship? Hardly.

Would I call this progress? Absolutely.

Chapter 17
Aspen

Lillian sighs happily beside me. I look up to see Jackson and Simon approach us. Jackson waves eagerly at us, or more than likely at Lillian, like it's been days instead of hours since he last saw her.

"When he waves like that, do you ever imagine him as a dog wagging his tail?" I ask.

"Yeah, sometimes. He doesn't understand why I call him a golden retriever boyfriend, but when he's practically vibrating with happy energy, it's hard not to."

"As long as that puppy is eager to please, you can't complain." I know my comment will make her squirm, and it does. Lillian's face turns the same shade of pink as my bikini as she swats at my chest.

It's not warm enough to be wearing almost nothing like I am. Lillian is wearing one of Jackson's old sweaters and cotton shorts, yet she still looks cold. With the rate my belly is growing, I don't know how much longer I will fit into anything in my closet. I have so many cute summer outfits that I will miss dearly.

I raise an eyebrow, waiting for a response to my statement.

Lillian sighs. "Yes, he's eager," she concedes. I can tell she's trying to keep a straight face to pretend she is annoyed with me, but within seconds, she breaks into a fit of giggles that I can't help but join in on.

By the time the guys reach us, our laughter has mostly died off. That bubbly feeling in my stomach is quickly replaced by dread-filled knots. When Lillian invited me over for a picnic on the beach, I knew the same invitation had been extended to Simon, yet I'm still annoyed he's here.

He's everywhere.

He's at home.

He's at the office.

He's with our friends.

He's in my head.

I hate it.

And what do I hate even more? I hate that I don't hate it.

For the last couple of months, since I found out I was pregnant, I've been on edge. I'm just waiting for something to come out and ruin my life. I can't even understand it.

Am I worried something is going to happen to the babies? Maybe.

Am I scared I'm going to mess up something at work, lose my job and not give my babies a good life? Not really. I am very good at my job.

Am I worried I'm not going to be a good mother? Sometimes. I love children and have always wanted to have them, but I don't have a relationship with my mother. Who do I go to for advice?

Honestly, I could handle all these worries fine if I had a healthy mechanism to cope with them. Currently, the only thing that puts me at ease is the tall brunette who won't stop feeding me and is making himself comfortable on my towel right now.

I'm convinced the babies know he's their dad. It's the only explanation. They feel his presence and send calming energy through my body.

The only other explanation is that I am going insane, and Simon Cadwell is a calm presence in my life.

Doubtful.

And yet, all he has to do is gently wipe some sand on my shoulder before leaning back on his elbows, sitting way too close to me and suddenly I'm taking my first full breath of the day.

Asshole.

And I even feel guilty thinking that in my head when a couple of months ago I would have said it to his face. The problem is, he isn't an asshole. At least not anymore.

We used to have this thing where we would both hate each other from a distance and then, when we were forced into a room together, we would either ignore each other or be openly rude. I would make a snide comment to him, he would throw it right back at me and this would continue until one of us either took it too far - usually me- or someone would come to break it up. Then we would move on from the whole exchange, hating each other a little bit more.

But he isn't doing that anymore.

He's thoughtful, considerate, caring. I had been avoiding him until he called me out on it and now, I'm stuck with his unwavering support.

It makes me sick.

Although that could be the morning sickness, which does not, in fact, only occur in the morning. Can we just call it pregnancy nausea and move on?

I must admit that it isn't as bad as it was in the beginning. My second trimester has me feeling a bit better overall. It certainly isn't the biscotti Simon made with candied ginger on top. I've been eating about five a day, every day, for the last week. But that's just a coincidence.

Jackson hurries to help Lillian lay out the food for our picnic as I catch Simon's eyes on me while he wears a smug smile.

"What?" I mouth at him, not wanting to disturb the whispering Lillian and Jackson are currently doing on their shared beach towel.

"I did something you're going to love," he says quietly to just me.

"Doubtful, but tell me anyway."

He leans in close, putting his face practically in my neck. I try not to inhale. I swear I do, but I'm assaulted with the rich smell that is all Simon Cadwell. He always smells like a rich leather. I assumed it was coming from his dress shoes or matching belt but given that he's wearing swim trunks and a plain t-shirt, the leather is all him. There's always something herb-like there. I don't know if it's sage, oregano, or basil, but if you told me all those days cooking alongside his Nona altered his body smell to resemble her pasta sauce, I would believe you. His smell is comforting and homey, and it is currently making my entire body tingle.

"We have an appointment with a family practitioner in Saintrich next week. She works at the clinic here in town a couple of days a week during the summer, so she's local, but the equipment is newer in Saintrich, so she suggested we schedule there."

I'm not sure what I was expecting, but Simon removing the biggest stressor in my life so easily was not it. The tingles I was feeling just a moment ago are now feeling a little more like an ache, and instead of being all over my body, they are only below the waist.

For fuck's sake, Simon booked me a doctor's appointment and now I'm horny.

Not that that's anything new. They warn you that pregnancy hormones can be wild, but I was not prepared for how turned on I would be all the time. Simon passed me the salt at dinner last night and when our fingers touched, I almost moaned. From his fingers! And they weren't even where I wanted them!

I need to be sedated.

Rule # 9: Do not let your baby daddy get you hot and bothered in public.

I'm just about to put some space between us so I think can think properly before I do something crazy like mount him in public when a sudden movement in my stomach forces my attention. Now I've felt some flutters and bubbles that aren't gas for the last couple of weeks, but this is more. This is sure and honestly a bit aggressive. I wish I could stick my face to my belly and say, "Hey, I'm growing you inside me, please don't kick."

Kick.

Oh, my god. That was the first kick.

One of my babies just kicked me while I was thinking about doing dirty things with their father. I've always skirted on the side of inappropriate, so why would my children be any different?

I must have gasped because Simon is somehow even closer now and Lillian and Jackson both have worried looks on their faces.

"Are you okay?" Simon asks. Panic laces his voice as he hovers his hands over my face and body.

I nod and let my hormones take over, grabbing his hands and placing them on my belly, right over the spot I felt the kick. Within seconds, I feel the bump against my skin again. Simon drops his face straight to my stomach and starts mumbling against my skin. I would laugh at how much it tickles, but the small pool of tears running down his cheeks to my skin stops me.

Simon is crying.

I sniffle a little. Shit, I'm crying too.

We are quite the pair. Every time there is a big moment, we both dissolve into tears. I stroke the hair on the back of Simon's head as he continues to talk to our babies. Lillian, having held herself back as long as she could, scoots over to my other side and leans her head against mine. Jackson sits beside Simon and rests his hand on his shoulder.

I know they say it takes a village, but our babies are so fortunate to be brought into a world with people in it that already care so much for them and us. I know we have a lot of milestones ahead of us, but I think I will remember this moment with Simon and our best friends for the rest of my life.

After a couple more moments, we all compose ourselves and dig into the delicious lunch Lillian prepared for us. With it being just the four of us, it feels suspiciously like a double date. Up until this point, Lillian and Jackson typically included a buffer friend in our group activities. I guess considering Simon and I are successfully living together, this isn't a worry for them anymore.

When we get home after lunch, there are three things I notice.

One, the yard looks immaculate. Simon must have hired a lawn care company. That sounds like something he would do.

Two, there is an ugly bouquet of flowers on the front step. Typically, John has waited a couple of weeks between sending them. Maybe me moving has him escalating. I meant what I said to Simon. John is harmless, a dud really. The man is clearly asking the florist to put together the ugliest arrangements they can just to piss me off at this point. I'm not worried.

Three, there's a large gift basket, wrapped in cellophane, with a card attached to it blocking the front door.

Simon parks his car in front of the garage before we both get out. I have hardly used my car since I got to Bluefield. Simon better be prepared for the car seats in his fancy car.

Simon stomps to the front door and grabs the flowers before he takes off to the backyard. I follow him as best I can, but his legs are ridiculously long, and I do not feel like running. Before I can ask him what he's doing, he rips the flowers out of the vase and throws them in the river. I'm not overly upset that he got rid of them, but I am a bit worried that the yellow and purple dye might pollute the water.

"No more flowers," Simon spits out before storming back to the front of the house. We had such a nice day today, but it seems as though Simon's mood has officially soured with the presence of my ex's failed attempt to get my attention. I follow him again, this time slower, so that he can get his emotions in check. I'm supposed to be the unhinged one, not him. But no, Simon, the ever level-headed and calm man that he is, has turned into a little green monster fuelled by jealousy. It would be hot if I was even remotely attracted to him.

But I'm not.

Not at all.

It's not like I was about to jump his bones an hour ago or anything.

Nope.

By the time I make it to the front of the house, Simon is already inside, mumbling to himself.

"You good?" I ask.

"Do you know this guy?" he asks, shoving the card from the gift basket in my face. I pull the card out of his iron grip and read the note.

"It's a welcome message from Leo."

"And who is Leo?" Simon asks. I don't think I've ever seen him so worked up.

"Leo is a local real estate agent that I met this week." He was behind me in line at the café and figured out I was new to town, or at least not a local. He claimed he makes a point to know everyone in town, especially the women with beautiful eyes. I would have been flattered, but I am noticeably pregnant, not interested, and of course I need to follow the rules.

Rule # 4: No men and their bullshit

We chatted for a total of ten minutes before my order was ready and I left. It really wasn't a big deal, and I hadn't thought about our interaction once since. Clearly, Leo didn't share my sentiment.

"Aspen." Simon's voice almost cracks as he says my name. "I am a real estate agent. Why are you talking to other real estate agents? We work together at Mane Construction. Are you looking elsewhere?"

"What? No." This man is delusional. "It was a random conversation with a stranger in the café. It's no big deal."

"Why is he sending you gifts?"

"I don't know, but I'll share the chocolate with you if you drop the subject." I need a bath, a trashy TV show and my bed, now.

Simon's shoulders finally make their way away from his ears and back to their normal location on his body. "This day has been a lot for me. I think I need to lie down." And with that, Simon stomps his way up the stairs and out of sight.

Men, so emotional.

Chapter 18
Simon

JACKSON:

Are you done sulking yet?

SIMON:

What are you talking about?

JACKSON:

Lillian is a big fan of the speakerphone function. I know everything...

SIMON:

Leave me alone

After my emotional breakdown on Saturday, I steered clear of Aspen while we were both home on Sunday, and then worked from Jackson's truck on Monday and Tuesday. I am now the one doing the avoiding and I'm man enough to admit it.

I'm also man enough to display my emotions in front of my friends, clearly.

The moments at the beach were a lot. We had such a great day only to come home to not one, but two men trying to make a move on my pregnant...Aspen.

Yeah, she's my Aspen, and they need to back off.

I asked around about this Leo guy. Dylan gave me absolutely zero information. The guy doesn't know how to gossip. Julia, on the other hand, has a wealth of knowledge when it comes to the citizens of Bluefield.

Leo moved here at the beginning of this year and took over his uncle's brokerage. They are the only real estate firm in town, so I am most likely stepping on their toes by working here. He is the definition of a lady's man, Julia's words. Apparently, there is a correlation between couples he sells houses to and suddenly divorced women who recently bought a house. Julia says he's a charmer, I say sleazy.

I know Aspen would be able to hold her own against a guy like that. Hell, I would pay good money to see her put him in his place. But I can admit that I am not secure enough in our relationship to want other guys snooping around. And right now, there are two.

Aspen may be the mother of my children, but beyond that we are hardly friends. When she packs up to head back to the city for the winter, I have no idea what her plans are. Worst-case scenario, we co-parent, live separately and eventually Aspen finds her dream guy and I'm just a sperm donor. Best-case scenario, she falls in love with me, and we live happily ever after with our two beautiful children, a dream home and maybe a dog.

Should I get Aspen a dog? I probably should.

Now that it's Wednesday, the day of our twenty-week doctor's appointment, I can't avoid Aspen anymore. I also don't want to. There's always been something about Aspen that's intrigued me and now that we are sharing a space, I feel like an addict, waiting for my next hit. I thought my goal for us was to not kill each other, but I want more. I thought my impending fatherhood would be derailing my plans for finding the one and settling down. Turns out I was blinded by the shock to see what was in front of me.

Aspen.

She is perfect and so imperfect I can't wrap my head around it. I don't want to wrap my head around it. I just want her. All the time. Her quick wit, the sass. Her thoughts on anything and everything. Give me all of it.

Considering all of this, hiding from her is not what I should be doing.

When I said I got us an appointment with a local doctor, I played it off that it was easy, no big deal. What really happened was I asked Dylan for some insider info, the hookup in the first responder/public servant department. Where he may not have had any goods on Leo, he did on the medical situation in Bluefield. The current family practitioner is very old, like most of Bluefield's full-time residents, and he had brought in a younger doctor to slowly take his place.

The thing about the folks that live in Bluefield is, they don't like change. When Jackson and Lillian were targeted last summer, Dylan's initial theory was that it was locals who were mad about new cottages being built in the place of the ones that were falling to pieces. They have since opened their hearts to Jackson. Everybody loves that guy, and all is peaceful on that front, but they can still be reluctant. That is why Dr. Faith Azarian is slowly taking over the clinic while still working part time in Saintrich, a town forty-five minutes outside of Bluefield.

I begged Dylan and threatened to take away his use of my garage gym if he didn't help me. Dylan worked some magic, probably used his constable voice, and got me a direct line to Dr. Azarian and now I am a problem solver in Aspen's eyes. Hopefully.

Aspen and I load into my car in silence. I made breakfast for both of us, which we also ate in silence. Us not talking is starting to drive me crazy, and I have no one to blame for it but myself.

Her grapefruit and eucalyptus smell is now surrounding me and if it wasn't pouring rain outside, I would have the windows all the way down. If Aspen is going to continue to smell so fucking good, I'm going to need to invest in a convertible for all the long-distance trips with her.

I know there is always a lot of talk about the changes in hormones throughout pregnancy. Is there a chance I'm experiencing that too? I mean, I've always found Aspen beyond attractive. And not just her looks. Her personality is everything. She's driven, outgoing, confident and witty. She is a literal dream, and I used to be better at controlling my thoughts about her, especially while I was around her.

Now not so much.

Living with her is a test of my will. One I would take over and over again because I am living and having babies with Aspen Arthur. I'm a lucky bastard.

I am also a horny bastard.

I thought about asking Jackson if your sex drive goes up when you live with a woman since I have never done this before, but I know the second that sentence left my lips, he will accuse me of having a breeding kink or something.

Maybe I do.

All I know is Aspen Arthur is in my space, warming up my home, growing my children, instant hard on. Yeah, I'm going to keep that thought to myself for the time being.

"Okay," Aspen huffs out. "Are you done avoiding me? I know I avoided you at first, but this is driving me crazy. I don't think I've ever existed in this much silence, and I've lived alone for a lot of my adult life."

I let out a breath I didn't know I was holding.

"I'm done. I'm sorry," I sigh out.

"Good. Now I'm nervous, so I need you to listen to me vent out all my worries and tell me I'm amazing," Aspen says.

I feel like even more of an asshole now. I've let myself get in my head and left Aspen feeling alone and probably vulnerable.

"You are amazing," I tell her. "You've been eating well. You take your vitamins. You are staying as active as you are able to. You're killing it at Mane Construction, and you are putting up with me. Aspen, you are amazing."

"Thank you," she says quietly. "I feel like I should still be doing more. I'm hoping this doctor has information on classes and stuff we should be doing. Julia mentioned birthing classes a couple of weeks ago and I've completely let it slip from my mind. And we are almost halfway through the year and I don't have a hobby yet."

A hobby? I get everything else, but I have no idea what that's about.

"We will ask Dr. Azarian about classes and make sure we are doing everything we can. It's only been a month since our last appointment and a lot has been going on. We will figure it all out." I hope my sentiments help. Aspen acts like she's got everything together and it's all going to be fine all the time. She rarely lets her true feelings be seen by others. I'm glad she is comfortable enough with me to talk about this stuff, but I also hate that she's worrying so much. The last couple of days I have been thinking about my feelings, emotions and other guys. I need to get my head back in the game and be the world's best baby daddy.

"I'm amazing," she repeats to herself, a bit quieter. "I'm amazing." She takes a deep breath then fiddles with the music controls for my car. After a minute, she has my phone disconnected and hers playing out of the stereo. I will listen to almost any type of music, so if Aspen needs to blast a pump-up playlist at 9 am on a Wednesday morning, who am I to stop her?

Aspen is not a good singer. Not that she ever claimed to be, but after thirty minutes straight of her scream singing lyrics in my car, I'm more than happy to be entering the doctor's office.

I check us in at the reception desk, but before we can even sit down, we are directed to one of the three examination rooms in the back.

"How are you feeling now?" I ask.

"Not sure, to be honest. Distract me."

Why does my mind immediately go to all the dirty ways I could do that? Instead of letting that part of my brain run wild, I give Aspen an update on work since we haven't done that yet this week.

Just as I'm wrapping up, there's a knock on the door and then it opens.

"Hello Aspen, Simon. I am Dr. Faith Azarian. I know this can be a wonderful and scary experience, so I want you to be as comfortable as possible."

I can visibly feel Aspen's nerves leave the room. Dr. Azarian has a calming presence that I appreciate. She looks to be about the same age as us, maybe a year or two older considering she's a doctor and that requires at least nine years of schooling.

We both shake her hands before she gets started with the examination.

Both babies are measuring where they should and there isn't anything to worry about at this point, but because we are having twins, we do need to continue to schedule frequent appointments. Every four weeks through the second trimester, increasing to every two weeks in the third. If we make it to thirty-six weeks, fingers crossed, we then will check in every week until delivery.

In my mind, I had until the end of September to get ready to be a dad. From the sounds of it, the end of August or early September is more likely.

Deep breaths, Simon. Keep it together, dude.

I'm not sure what flipped since the car, but I think Aspen and

I have reversed roles. She's calm, joking with Dr. Azarian, while I sit in silence trying and failing to stop my leg from nervous bouncing.

There is so much to do and so little time.

When we finish with the appointment, new ultrasound pictures and all, I schedule the remainder of the appointments we will need up until the birth, while Aspen heads to a café down the street to order her mid-morning meal. I need to make sure I have snacks on hand from now on.

Once she is all full again, we get back in the car and head for Bluefield.

"Do you have any reason to be in Toronto this week?" I ask Aspen, seemingly out of nowhere as we sit on the couch after dinner. But the nonstop text messages from every member of my family are clogging my phone and I need to do something about it.

"Um, yes, actually I do. I need to get some decorations for the fundraising event and check on tile samples. Why?" she answers.

"I need to check in on some things and I wouldn't mind meeting with my parents for lunch."

I would normally see them once every other week or so, but since I've been in Bluefield, that hasn't happened. They've offered to come see me there, but what they really want is to meet Aspen. Now my parents are great, awesome, really, but I have no idea how Aspen is going to handle all that they are. They are very excitable people, warm, loving, supportive, but excitable. When I told my parents they were going to be grandparents, I'm pretty sure my mom peed her pants. Do you know those dogs that pee when they are excited?

That's my parents.

"Why do we need to go to Toronto to see them? I'm okay having them here if they want to spend the weekend." Aspen seems very calm about all of this, which is a good sign. I don't want to worry her, but also, she needs to be prepared.

"We need to have an exit strategy," I state. Aspen lets out a chuckle like she thinks I'm joking, but the look on my face must convey otherwise because she sobers up quickly.

"Why?" she asks warily.

"If we invite them here, they may never leave. My parents make themselves comfortable everywhere they go, and I think if we give them an opening, my mom would move in here and raise the babies with us."

Aspen snorts but covers her mouth when I raise my brow to her. She thinks I'm kidding.

I wish I were kidding.

"You're being serious? You haven't mentioned how they reacted to the news once, so I assumed they weren't happy." Aspen looks away from me to hide whatever emotion is clouding her eyes. I should have known I needed to be upfront about this. Aspen never mentions her parents. If she ever talks about family, it's Lillian's parents, not hers, so I've never broached the topic with her. Clearly, having my parent's support means something to her.

If she wants me to unleash the love monsters that are my

parents, I guess that's what I'll need to do.

"Aspen." I take her hand, and she only flinches slightly.

Progress.

"I have been holding my parents back from us ever since I told them. They call and text me almost constantly for updates. I had a cousin ask if I got married and didn't invite them to the wedding because my dad is referring to you as his other daughter. I don't think you understand how much they want to support us."

"Why didn't you say anything?" She asks, emotions clear in her voice.

"They are a lot, and I didn't want to overwhelm you?" I'm not sure why it comes out like a question. I don't want to overwhelm her any more than she already seems to be, but clearly, I've made a mistake.

Aspen's face grows serious and hardens in front of my eyes. I'm getting whiplash from all the emotions she has experienced since we started this conversation. My feelings for Aspen have been giving me whiplash since the moment we met, so I really can't complain.

"Simon, I want to meet your parents. Parents that are not my parents, they love me. I'm not some fragile thing that you need to shelter. Let me make these decisions for myself. I'm meeting your parents."

"You're meeting my parents," I repeat. That is exactly the reason why I started this conversation, but I am not going to point that out now. When Aspen gets this heated, it either ends with her storming off or crying and I would love to avoid both of those emotions. "So, we could head to the city on Friday night, get all our work out of the way the next morning, and then meet my parents for lunch? Does that work with you?"

"I suppose," she responds before pushing her way off the couch. I try to help her up, but she swats my hands away. Her stomach isn't that big yet, and I saw her get up from the couch just fine yesterday. I have this theory that she pretends to struggle just to refuse my help. It would be a very Aspen thing to do. I wonder if I tell her that it turns me on if she would stop.

For some reason, the more stubborn she is, the harder I get.

Chapter 19
Simon

MOM:

I can't wait to meet Aspen!!!!!!!

SIMON:

Less exclamation marks please

MOM:

I'm excited. Don't take this from me

DAD:

What your mom said

J
ust as I'm about to get off the highway, Aspen says, "You can just drop me off at Billy and Jackson's place. I'm going to stay there."

Shit.

"Why aren't you staying at your place?"

"I have someone subletting it while we're in Bluefield. You

know this. Speaking of, you haven't accepted my e-transfer to cover my rent in Bluefield yet."

Shit.

I ignore the comment about her rent in Bluefield. I don't want to accept the transfers.

"So, funny story," I begin, "I'm also staying at Lillian and Jackson's place."

Aspen's head whips towards me.

"WHY?"

Yeah, Simon, why don't you tell her why you can't stay at your place?

Well, Simon, I would, but it will freak her out and probably cause a fight.

"My place hasn't been cleaned recently," is unfortunately the first thing to pop into my head.

"Your place isn't clean?" she asks, giving me the up-down because she is firmly judging me right now. "Do you have someone come and clean your apartment? I've never met someone as tidy as you. Why are you wasting your money on that?"

I'm not, but we're in too deep now.

"Yes, my cleaning lady...Cindy has been sick and hasn't been cleaning my place. There's no way I can stay there."

I sound like a douche.

"Oh Simon," she practically laughs out, slightly horrified. "You are something different, aren't you? I'm not sure why I'm surprised. The lawn care service you have in Bluefield must cost a fortune, considering how nice everything looks constantly. Or are the owners taking care of it?"

She's right, our lawn does look immaculate. Surprisingly, I

hired some university kid to do it and he's better than most professionals.

"It's just some kid I met in town. He probably should start his own company. The guy has talent."

"Hmmm," she hums. "Are you going to help him make a business plan, Mr. Suit and Tie?"

I know she's making fun of my wardrobe again. I dress for the job I have, which is professionally. And I don't wear a tie all the time, so that's an exaggeration. I'm not going to take the bait.

"Maybe I will." He already told me that Leo was recommending him to all his new homeowners. The kid's got talent. I don't want to see him learning the ways of the world from scum like Leo.

Aspen drops the conversation as I see her silence her phone for what seems like the hundredth time since we got in the car. I noticed she does that a lot, but I can never see whose name or number is on the screen. I don't want to sound like a jealous ass, but if it's John, I may lose my cool.

"Whose calls are you avoiding?" I ask, hoping to sound unaffected even as I grip the wheel so hard my knuckles turn white.

"Hmm," Aspen responds, clearly trying to brush me off. This just makes me more suspicious. Maybe I'm on edge given that before we left, Dylan mentioned that they thought they might have another missing person case in Bluefield, but I feel like any secrets between Aspen and me are hindering my ability to protect her.

"Aspen." I take a deep breath, knowing if I don't come into this conversation in a calm manner, she will shut it down. "I know you are avoiding someone's calls. Would you please let me know who it is so I don't worry? I don't want anyone bothering you or adding stress to your life."

Aspen's shoulders, that had been creeping towards her ears as I spoke, drop back down as she slumps into the seat. Her body language tells me she's going to let me in before she even speaks.

"It's my sister, Sidney."

I don't respond right away, giving her space to continue because not only was I not expecting that to be her answer, I also don't really know what to say. Aspen never talks about her family. The only reason I even know she has a sister is because I've casually been trying to get information about her from our friends ever since Aspen reappeared in my life. Noah, Ben's son, is a wealth of information. I do feel a bit bad using a child to feed my curiosity about the woman beside me, but the kid loves to talk and loves Aspen. I barely have to ask a question before he's giving me her life story. Obviously, some of the details are a bit skewed because he doesn't understand everything he's observed in his young life. Based on what he's told me, and what I've gathered from Jackson, Lillian and Ben, Aspen was never close with her parents. They never saw eye to eye. She was close with her sister Sidney throughout their childhood until they had a falling out around six years ago. Aspen has basically inserted herself into the Shaws' family from day one of her friendship with Lillian, and they welcomed her with open arms.

Would I love to know all the nitty gritty of what happened? Kind of.

But honestly, it doesn't matter to me. I will always be in Aspen's corner. What happened is irrelevant because I've already picked my side.

Aspen breaks my rambling thoughts. "She normally reaches out on my birthday each year, but that's it. About a month ago, she started blowing up my phone. I think she knows I'm pregnant. I have no idea how she would know, but it's the only reason I can think of that she would suddenly make more of an effort to reach me."

"Do you think something is going on with your parents and she's trying to reach you?" I offer as an explanation.

Aspen scoffs. "No, they still send me their monthly newsletters, even though I've unsubscribed multiple times. They are sailing through the Mediterranean this summer. They're fine." There's a lot to unpack there, but I don't want to change the subject.

"You don't want to answer and hear what she has to say?" I already know the answer to my question. If anyone knows how stubborn Aspen Arthur is, it's me.

"Not even a little bit. She's not a good person. I don't want or need that in my life." Aspen's tone makes it clear that that's the end of this conversation, so I let the sound of traffic fill the car as we take the final few turns into the city.

We get to Jackson and Lillian's place, avoiding most of the city traffic, and I bring our bags up while Aspen figures out where she wants to go for dinner. She wanted to order in, but I pushed that we had been in the car for hours and walking somewhere for dinner would be nice. Aspen surprisingly agreed. So, now I have to get ready to have a date with someone who doesn't know they are on one.

Aspen picks a nice Turkish restaurant a couple of blocks away. It is a surprisingly warm night, but the air is still fresh as the summer heat hasn't hit the city yet. There's nothing like exiting the comfort of your air-conditioned office for Friday afternoon drinks on the patio just to be hit by the smell of cooking garbage and sweaty bodies. August in the city is kind of the worst.

We chat, we eat, we eat some more, and then we head back to Jackson and Lillian's place.

"Tonight was nice," Aspen says as we enter the condo. I try to ignore the slightly shocked tone in her voice. We eat dinner together most nights. She should know by now that I'm not terrible company.

"Did you really think I would be a terrible date?" I ask. I may sound cocky, but nothing about me is a sure thing when it comes to the beautiful women in front of me.

"A date?" she practically laughs out. "Simon, that wasn't a date." Aspen tries to step around me and head towards the living room, but I stop her, boxing her in against the entryway wall.

"What about taking you out to dinner and getting ice cream is not a date?"

"Well, for starters, we eat dinner and dessert together every night, some of those times at home and some not. In fact, we eat most meals together, so let's take that out of the equation entirely. Also, I would have split the bill, but you paid while I was in the bathroom."

"This wasn't me making a meal at home or us both craving something from Ron's. It wasn't assumed like every other night in Bluefield. Why can't it be a date?"

"You didn't ask me!" she yells, cutting me off. "You have to

163

ask someone to go on a date with you for it to be a date. You didn't ask!" She's got me there, unfortunately. Easy fix.

"Aspen, will you go on a date with me?"

She doesn't even take a second to think about her answer. "No."

"What do you mean, no?"

"No. I mean no. That is an entire sentence."

"Okay, I agree with you there. Why, then?"

"Why would I?"

"Why wouldn't you?"

"Stop answering my questions with questions."

"You started it."

"Are you five? Am I going to have to raise you with our babies, you man child?"

I take a deep breath before continuing. I know for a fact Aspen can keep this up all night. I don't want either of us saying something hurtful that we can't take back.

"Aspen, I would like to take you on a date. I would like it if we tried dating." We get along, sometimes. We have things in common. We are attracted to each other. Why shouldn't we try dating?

"Simon, I cannot date you. I cannot date anyone right now. Please drop it." I know I should drop it, but I've already put myself out there. Let's see how much I can hurt my own feelings.

"You can date me. I'm very datable. I'm dateable for you. No one else. I want to date you."

"I don't think dateable is a real word. And besides, I can't date you."

Can't. She's used the word can't, or cannot, instead of won't.

Something about that is bothering me. What's holding her back? "Can't or won't?"

"Both?" it comes out of her mouth like a question, so I know I'm getting somewhere. Getting Aspen to open up to someone that isn't Lillian takes expert level skill. I think I'm slowly making my way there.

"Can't or won't?" I ask again.

"Can't!" she concedes. "I made a promise to myself. I have rules..." her voice trails off, but unfortunately for Aspen, I have even more questions swirling around in my brain than I did a second ago.

"What rules? Did you take a vow of celibacy?" The second the words are out of my mouth, I wish I had stopped before I even started. "What rules?" I repeat.

"Life rules," she huffs out. "I have a lot of goals to accomplish in the next couple of years, so I made myself rules to help stay on track. And what if I was celibate? Would that be a problem?"

"NO. No. There's nothing wrong with celibacy, and I can respect your rules. Just tell me what they are." I need to know her rules to find my loopholes, of course.

"They've changed a bit since the year started. The only one you need to concern yourself with is my no dating rule. You cannot take me on dates. We will be doing no dating."

Kind of annoying, but I can work with this. Just because this wasn't a real date doesn't mean I'm not getting my good-night kiss.

I press us further into the wall and drop my lips to her ear. "No dating, okay. What are your rules on touching?" I drag my nose down Aspen's throat and feel her shudder. Knowing I can affect her this way makes me so hard, but I have to ignore that until I send Aspen off into a cozy sleep and I'm alone in the shower.

Aspen doesn't answer, so I drag my lips across her collarbone, scraping my teeth against her skin as I go. "Can I touch you, Aspen?" I can feel her nod her head into my shoulder, but that's not going to cut it. "Words, kitten. Give me your words."

"Yes," she breathes just above a whisper.

"Good girl," I coo. When I pictured touching Aspen again, I had hopes for a bed, or even a couch, but she's like putty in my hands right now so the wall will have to do. "This isn't the romance I want to give you, but we have plenty of time for that." I can feel her argument in the air, so I clap our lips together in a punishing kiss, stopping her from ruining the moment. Our tongues battle for dominance, swirling around in each other's mouths until I nip Aspen on the lips, causing a shocked yip from her. I take the moment of distraction as my chance and work my hand down between us until it's breached the waistband of Aspen's long skirt.

I gently scratch my thumb down her sensitive skin until I reach to the damp scrape of fabric between Aspen's legs. "You're soaked," I rumble. "Is this all for me?" Aspen is now nibbling on my ear, so I don't wait for an answer. I push her panties to the side and swipe my finger through her wet folds. Aspen jerks from underneath me. Pregnancy has made her ultra-responsive to my touch. I dip two fingers into her while my thumb gets to work on her clit. Aspen fights to get her hands between us, reaching for my belt.

"No touching," I mumble against her lips. "I'll make you

feel so good, but you keep those hands on my shoulders or to yourself."

Aspen whines, but it quickly turns into a moan as I angle my fingers just right against her walls, causing her to cry out with pleasure. I'm impossibly hard, but I need to follow my own set of rules. I can make Aspen feel good as much as she wants me to. I need to hold myself back until she's open to more with me.

Before Aspen can fall to the ground on her wobbling legs, I grab her waist and hoist her up, wrapping her legs around me. Aspen must be in a post orgasm haze because she puts up no argument as I carry her back to the bedroom and cuddle her into bed with me.

One obstacle mostly conquered. Now I just need to make sure Aspen makes it out of my parents' house alive.

The second we step foot into my parent's place, I am invisible. Both of my parents gave me a quick greeting before ushering Aspen into the sitting room and waiting on her hand and foot. Not that Aspen let them, but if she wanted loyal servants, Caroline and Tony would be first in line. Aspen was open and answered any and all questions, even ones that seemed a bit too personal to be asked by someone you just met. Did my parents need to know about Aspen's bowel movements? Definitely not. Did we discuss them for over ten minutes? Yes.

Nothing is too personal for my mother and the dirty looks she shot me every time I tried to steer the conversation away from bodily fluids was deadly. I think Aspen has stolen the favourite child title from this momma's boy. She said parents love her, and I should have taken that piece of information a bit more seriously.

Lunch went on for hours, my parents making us excuses to get us, or more accurately Aspen, to stay longer. When my mother casually dropped the idea of them moving in with us, I got Aspen out of there as fast as I could. Aspen thought it was a joke.

It very much wasn't.

"How do you know that my sister was in P.E.I. last week?" I ask when we are back in the car. When my parents brought up that my sister, Claire, had been travelling a lot recently and wished she had been able to make our lunch date, Aspen dove right into a conversation about my sister and her career as a wedding photographer, a fact I'm sure I never shared with Aspen. Not that I'm not proud of my sister and all her success, but I don't want to mention weddings around Aspen in general. I don't need her thinking that I'm thinking about marrying her.

I am.

But she does not need to know that yet.

She would think it was for the babies. And it would be. But only partially.

It would be for us too.

We are probably soulmates. She just doesn't know that yet.

"I follow her on social media," Aspen says with a lift of her shoulder.

"You don't even follow me on social media." I've checked. Multiple times. I'm grateful I'm not blocked altogether, but she does not follow me back.

"Yeah and? You aren't an amazing photographer. Do something with your life and maybe I'll follow you."

Do something with my life?

"Is fathering your children not enough?"

"Meh."

Chapter 20

Aspen

LILLIAN:

> Hand holding??

ASPEN:

> I don't know what you're talking about

JACKSON:

> I saw it too

ASPEN:

> Who invited Jackson into this conversation???

W hen we get home, Lillian and Jackson are waiting for us. Calling this place home feels strange, yet comforting. As an interior designer, I have, of course, dreamed of living in a place as beautiful as this. I just never thought it would be with Simon Cadwell as my roommate. Something about living with

Simon feels so wrong. Mostly because it feels all too comfortable.

Simon grabs our bags, dropping them in our bedrooms, separate bedrooms. I may have let Simon cuddle with me last night, but that won't be happening again. He joins the three of us in the living room. We all sit on the couch, staring at each other. It's not weird for them to just be at our house, or to invite themselves over, but usually there's a reason.

It's not until I see Lillian's eyes go from Simon's hand on my shoulder to mine on this thigh that I notice that not only are we sitting way too close, we're practically cuddling. I want to blame this on pregnancy brain, but I think pregnancy libido is more accurate. I remove my hand from Simon's leg and scoot away from him. There's no way to be subtle about this, considering the room is silent and everyone is now staring at me.

I clear my throat, about to direct the attention away from us, when Lillian gasps.

"You two are sleeping together!" Jackson all but yells, pumping his fist and reaching toward Simon for a high-five. Simon knocks Jackson's hand away, ignoring him. I would give Simon props for his non-reaction, but the smile he's trying to hide is getting the best of him.

"We are *not* sleeping together," I say firmly.

"Oh, I think you are," Lillian says with a huge smile.

"This is awesome," Jackson adds.

"We aren't sleeping together." This time, Simon is backing me up. The smile on my face drops the second I hear him mutter "yet" under his breath. That cocky shit. I know who is not getting laid now.

"Simon's penis has not entered my vagina since New Year's Eve. Let's move on," I state.

"Way to make it clinical, Aspen," Simon says at the same time I hear Lillian whisper to Jackson, "She didn't say anything about other body parts."

"Is there a reason you guys are here?" I ask, trying to steer the conversation away from what Simon and I may or may not have done last night.

"Right, sorry," Lillian says. She at least has the decent to look sheepish about it. Jackson looks smug. "We were driving by after stopping at Mrs. Langley's place and noticed Sam was snooping around. Jackson asked him to leave since you guys weren't home and then we thought we should stay in case he came back."

Mrs. Langley is an older woman who has lived in Bluefield her whole life. My younger sister was friends with her grand-daughter, Alexandra, for a bit and we all hung out one summer during university. Alex doesn't live in the country anymore, so Ben would often check in on her. Now it's something we all do. She makes the best peanut butter cookies and butter tarts I've ever had.

The mention of Sam immediately puts me on edge. I met Sam last summer after Lillian said he followed her to the park and made her feel awkward and uncomfortable. She even faked a phone call to get away from him. I wanted to reassure her that it wasn't all in her head, so we went to the General Store, where Sam works, so I could scope him out.

The kid is weird. He may be harmless, but no one should be holding eye contact that aggressively. He also likes to call Lillian Lilly, which she hates, and he's never liked Jackson very much.

There's not explicitly wrong with him, but the red flags are waving. He's a nineteen-year-old kid, was the star of Bluefield High's football team and lives with his grandma. There is no reason for his social skills to be so off. There's also no reason for him to be snooping around our house.

"I gave Sam permission to be here," Simon says, shocking us all.

"You what?"

"Why?"

"Dude, no."

"He's our landscaper," Simon states.

"Weird Sam from the General Store is the one who's been taking care of your lawn?" Jackson asks.

Simon looks like Jackson just called him the weird one. "Weird Sam? Are you guys bullying the poor kid?"

"He gives me the creeps," Lillian whispers.

"You guys are overreacting. He's starting up a lawn care and landscaping business, and I'm giving him business advice and letting him use our property to build his portfolio. He's not weird at all."

"He's a bit weird," Jackson argues.

"Funny you should say that, Jackson." Simon has a coy smile on his face now and I just know he's about to drop something on Jackson. Normally, I'm on the receiving end of his wit. It's kind of nice watching the show instead of participating for once.

Growth.

"Sam actually asked about you, Jackson. He knew we were related and wanted to make sure you were a good guy. He was convinced you were stalking Lillian last summer and were praying on her for being lonely."

"I wasn't stalking her," Jackson sputters out. "We ran into each other naturally, no stalking."

"I remember a specific conversation where you told me you wanted to wander around Main Street until you ran into her. You also showed up at her house unannounced multiple times."

"I was making my intentions clear. And besides, Wildflower likes my persistence."

Lillian giggles at that. Our girl is lost forever to love.

"Back on topic, please," I prompt.

"Right," Simon says. "I was chatting with Sam at the General Store, asking about school, his grandma, girls." Only Simon goes in for bread and comes out with someone's life story. "He found out where we were staying and asked if I would like him to manage our lawn and garden for the summer. He's in school for it, so I gave him a shot. He needs some guidance, but he's got a good business head on his shoulders. I've been recommending him to everyone in town. Now, if you'll excuse me, I need to call him to tell him it was a misunderstanding and to ignore our overprotective friends." Simon grabs his phone from the coffee table and heads out back through the patio doors.

Jackson shakes his head but follows Simon outside.

"Whoops," Lillian says once we're alone. "But can you blame us? Two women are missing, and we find him lurking around your home. I talked Jackson down from calling Dylan."

"I guess I should have asked more questions when Simon told me some kid was doing our lawn care. Whatever. Let's give him a chance, I guess?"

"I guess," Lillian says, shrugging. "So, what's going on with you and Simon?"

I roll my eyes; I knew this was coming.

"Nothing really, we're just trying to get along better."

"Does getting along involve...how did you phrase it? Him putting his penis in your vagina?" I cringe hearing my words out of Lillian's mouth. Not very sexy at all.

"We called a truce or something. I told Simon we couldn't date because of my rules."

"Can't you break the rules for him? I mean, he's your baby daddy. Exceptions should be made."

"No exception... But there are no rules against touching..."

Lillian screeches so loudly you must be able to hear it from outside. Both Simon and Jackson's heads whip in our direction. I wave them off all while Lillian blushes. "Whoops... Okay, what kind of touching? Friendly, or *friendly*" she asks while raising her eyebrows suggestively.

I give her a brief play-by-play of our heated kiss and the heavy petting involved. I've never been shy about sharing my sexual encounters with Lillian. I called her seconds after I lost my virginity. She called me seconds before. But for some reason, I leave out the details of the cuddling we did and the light kisses and touches we've shared today. Something about them feels special, maybe even sacred. Surely I need to revisit my rules and make some changes to keep him away. And probably see a therapist since this is Simon and me we're talking about, but there's a part of me that wants to lean into the warm and sparkly feeling I feel inside.

I watch as Lillian and Jackson make their way to Jackson's

truck. Lillian's battery died in her car and instead of replacing it, she's decided she can bike everywhere or make Jackson drive her around. I think it's just an excuse to spend as much time with him as possible. Those two are obsessed with each other in the best way possible. "Jackson and Lillian are wearing matching shoes; did you see that?" I say to Simon the second we close the door. They have on those leather clogs we wore in middle school that might be back in style.

"I did," he responds coolly and without looking at me. His response shocks me only for a moment before it hits me.

"You like that they're wearing matching shoes?" I expect him to laugh at them with me, but no, of course not. Simon would love all the weird couple shit they do. Don't get me wrong, I love that my bestie is happy. But matching shoes? In public? Who are these people?

"Why should we care if they're wearing matching shoes?" He asks, pulling me out of my thoughts. I was so distracted in my own head that I didn't notice how close he had gotten. Somehow, I'm pushed up with my back to the door, Simon and I toe to toe. If it wasn't for my protruding belly, our chests would be touched as we breathe in sync. "You wouldn't match with me? You wouldn't want to be cute with me?"

His voice is much huskier now, and I hate the way my body reacts. My nipples immediately harden, and I don't even want to think about what is happening in my panties. I want to blame it all on my sporadic pregnancy hormones, but I think at this point, it's just Simon. There's something about him that lights my whole body on fire while calming my mind.

I try to come back at him with a witty remark, but my brain

is empty of all thoughts except how I can get Simon's hands on me. I should never have let him touch me last night. Now I'm addicted. I knew the second I opened the door to this, it would be hard to stop. But what's a girl to do? The pregnancy hormones are not only making me crave touch, but they want the touch of one person, Simon.

"Simon," I whine as he runs his nose down my throat ever so lightly. I need more, but I know he's toying with me.

"Tell me what you want, kitten."

I am no longer able to think coherent thoughts. I think I respond, but it also might have just been a moan.

"You want me to touch you?" he rasps. "Are you going to purr for me as you come on my hand?" He nibbles on my neck, then my collarbone before he reaches the dip in my shirt. I reach up to rip the buttons of my shirt apart to get him closer to where I really want him, but he grabs my hands and stops me. Grabbing the belt from my raincoat hanging on the hook beside me, he wraps it around my wrists a couple of times before tossing the wreath hanging on the door to the floor and looping the belt to the hook it was hanging from.

I've never been tied up before, but I would be lying if I said it didn't make my whole body feel like it's on fire.

"That's better. Now stand there and look pretty while I make you squirm." If I weren't two seconds away from combusting, I would lay into him for telling me what to do. But, as Simon's lips finally reach my sensitive nipples through my shirt, I'm pretty sure all femininity has left my body.

Simon sucks and nips at me through my shirt. I don't think I've ever hated a piece of fabric more in my life. I need more.

I need skin-to-skin, preferably his lips on my skin. He must be able to read my thoughts because he chuckles against me before finally unbuttoning my shirt.

"I know, I know, Aspen. But you need to trust me. I will always take care of you," he says. I know he means physically, in this situation, but there is a part of me deep inside that wouldn't mind if he meant it in every way. These thoughts aren't rational, and they seem to pop into my head as quickly as they leave.

Simon pulls my breast free from my bralette. Not a hard task, considering it's time to upgrade to something bigger. Simon circles one nipple with his rough fingers as his mouth licks and pulls at the other. You would never guess that suit-wearing Simon would have working man's hands, but whatever he and Jackson seem to get up to in their spare time is clearly physical. I didn't know manual labour turned me on until now.

"I know I said I'd make you come on my hand, but I've been dying to taste you again for months," Simon says as he trails kissing down my stomach and reaches for the waistband of my linen pants.

Yeah, I could get on board with that.

"Please," I say instead. I don't even know who I am right now. Aspen Arthur doesn't beg a man for anything. These babies have body-snatched me and wiped my brain of all logical thought.

Sweet, sweet relief is all I want now. I'm not saying I haven't been touching myself lately, because I have. But I have been limiting my self-care to my fingers only. I'm paranoid that Simon will hear my battery-powered friends and think I have some sort of addiction, considering how often I feel the need for a release these days.

Simon drops to his knees and pulls my pants and panties to the floor before grabbing me by the waist to get my bottoms fully out of the way.

I'm currently tied to the door and being manhandled by Simon Cadwell.

New kink unlocked.

He wastes no time dropping his mouth to my clit and sucking. Hard. I cry out as the sensation travels through my body. I swear I can feel it in my toes. He slips his fingers into my slit and just rubs my juices around. It feels a bit dirty and a lot hot.

Simon plunges two fingers inside me and scissors his fingers, stretching me out. If he keeps up this pace, I will be crumbling before long.

How is he so good at this?

I must say it out loud because he responds, "I excel at the things important to me. And pleasuring you, that's at the top of the list."

My knees are weak. WEAK!

Simon must be able to tell by the dumbfounded expression on my face that I am about to melt into a puddle because he chuckles against my clit, sending vibrations through my body. Just when I think it can't feel any better, Simon curls his fingers and hits the sensitive stop deep inside me that sends me off the cliff.

"Simon," I gasp out, suddenly parched for air. "Holy shit."

He slows his pace but continues to lick and suck, letting me ride out the wave. When my body finally stops glitching, he gathers my bottoms from the floor and guides my legs into them. He then rights my bra into place and buttons me back up before untying my hands from the door. I'm about to pull him in for a kiss I feel desperate for. What he just did was great, but I want more. More of him, more of us. More, more, more.

Instead, he plants the lightest kiss on my lips and turns towards the kitchen.

"I'll start on dinner. How do you feel about burgers? It's a nice night for a barbecue," he says as he strolls casually to the patio doors, peeking outside. When he looks up to me for an answer, all I can do is nod. If it wasn't for the obvious bulge in his pants, I would think what we just did left him completely unaffected.

Something about this whole situation is making me feel like he has the upper hand somehow. Not going to happen. *Not again.* I straighten my spine, drop my shoulders and march up the stairs to get myself cleaned up for dinner.

Rule # 10: Get the power, keep the power

Chapter 21
Aspen

Age 17

ASPEN:

We need to debrief tomorrow!!!

LILLIAN:

Good or bad???

I t's been more than five minutes.

I would know because I've been obsessively checking my phone for the last ten minutes. He said five minutes, right? I didn't imagine that. I don't think he's blowing me off. He's spent the last hour in a sticky, saturated shirt because of me. He didn't have to do that. He could have yelled at me for ruining his shirt. He could have kicked me out of the party. He could have pretended like I didn't exist. But he didn't do any of those things. No, he took me somewhere private and spent time getting to know me. All while keeping at least one of his body parts touching me at all times.

Holding my hand. Squeezing my thigh. Tucking a stray piece of hair behind my ear.

Simon Cadwell could have spent the night with any girl here, and he chose me.

But now I don't know where he is.

I check my phone for what feels like the hundredth time since I walked away from Simon in the hallway. Someone taps me on the shoulder. I turn around with a big smile on my face, expecting Simon to be standing there, but instead, it's Maddie, one of the girls I came here with. I try not to let my disappointment show, but the look of concern on Maddie's face is evident.

"Hey," she says. "Everything okay? I think we're going to head out soon."

"Everything's fine," I assure her. "I just thought you were someone else."

"Who?" she asks eagerly.

"Oh, just some guy." The hottest guy at this party. "He had to handle something and asked me to meet him here."

"Do you want to stay?" Do I want to stay? I mean, yes. I want to hang out with Simon more, but he isn't here, so how do I ask him that? Maddie must be a mind reader or something because she says, "I can have the girls wait out front while you go find him. If we don't hear from you in like fifteen minutes, I'll assume you are too preoccupied." She raises her eyebrow suggestively and I can't help but giggle. Of course, the thought of getting busy with Simon has crossed my mind, but I did just meet the guy. I think a good-night kiss isn't out of the question, but I don't want to take things too fast with him. This feels special and I don't want to skip any steps.

I don't want to keep the girls waiting, but I also don't want to just disappear on Simon. I should have asked for his number or given him mine. A casual text to see where he is seems way less desperate than following him upstairs, but I guess that's my only option right now.

"I'll be quick," I assure Maddie before practically sprinting toward the stairs. I get a couple of dirty looks from the people I push past, but I don't really care. If they knew I had a chance with Simon Cadwell, they would be applauding me for my effort.

I'm trying not to think about how silly this all is. He's just a boy. A high school boy. It's not like he's some celebrity or something. It's just that the small amount of time we spent together tonight felt really good. We just clicked or something. Maybe it was a fluke, and after a couple of weeks of talking, things will fizzle out or he'll actually be boring. I don't know. But I do want to find out.

When I reach the top of the stairs, there are way too many closed doors to choose from. I'm ninety-nine percent sure Jackson is an only child, so I have no idea why this house needs to have so many bedrooms.

I quietly creep through the hallway, stopping in front of each door to see if I hear anything inside. Most of the doors are locked, which is probably smart with the amount of people downstairs. With only a couple of doors left to check, I hear voices coming from the door to my left. One of the voices is deeper. It's slightly muffled, but I'm pretty sure it's Simon. I don't want to intrude on whoever he's talking to. But I'm on a time crunch and I either need to confirm that he wants me to stay or catch a ride home now.

I stick my ear to the door to try to listen. It's Simon's voice in there, but he's not alone.

The door isn't fully closed, so I give it a small push so I'm able to see inside. I'm not expecting the scene in front of me, maybe I'm too naive.

Simon is half-dressed, a soiled shirt discarded on the floor as if he took it off in a hurry, but that's not what causes my alarm. It's the girl he's wrapped his half-naked body around. I can only see her hands. Bright red nails clinging to his muscular back like a lifeline as he directs her toward the bed in the middle of the room. For half a second, I'm jealous of this girl, but then I remember who the fuck I am.

THAT PIG. He had me waiting downstairs for him while he hooked up with someone else. Was that the real reason he wanted to get away from me? Was she waiting up there the whole time? Did he think I was going to be next in line? No way, no how. I may not be some hockey-jock cool guy, but I'm Aspen Arthur. I am no one's second choice. I am smart, pretty and confident and I will not be made a fool by some guy who gave me an hour of attention. No. Not happening.

I spin around, leaving the door ajar. What do I care if someone walks in on them? Not my problem. I make my way back down the hallway as quickly as I can without breaking out into a sprint. If anyone finds me up here, they won't see any emotions on me.

I get back down to the party and shoot off a text to Maddie, letting her know I'm on my way to meet them out front. I'm getting the hell out of here. I've experienced a Jackson Mane party, and I can't say I ever want to come back. Lillian had the right idea. I should have stayed home with her and binged movies. That would have been a better use of my time. This is a night to forget.

Fuck Simon Cadwell. He's no one to me now.

Chapter 22
Simon

JACKSON:

This is getting out of control

SIMON:

Anyone checked on Dylan?

BEN:

Dylan???

DYLAN:

I'll call you in the morning

I *am in so much trouble.*

That thought has run through my mind no less than ten times since we got home from the city two weeks ago. If I know Aspen, and I think I do, she is purposely torturing me.

It's not her typical brand of torture.

I'm not being ignored. She isn't making jabs at my clothing. I don't feel like anything I say or do will set her off. No. It's worse. Much, much worse.

She's trying to seduce me.

A dream come true, right?

Wrong.

I would love to give into it. I want Aspen more than I want anything, aside from healthy babies, but I don't want her like this. I don't want what she's offering, which is only her body. I want her mind, her wit, her humour, her laugh. I want her good days, her bad days and any in between. I want her warm hugs, her cold shoulders, her happy, her sad. And most importantly, I want her heart.

To get her heart, I can't give in to temptation.

I'm using my package as leverage.

That's right, my manhood will not be entering her honeypot until she drops the stone walls that surround her heart. That sounds so much better than penis entering vagina.

That doesn't mean that other parts of my body are out of the game. Oh, no, no, no. I'm getting Aspen off every chance I get. I won't know until postpartum if Aspen's horniness is due to pregnancy hormones, or if she just has a high sex drive. My dick may be screaming at me to let him come out and play, but he'll be thanking my heart and brain in the long run.

It's been two weeks since I had Aspen tided to the front door and Aspen has been pulling out all the stops. I used to love working from home when I could, not anymore. I've started going into the office to avoid Aspen and the lack of clothing she's been wearing. It's June, the weather is warming up, sure, but I'm pretty sure the summer dresses Aspen has been sporting lately are actually lingerie.

She makes excuses to walk past me as she runs her nails down my back. She bats her eyelashes every time we make eye contact. I tried to escape her in my bedroom, but I think she sprayed her perfume on everything I own, my pillow included. I'm glad her centre of gravity is a bit off. She tried to drop something in front of me so her ass would be in my groin when she stood up. After almost face planting in the kitchen last week, she gave that one up.

Small victories.

I don't know how much longer I'm going to be able to handle it all, so I need to make a move. I'm asking Aspen on a date. One she knows she's on this time.

"What are they listening to?" I ask as I drop a plate of sweet potato gnocchi in front of Aspen. I bought small sweet potatoes since I don't think the twins are quite that size yet.

Aspen has her headphones resting on her belly. We have been trying to play music for them as much as possible. Multiple baby books suggested it, so we're giving it a try.

"The queen," Aspen responds as she digs into her food. The queen? Is she playing old speeches the Queen of England made? Are we supposed to be exposing them to different accents, maybe? That might make sense if I don't think about it too much.

"What's she speaking on?"

"What?" Aspen asks over a mouth full of food.

"What was the occasion for her speech?" Aspen is looking at me like I've never said an intelligent thing in my life, and I just know I've read this whole situation so wrong.

Aspen wipes her face with a serviette and then clears her throat. "The topic," she says, "is men being trash." My thoughts spiral as I try to think of any reason The Queen would ever publicly speak about that and then it clicks. Not the literal queen, but Aspen's queen.

"Joe, Joe, Harry, John, or Matt?" I ask.

She lifts glances at her phone to see what song is currently playing. "The most recent Joe."

"Ahh," I respond. I'm going to be raising second-generation Swifties.

I let us both get the majority of our dinner off our plates before I make my move. "So, do you have any plans this weekend?" I ask. Aspen pauses to think. This isn't an unusual question for me to ask. I have a digital and physical calendar for us. It has everything from work meetings and events, and doctors' appointments, to get-togethers with our friends, and preplanned workouts with the guys. I'm determined to have some level of organization in place before the chaos of babies flips our world.

"Julia and I are meeting on Saturday morning to do some event planning. I'll probably be done before lunch." Aspen explains that Julia hopes to host events to give locals the opportunity to have social lives outside of tourism and possibly draw more people to consider living here full time. This coincides quite nicely with the housing project we are working on. Everyone here agrees it's a great place to live. We just need more people to support the economy on a year-round basis. "What are your plans for this weekend?" Aspen asks, probably just trying to be polite.

I clear my throat, suddenly nervous. "I was hoping we could go on a date on Saturday."

Aspen spits out a mouthful of butter tart. This is not the reaction I was hoping for. She quickly gets up from the table to get a cloth to clean up her mess. I sit there silently, trying to figure out what to say. She hasn't turned me down, not in any words, but maybe I've read our situation completely wrong. We've been getting along well, I consider us friends now, which is a big step for us. Our chemistry is certainly there. Why wouldn't we try dating? Why is she so against dating me?

Aspen sits back down at the table, clasping her hands on the surface like we're in a business meeting, not at home sharing a meal.

"I'm sorry for my reaction," she begins in a calm voice. "I was genuinely not expecting you to suggest we go out. I know we may be blurring some lines, but I think it's best we work on our friendship, not anything more."

And there it is—I'm being friend-zoned by my baby mama.

"Why?" I ask. I've already put myself out there, might as well go out in flames at this point.

"Why would we?" she volleys back. "We couldn't stand each other until recently. There is no need to rock the boat by adding a romantic element to our situation."

"You couldn't stand me," I argue. "I've never felt anything ill towards you in my entire life. Our entire feud has been based on your feelings towards me. I wanted to ask you out when we met in high school, but you disappeared before I had the chance. I would have asked you out the second we saw each other again last year, but you already had it out for me. I've always liked you,

Aspen. We're getting along well, and you're one of my closest friends at this point. Why can't we give it a try? If it doesn't work, we go back to making sure we can successfully co-parent together. But if it does work out..." You're it for me, is what I want to say, but I don't. Not yet.

Aspen opens her mouth, probably to argue I'm full of shit when both of our phones begin to ring. This can't be good. Jackson's name flashes on my screen, Billy of Aspen's.

Aspen grabs her phone and heads for the stairs as I answer Jackson's call.

"Dude," he says before I can get a word in. "There's another missing person reported. Lillian and I were grabbing dinner when we saw all the police cars peel out of the station parking lot."

"Shit," is all I can come up with. Three missing women and the span of a couple of months is huge. Two we could say was a very strange coincidence, but this can't be ignored. I need to make sure I can keep Aspen safe.

"I'm getting some security for our place. You want in?" he asks, reading my mind.

"Yes, top of the line, whatever you can get your hands on quickest too. Is Lillian shaken up? She's on the phone with Aspen right now."

"A bit, yeah. I think being out in public when we heard the news put her on edge. All I wanted was to have a normal summer with her, truly relax this year. Is it selfish that I want to hide her away from all of this? I feel helpless."

"I know what you mean. I'm constantly trying to free Aspen from stress. I don't want anything to upset her and negatively affect the babies. It's a constant battle." Part of me wants to pack us up and head back to the city.

Jackson sighs loudly. "I shouldn't be complaining; you've got a whole family to worry about now. Plus, I can't imagine what the loved ones of the missing women are feeling." I don't think the guy is capable of having negative thoughts towards someone else. He's good to his core. Hard on himself too.

"Don't sweat it, man. We'll figure out a way to help. I'm sure of it."

I hang up with Jackson and wait for Aspen to come downstairs. After ten minutes and not hearing a peep, I go to find her.

Her bedroom door is cracked so I can see her sitting on her bed with a stuffed bunny from the nursery hugged to her chest. I knock on the door once before pushing it open and sitting on the edge of the bed beside her. We sit in silence for a couple of minutes. Aspen puts the stuffed animal on her nightstand, then bumps her shoulder to mine. A silent communication.

Aspen doesn't let a lot of people see her like this. Introspective. At a loss for words. She doesn't want to talk, and that's okay. I just need her close right now.

A tear drops from her eye, splattering on her bare thigh below her shorts.

Aspen goes to open her mouth, to apologize probably, but I shake my head and place a light kiss on her lips. It's delicate at first, like we haven't done this a dozen times before, like we're rediscovering what turns each other on. My blood starts to thrash as the slow kiss grows quicker, hungrier.

We're a mess of teeth, hands, fingers, nails, as I fight Aspen's clothes off her body. We need to be closer. To not feel helpless right now. To give in to this. To us.

I bring her all the way to the edge just to stop before she reaches her point of release. I know what Aspen wants, but I want something too.

So, I do it again, and again, and again, until Aspen is a blubbering mess.

"One date. You want my cock? Give me one date."

"Fine," she practically screams. "One date."

Chapter 23

Aspen

Julia, are you sure you don't want to stay with us for a bit?

I'm fine, but thank you for offering

We have a spare room ready for you!

In light of last night's news, Simon decided to forgo his morning workout with the boys and instead escort me to my meeting with Julia. He's been sitting in the back of the bookstore for the last hour sorting through children's books to see which ones we haven't bought yet. I would love to say he's being dramatic and overprotective, but I appreciate his hypervigilance.

According to Dylan, they are bringing in a special task force to help with the case. I'm honestly surprised it took this long. Most of the crime in Bluefield is exclusive to drunk tourists and speeding tickets. Dylan is a great officer, but this is out of his realm of experience.

Julia glances out the window at the almost empty street. Since the children aren't out of school for another couple of weeks, it's normal that there isn't a complete rush of tourists out there. The fact that the street is empty feels ominous.

People aren't lining up to bring their families to a town with multiple missing persons cases open. I don't blame them, but I do feel for the businesses that rely on tourism as their main source of profit. It's started to affect Mane Construction. We aren't completely on hold, but Jackson has put a percentage of the builds on pause. The new build subdivision is continuing as scheduled for now. Most of the houses will be going up for sale or rent in the fall, when hopefully this is all behind us. The custom builds, like the property Jackson and Lillian live in right now, are taking the biggest hit. It's hard to convince people to spend over a million dollars on a property in a town that currently has a crime spree.

I hope they find the women safe soon.

"Maybe we should wait until fall," Julia says. "Planning anything fun seems vain with everything that's going on." Julia's grandmother owns the bookstore and has recently given her a bit freer rein to do as she pleases. Last fall, she started a romance book club after fighting her grandma for years to get it approved. Now we are thinking about hosting book cover wine and paint nights, and audiobook yoga. I understand her apprehension though. How do we ask people to come and indulge in a night of fun when some are scared to leave their houses?

"Why don't we plan everything out and then wait until it feels right to start advertising?" I offer. Julia has put a lot of time and energy into both events. I don't want her to get discouraged.

"That's probably the right move," she agrees. "Thank you for your help. I have all these ideas in my head that feel really daunting to handle on my own."

"I got you, boo." I give Julia a hug after she gives my belly a little 'pat pat.'

"Have you heard anything about the Retirement home fundraiser? Do you think they'll cancel it?"

"From what Lillian has told me, the town council wants to move forward with the event. There's already a waiting list for residents, so the timeline doesn't leave any room for setbacks." If they don't raise the money, the whole project will be pushed back a year, and some people are relying on the facility opening by this time next year. "Jackson is stuck here and doesn't have the final say."

"Then I guess we go and try to have fun? At least it's for a good cause," Julia shrugs.

It's certainly not what we all want to be doing when the safety of the town is at risk. I know Dylan has advised against it. Jackson's bringing in a private security company that I'm pretty sure he's paying for out of pocket.

I signal to Simon that I'm ready to go, and he joins us near the cash register.

"I think we'll place a bulk order. I don't want to buy out your entire children's section." I can't help the laugh that escapes. I've talked Simon out of buying two of every single thing we need, but I haven't been able to stop the buying all together. He's excited. I'll let him have that.

As we make our way to Simon's car parked on the street out front, nerves begin to float through my body. Meeting with Julia was a good distraction, but I know we are heading home to get ready for our date today.

I'm going on a real date with Simon Cadwell. Who even am I?

When we get home, Simon instructs me to get changed into the outfit he has left out on my bed. It's a maternity tennis skort—I didn't know that even existed—and a matching tank top and sweater. I can't say I was expecting an athletic date considering the current state of my body, but I'm excited, nonetheless.

I have been on dates before. I've had what feels like a million terrible relationships, so dates have happened. None of them were any more impressive than dinner and a movie, and typically I was the one to plan it.

A man planning a thoughtful date is officially a turn on.

We drive over to the hockey arena in town, where Simon leads us into a gymnasium where Leo is waiting for us. Not what I was expecting.

Apparently not what Simon was expecting either. "What are you doing here?" he asks Leo.

"I'm your pickleball teacher."

"No, you aren't. I spoke with a woman named Sandra. You aren't Sandra."

Leo steps toward us, taking the hand I didn't offer him and dropping a kiss on it. A bit much, but I think that's his style. "Sandra's kid is sick, so she asked me to fill in. I've been playing for years. Great way to meet new people." Simon steps in between us and steps forward until Leo is a couple of feet away from me.

"Who is Sandra, and what are we doing here?" I ask Simon. He turns to me, blocking Leo from our conversation.

"I signed us up for a couple of pickleball lessons. I know you aren't your most agile right now, but we're both beginners. We could take it slow and then it would be something we could improve on after the twins are born. It's like a hobby." Simon looks into my eyes warily. Planning a sports date is definitely a risk, but it's also thoughtful. Simon took a common interest, exercising, and found a way for us to learn something new together. He knows I want to get a new hobby, so he found one for both of us. I swear I'm not swooning over a man for listening and making an effort.

"Pickleball sounds fun," I reassure him. "Let's get started."

"Yes, let's get started," I hear Leo call from behind Simon.

"Not with him," Simon whispers. "I don't like the guy." I've only had a couple of interactions with the guy. He's a playboy, but he seems nice enough. I don't know if this is Simon's ego talking or if he knows something I don't, but I don't want this to ruin our date. Simon's in charge. I'm just along for the ride.

"Okay, it's your call."

Simon looks instantly relieved; his shoulders drop, and he gives me a small smile. "No lesson needed after all, Leo." Simon pulls out his wallet to offer Leo payment for the non-lesson, but he refuses.

"It's fine. You guys have fun. The high school basketball team will be in after you." Leo leaves us alone as Simon pulls out his phone. I hear a video message ringing before he's greeted by a familiar voice.

"Simon! Shouldn't you be wooing our girl?" Linda Shaw, Ben and Lillian's mother asks. I ignore the 'our girl' comment because I'm so confused. Why does Linda know I'm on a date with Simon?

"Slight change of plans Linda, we're going to need some pointers."

"Bruce!" Linda calls through the phone. "We're teaching a virtual lesson. Come in here."

And that's how I found myself being taught how to play pickleball, via video call, by Bruce and Linda Shaw. I didn't even know they played, but based on all the tips they gave, they seem like professionals compared to us.

Simon was right. We were able to learn the basics and 'dink' the ball back and forth for a bit without me having too much trouble. The game seems super fun, so I think this could be something we make a habit of doing. I have half a mind to get Lillian and Jackson into this so we can play doubles. Lillian would probably kill me though. Maybe Jackson and Dylan instead.

Simon has a change of clothes ready for me to change into for the next portion of our date. We manage to get in a lunch at the café in Bluefield and strawberry picking before heading to the marina around dinner time.

Jackson and Simon co-own a sport boat. It's way fancier than they probably need but fits everyone comfortably and is great for water sports. The vessel is named "Wildflower" after Lillian. This was a post-Lillian-getting-kidnapped-on-Jackson's-old-boat decision.

"You know you didn't have to do this much. We could have probably done one or two things, and it still would have been a great date," I say as we cruise the water of Lake Huron at an easy pace.

Simon blushes under my compliment. "I know. I just had so many ideas and if you didn't agree to another date, then I wanted to make sure we did them all."

I don't have a chance to process what Simon said as my phone vibrates in the pocket of my leggings.

"She's still calling you?" Simon asks as I silence the call. We're having such a good time today; I hate that my sister and the sour mood she is causing could ruin it.

"She is, but I don't want to talk about it." I don't mean to be harsh, but I need to draw a boundary here. I don't want Simon anywhere near the mess that is the relationships I have with my family. He'll try to fix it or something, but it's not possible. And I don't even want it to be. I've made my peace. Sidney needs to move on. "She did something I consider unforgivable. I'm not being dramatic here. I'm not allowed to talk about it, but she could and should have gone to jail, in my opinion."

Simon lets out a breath. "Woah, okay. I don't need the details; I just wonder if we should be getting Dylan or Ben involved. I don't want any added stress to your life right now. Or ever."

"Not Ben," I cut in. "He has enough on his plate. And so does Dylan. I'm sure if I keep ignoring her, she'll eventually go away." I hope.

"It's obviously up to you, no pressure," he says quietly. Sometimes it surprises me how gentle Simon can be. Not that

I didn't see him that way with others before we lived together, but he was never like this with me. I can say that was most likely my fault. I didn't let him be soft or gentle. It's kind of nice. *I'm losing my mind.*

We cruise to what feels like the middle of the lake. I can still see the shoreline behind us, but nothing else. Simon pulls out premade sandwiches and sparkling water from a cooler, setting up a small picnic for us as the sun starts to set.

Peace.

I feel at peace right now. I'm not sure I've ever felt this way before and, all things considered, I probably shouldn't. I'm still getting my feet under me at Mane Construction, even though I'm killing it. I'm living with and planning on raising children with a man I swore I would hate for the rest of my life. There is someone in Bluefield kidnapping women. And I'm dating Simon Cadwell. Nothing about any of this is in line with the rules I set for myself at the beginning of the year.

Fuck the rules.

Simon must have tapped a line in my brain because he breaks our silence and asks, "How are you feeling about the disappearances? I noticed you and Julia didn't seem as excited about your event planning as you normally would be." Of course he did because he notices everything, apparently. Simon should be a spy, not a realtor.

"It's not good timing. We aren't going to plan a date for anything until things are more comfortable in town. Julia is a bit down about it, but it's the right thing to do."

"But how are you feeling, kitten?" he asks.

I ignore the thrill Simon calling me kitten outside of the bedroom causes. "I'm a bit unsettled. Not as relaxed as I assumed our summer would be here. I know there are loads of crime in Toronto that we are privileged enough to ignore a lot of the time, but it just feels so much closer here. It's affecting the whole community in a lot of negative ways, and I just wish we could do more to help, but it's up to the police at this point." I'm one woman. Even if I wanted to go searching by myself, not only could it be potentially unsafe, but pointless. I hate feeling helpless. I've made sure I have a purpose in as many facets of my life as possible. Not helping now feels wrong.

"That's understandable. I wish there was more we could be doing too. I've been thinking about it, and I think we should install a security camera doorbell and put an alarm system in the house."

Would that make me feel better? Probably. It may not be necessary to have it alarmed all the time, but it would add some peace of mind. "You and Jackson doing a joint order?" The conversation has brought down the mood drastically. Between this and my sister's constant phone calls, we need to keep things light.

Simon rolls his eyes. "You know what? Yes, we made a joint order. We even got one for Julia's apartment since she only has a system in the store, thank you very much. And I'm not even going to take credit for this idea, Dylan made the suggestion."

Fair enough, can't argue with any of that.

Having a security system is one thing, remembering to arm it is a whole other. "I might need a reminder on my phone to set the alarm when I leave the house...Wait." A thought pops into my head that may damper Simon's Fort Knox plans. "Are the owners of the house okay with us installing technology and stuff? It's a bit much if they won't need it when we leave in the fall?" Simon shifts beside me awkwardly and looks out to the lake, avoiding my stare. If I've ever seen a man who is hiding something, Simon is ticking all the boxes right now. "Simon, what aren't you telling me?"

He glances my way for a split second. "The owners are fine with it," he mumbles.

Liar. "Since you just brought it up to me, when did you get their approval? Simon, whatever you're hiding, tell me now so I'm not as upset as when I find out later." I cannot imagine why he's being so shifty. Who could own this house that he wouldn't want me finding out about?

"Iownthehouse," he blurts out, unintelligibly.

"Try again, Simon."

He finally looks at me and grabs both of my hands in his. "I own the house," he says quietly but confidently. Simon owns the house. The house we are currently living in in Bluefield, Simon owns. I have been paying Simon rent for a house that he owns. What?

"You own the house?" I confirm.

"Yes, I own our house."

"No, not our house, your house. The house is yours."

"Ours."

"My name is not on the deed, not my house. Why did you buy a house we're only living in for a couple of months?"

"Your name could be on the deed, if you want," he says, squeezing my hands. I pull them out of his hold, putting some space between us.

"Simon, answer my question. Why would you buy a house you won't be living in for most of the year?"

He grabs one of my hands back, lacing our fingers together. I allow it, hoping it will get me the answers I want. "There weren't any rentals that would have been big enough for the both of us. I was initially planning on renting a room at The Inn, but then you said we were having a baby, and then it became two babies, and we would need so much more space, so we needed a house. I remember driving past our house last summer and loving it, so I got Jackson and Dylan to convince the owners to sell it to me and now here we are."

"Here we are? No, I think there were more steps to that whole process than that. More details, please."

"I mean, yeah, there were. I sold my condo to help finance it. That's why I had to stay at Lillian and Jackson's place in Toronto. But none of that is really important. We needed a house for our family, and now we have one."

"And when we aren't needed in Bluefield for the winter, and we head back to the city? Then what?"

"We'll figure it out," he says simply. It's not that simple, but my mind is a bit too blown to think too much about all of this right now. I'm going to be mature.

I am choosing not to ruin our first date. I am choosing to have a relationship with the father of my children.

What have I gotten myself into?

"Okay."

"Okay? That's it? Just okay?" he asks.

"Yeah, let me know when you get the alarm system installed. I'll have to learn how to use it," I say, shrugging one shoulder.

"Okay," he says with a smile. He drops my hand and scooches closer to me, draping a blanket over our legs and wrapping his arm around me. I can't help but lean into his warmth and rest my head on his shoulder.

When we get home, I stop just inside the door from the garage.

"You own this place?" I say.

"Yes," he states, like buying a cottage on the river is a normal thing to do. Maybe for a real estate agent, it is.

"Why?" I know he already told me this, but I need to hear it again.

"I needed a place to stay. I wanted a place where you could stay with me. And I know Jackson and Lillian are going to raise their future children here. There's no way we weren't going to have a place in Bluefield for our kids too." This is a lot to digest. This whole time, Simon has owned this beautiful house.

The designer in me immediately starts redecorating every room and planning a mural for a nursery. Suddenly, so much makes sense. I was so set on not having the nursery overly decorated because it was only temporary, but it isn't. Dammit, open the floodgates. I wave my hand in front of my eyes, but it's no use. Tears stream down my face as I try to smile them away. I'm sure I resemble a serial killer right now.

"This is why you've been replacing furniture when I complain about it? You aren't storing the original stuff in the garden shed, are you?"

"Nope, I'm not," he chuckles. "I've been donating anything you don't like. I figured eventually I could replace everything this way until you had unknowingly redecorated the whole house." He pauses a moment. It seems like he's contemplating what he wants to say. Finally, he continues, "I hoped that if you liked everything in the house, I could convince you to stay here with me. Or just stay with me, period."

Vulnerable Simon is not someone I'm used to but am seeing more of every day. I can't promise him much right now. There's too much unknown. We've been on exactly one date and haven't argued in the last twenty-four hours. That is not enough evidence for me to believe this is forever. It's a nice thought, but we need to be realistic here. I can still give him some hope.

Instead of answering him, I slowly approach where he stands leaning against the kitchen counter. He must be able to tell what's on my mind because his soft smile turns into a smirk. We had a date. A successful date. A date that was required for Simon to let me touch him, finally.

When I reach him, I lightly place my hands on his shoulders and then trail them down his chest and torso until I reach the band of his sweatpants. His grey sweatpants. He came to play tonight.

I grab the band with both hands, ready to drop to my knees, when Simon grabs my arms, stopping me. "We had our date. Why are you stopping me?" I basically whine. I'm done playing cool with Simon. I want him. He knows I want him. Why aren't we halfway to orgasm town right now?

"The floor will be too hard on your knees and when you're

choking on my cock, I don't want you sliding around. I want you focusing."

I've been turned on since last night, but that just took it to the next level.

Simon crouches in front of me and scoops me up into his arms, bridal style. With any other guy, I would be worried, but I've seen how much he can lift. If he struggles with me up the stairs, I may have to start a fight.

Simon, of course, isn't even winded when we get into my room. The only reason I can tell he's affected by any of this is the obvious tent in his pants. Simon places me on my feet; I immediately drop to my knees. Did Simon have this in mind when he bought the extra thick underpad for my area rug? Seemed like a nice gesture at the time, but based on his response downstairs, he had less pure intentions when it came to this purchase.

I don't waste time pulling his sweats and briefs to his ankles. He steps out of them completely and pulls his shirt over his head, leaving him gloriously naked in front of me.

I'm not sure where I want to look first. Simon has been shirtless many times around the house, on the beach and the boat, but the only other time he's been truly naked in front of me was our rendezvous on New Year's Eve. Truthfully, I wasn't paying a whole lot of attention to anything but the way he was making me feel that night. Not now though. Now I have a chance to take him all in. his bulging biceps, the dark hair curling on his toned chest, the muscles leading to a glorious V-shape. And his cock.

Wow, he has a beautiful cock.

I know Simon claims he has super sperm, but I can't deny it. If anything was going to beat the effectiveness of a condom, it would be the delectable piece of machinery in front of me.

"You just going to keep staring? Or are you going to put that smart mouth to work?" he asks with a chuckle.

Licking my lips, I place my hand on his thigh to get myself balanced. Hopefully, I won't need to keep it there, but if I accidentally nosedive into Simon's crotch on the first go, I will never live that down. I grab his shaft with my other hand and drop my mouth to his tip, licking the bead of cum. Simon groans the moment I make contact. His hands drop from his hips to the back of my head, twining into my hair. He doesn't put any pressure on my head yet, but the anticipation that he will, soaks my panties. I suction my lips around his cock and begin to slowly suck up and down, my hand working him where my mouth won't reach.

My movements are sure, but soft. I know he wants more. I want him to make me give him that.

"You're teasing me," he grumbles. "Come on Aspen, I know you've got more in you." I raise my shoulder, feigning innocence. The hands in my hair finally apply pressure to my scalp, pulling me deeper onto him until I'm swallowing around his tip, choking. "That's it, that's what I want to hear. You wanted my cock so badly. Choke on it. Make a mess." Based on the saliva dripping down my chin as Simon sets a punishing pace, a mess is exactly what he's going to get. Now that he's keeping my balance for me, I take my hand off his thigh and take a firm hold on his balls.

Tears stream down my cheeks, but I refuse to blink them

away so I can hold eye contact with Simon. I can tell he's getting close. His movements become sloppy, and his grip loosens on me. I'm not ready for it to end. I want to feel his cum shoot down my throat, smear the salty taste on my lips.

Simon pulls away just as I'm sure he's about to lose control. I try to pull him back to my lips, but he steps away, out of my reach. "Not yet," his voice cracks. He grabs me under the shoulders, pulling me to standing. "Your turn first."

Chapter 24
Simon

I think Aspen just tried to exorcise my soul out of my body, via my cock.

God damn, the sight of her on her knees for me is something I never thought I would see. But here we are. Aspen gave me the date I wanted and now she's getting what she wanted. My cock.

Aspen looks annoyed that I stopped her, but she should know by now that I am a gentleman. Nice guys don't finish last when they ensure their women finish first.

I nudge Aspen backward until the back of her legs hit the mattress, and she falls onto her back. I drop one knee to the bed and cage Aspen in, my hands on either side of her head. I had every intention of worshipping her body, from head to toe before we got into it, but now that I have her willingly underneath me, I need to be inside of her now.

I drop my lips to her mouth and work it open with my tongue. We duel for control.

I rest my weight on one elbow so I can pull her leggings down and get her shirt over her head. Aspen helps, and she's quickly naked in front of me. When I have been pleasuring Aspen over the last couple of weeks, I've been intentional about not getting her to this point of undress. I knew I wouldn't be able to hold back if I did.

She truly is beautiful. Inside and out.

"I'm clean," I mumble between kisses. "There hasn't been anyone since I was last with you."

Aspen doesn't miss a beat, grabbing my length and dipping it into her entrance. "Me too, only you," she says.

She's soaked, so it isn't hard to push my way in until my balls are hitting her ass.

Heaven.

Aspen Arthur is my version of heaven.

Now let's make those angels sing.

Aspen's belly is a bit in the way in this position and I want to see her face when she comes around my cock, but we have time for that still. Aspen claws at my back, her nails digging in and I'm sure I have marks to wear with pride tomorrow. Might have to take an afternoon dip just to show them off.

I sit back on my knees and flip Aspen onto her stomach before pulling her up so her back meets my chest. From this position, I'm able to thrust into her while holding her upright. Aspen tries to grasp for me, grabbing at my thighs, my arms, my neck, before she settles them on my hands that are holding her hips. I lean forward to meet her for a passionate kiss. I can taste our sweat mixing on my lips and it's the most intoxicating flavour I've ever consumed.

"Simon," Aspen moans, and I know I need to flip her over. She can't hold me like she wants to in this position.

I flip her back onto her back and pull her legs apart so I can push her knees towards her shoulders to allow me to get as close to her as possible. "You are perfect, Aspen," I mumble between sloppy kisses. "Perfect for me. Just perfect."

I can feel her body start to tremble, so I slip my hand between us and Aspen goes off like a firecracker. I hope the neighbours have their hearing aids turned off for the night because between the scream coming out of Aspen's mouth and the groan leaving mine as I finish, we sound like a chorus of pleasure.

I drop down to the mattress beside Aspen and pull her body towards mine.

"Wow," she says, just wonderful things to my ego. I can't help but chuckle as I brush the sweaty hair from her face and place a kiss on her forehead.

"Think you'll go on another date with me?" I ask, only partly joking.

"If this is how our dates end," Aspen says as she snuggles into my neck, "I'm going to need daily dates."

Chapter 25

Aspen

LILLIAN:

> I want all the details

ASPEN:

> I don't kiss and tell

LILLIAN:

> Yes you do. Always.

S imon and I are having a slow morning, just the way Sundays in the summer should be. We made breakfast together. Simon made pancakes with a berry spread while I sat on the counter and continued to grow our children. Simon said that is my only duty while in the kitchen.

I can cook, I just don't like to. Plus, I don't have all these family recipes like Simon does. I can't be pulling up some random blog on the internet trying to find a recipe when Simon pulls out handwritten recipe cards that came straight from Italy. I'm sure I would be offending his entire family tree. Can't have them haunting us.

I'm about to clear the table when there's a knock at the door. We aren't expecting anyone, but it isn't unusual for people in Bluefield to show up unannounced. Last week, an elderly woman I've met in passing came by to perform some old tricks to determine the baby's gender. I didn't have the heart to tell her that science got to me first.

Simon heads for the door as I load up the dishwasher. I expect to hear a familiar voice, but not the one I do.

"Simon, Simon, Simon. You sure are yummy. Can't blame my sister for locking you down."

Sidney.

A chill runs through my body. I was wondering how long it would take until she tracked me down. I hoped she would give it up, but my sister is annoyingly persistent when she wants something. I just need to figure out what it is she thinks I can offer her.

Sidney must have pushed her way past Simon because she enters the kitchen before I can meet her at the door. "Aspen," she practically cries in a terribly fake voice. "I missed you, big sissy." Barf. I want to barf.

"Sidney," I say, in a much colder tone than most would when greeting family. "What are you doing here?"

"I'm here for you, silly! We have so much to catch up on." As she talks, Simon stands behind her with an annoyed look on his face. Before he has a chance to step in, I grab Sidney by the arm and steer her towards our home office.

Simon may like my crazy and my chaos, but I don't want him

to see the ugly side of it. This is my dirty laundry, and I want to keep it that way.

"Sidney. What are you doing here?" I ask again after closing us into the room.

Most of the fake happiness leaves her voice as she says, "Oh come on Aspen, you've been dodging my calls for weeks. Did you really think you could get knocked up and run away to some town full on bumpkins?"

I don't bother defending Bluefield because if she doesn't like the town? Good, I don't want her here. "Okay, you found me. What do you want?"

"How's the baby? You're pretty fat. Are you due soon?"

Wow, she's as charming as ever. Must have read the book on how not to talk to a pregnant woman. She even goes as far as to try to touch my belly without permission. Strike two.

"Sidney," I growl, my patience running thin. "What do you want?"

"A relationship with my sister. We should hang out or something. Maybe a spa day in the city and then hit a club."

Clubbing while pregnant sounds like a nightmare. What is she thinking?

"Try again, Sidney. Give me the truth or leave."

"I want to have a relationship with the baby!" she yells, clearly annoyed with my short patience. The baby, not me. She doesn't even know I'm having twins. How would she? My parents obviously know I'm pregnant but haven't bothered reaching out. And clearly my sister is here for her, not me. "Do you know how embarrassing it was when some random I went to high school congratulated me on becoming an aunt and I had no idea what she was talking about? Are you trying to make the family look foolish?" Someone must have recognized me when Simon and I were in Toronto. The city is too small for being so big.

"I'm not trying to do anything to you. This isn't about you! You don't care about me! You don't care about being an aunt! You care about your image. If people knew the real you, they would be sick with disgust."

"Oh please," she lets out a coldhearted laugh. "You're still not over it, are you? Are you jealous that we didn't let you in on our plan? You wanted a piece of him, I'm sure, and now you're acting like a scorned lover when he's never wanted you like that."

I lower my voice because I don't want Simon to hear this part of the fight. It's not something he needs to know. It's not my story to tell. But it's the fight. The one we've had so many times it makes my head spin. My sister has no morals and thinks I'm the weak one because of it. My parents took her side because it's better to hide the devil in your home than have them burn you. And that is why I've formed my own family. One based on trust, loyalty and love. Blood means nothing when you're expected to hide each other's demons. "Sidney, I am not having this conversation with you again. We can go in circles, but it will accomplish nothing. I don't want you in my life. You will not be an aunt to any children I have. They will never know you. Please take your bruised ego and leave me the hell alone!"

"You can't shut me out of your life," she yells, taking a step towards me. I turn away, shielding my babies from whatever fury Sidney is about to unleash on us. But it never comes. I slowly glance over my shoulder as a familiar embrace pulls me into their chest. I smell leather, good food...home. Simon Cadwell smells like home.

Some grunting sounds from the doorway as Dylan escorts a very angry Sidney out of the room, and hopefully out of my life. "You called the cops on me?" I hear her yell from the other room, but I ignore it and turn to Simon.

"You called Dylan?" I ask Simon.

He nuzzles his face into my hair. "I could feel her bad intentions the second she stepped foot into our home. I know you can handle any situation on your own, but you shouldn't have to. I just wanted backup."

Something calm settles into my bones amongst the chaos of the day. Simon is right. I could have handled the situation I have before, but I don't have to take on the world alone anymore. I may have only fully given into what is brewing between us yesterday, but this already feels more solid than any other romantic relationship I've ever been a part of.

"Thank you," I say, pushing to my tiptoes to plant a kiss on his lips. He licks the seam of my lips, commanding me open. My tongue mingles with his, tasting like maple syrup and the sweet latte he made this morning. There's so much more I want to do, so much more I want to say to Simon, but we need to go see how Dylan has handled this situation.

We make our way out to the front of the house just as Sidney's car roars down our street, leaving a cloud of exhaust in its trail. I hope that's the last we hear of her.

Dylan shakes his head as I pull him into a hug, grateful for both his friendship and muscles right now. "Thank you, Dylan. I don't think she's physically dangerous, but you stepped in at the right time."

"You know I do anything for you. Both of you," he says as he pulls out of our embrace and pulls Simon into a backslapping hug. "I can't guarantee that's the last time we will see her snooping around, but I may have planted some fear in my warning."

"What did you say?" I ask, a thrill running through me. Dylan is so by the book, it's fun to see him push his weight around when needed. The guy could use some fun—and probably some orgasms—to manage his stressful job. And since I can't help him with the latter, I'm excited to see how he messes with my sister.

"Nothing too crazy," he says, causing me to make an exacerbated pouting face that Simon tries to hide in as he pulls me into his chest. "I told her she was trespassing, and that Simon was prepared to place charges if needed. I made it clear that the charges would assist in a judge granting you a restraining order and that all of this would be public record that I could make sure the public saw. Her face turned the shade of a tomato before she slammed her car door in my face and took off."

I can't help but smile. Sidney rarely lets anyone get to her. Her sense of entitlement is so ingrained in every part of her life that the speech Dylan gave her would have left her speechless. I will forever be indebted to Dylan for accomplishing that.

Dylan says his goodbyes, needing to get back to the station for more official duties, so we make our way back inside. Simon insists we should relax on the couch for a bit, but I need a distraction. I have some work I can catch up on, so I head to the office, getting myself situated at my desk while Simon does the same. When we first moved in and he showed me this room, I thought it was so ridiculous, but now I find it beneficial. I can't let my thoughts wander too far away because Simon will catch me staring at him. His ego is big enough. I don't need him to think I enjoy looking at him as much as I do.

I do get some tasks done, but I can't keep my mind focusing as much as I want to. I would love to say that this blow up with my sister hasn't affected me, but I'm human and it should. My parents weren't the warmest to us growing up, but I always felt like I at least had Sidney in my corner.

I don't know when she turned into a vile person, or if it was always in her and I didn't see it. I probably wanted to see the best in her. She's my little sister. I knew I would never be close with my parents, so I held on for longer than I should have. I wish I had seen it sooner and cut her out clean enough that she wouldn't try to come back.

Simon must sense my inner turmoil, because he gets up from his desk and pulls me into him, planting kisses down my neck.

Home. I can't help but lean into the warmth he casts on me. I rock my hips against his and without warning, he lifts me up so my legs can wrap around his waist. We stumble around, messily making our way to his desk where he drops me to seating and spreads my legs to make space for himself. I stare up at him through my eyelashes, grinning with anticipation. He slowly takes me in, unbuttoning his white linen shirt while his eyes travel from my hard nipples poking through my dress to where my panties peek out from under the hem. My eyes catch the smattering of hair on his chest. Why is everything about him so sexy? No matter how many times I'm in this position with Simon, I am always left breathless at how my body reacts to him.

He leans over me on the desk and pulls at the hem of my dress, letting it flow over my head in one swift movement. It's only been a minute since my lips were last on his, but it feels like too long. I grab his neck and force his lips to meet mine in a hungry kiss. A soft moan leaves my lips as he lowers his body over mine and again, I am reminded that there is too much between us, too much space, too much fabric. I reach down and unzip his pants as he leaves a trail of wet kisses down my neck. Taking my nipple in his mouth, I can already feel the tension building in my core. The wild glint in his eyes sparkles as he must feel the way my body is reacting to him and bites down hard. They're so sensitive that if he were anything but rough with me right now, I would scream. He bites me, licks me, sucks me. I bask in the sensation as he loses control. "Simon," I moan, "I need you, now."

With that, he pulls my underwear down my legs and rids himself of any remaining clothing. While he gets naked, I take the opportunity to take control and slides off the desk, flipping over so my ass is in line with his cock. He lifts my hips slightly and pushes in all the way, taking a second to allow me to adjust to his size. He makes use of his hands and begins rubbing his finger against me, as my head falls forward to meet the solid oak, he increases his speed, I'm unable to hold on much longer, I screw my eyes shut as pleasure takes over my whole body.

"You're so beautiful," He whispers against my neck. I look into his eyes and meet his lips again. Simon pulls me against his chest, supporting my unsteady legs, and turns us so I'm in front of the mirror in the corner. Making eye contact with me through the mirror, he places light kisses down my neck and shoulders. I grab his neck from behind me, needing to be touching him as he grips his hands on my hips and thrusts into me. He swears under his breath as his thrusts get more rapid, never breaking eye contact with me. I can't believe how quickly I am becoming undone again, but the tension is building quickly, and I don't know how much longer I can last.

His stubble runs slightly against my cheek as I hear him whisper in my ear, "You're mine."

I can see in his eyes he's waiting for a response, and I can't help myself. I respond with the truth. "I'm yours."

Chapter 26
Aspen

"Do you think Dylan could get me a copy of his body cam footage so I could watch Sidney have a meltdown? It would be so satisfying to watch."

Lillian rarely gives in to anything petty, but I know she hates Sidney just as much, if not more, than I do. It's been two weeks since my sister's surprise visit. This is the first time Lillian and I have had a chance to sit down and really talk about it.

"Ugh, I wish." I would add it to my Christmas movie roster. There would be no better gift than waking up on Christmas morning and watching Sidney finally get the lashing she deserves.

"But in all seriousness," Lillian says, flipping over on her side to face me as we lay on the lounge chairs on her back porch, "How are you feeling about everything?"

"I'm not totally sure. Bittersweet maybe? I'm glad I shouldn't have her popping up in my life anymore, but sometimes I think about what a sweet little girl she was, and it makes me sad. Like, how did we get here?"

"That makes sense," Lillian says while nodding. "I think you're allowed to grieve the relationship you want with your sister, the one you thought you would have and deserve to have. But I also think it's okay to feel like you need to move on with your life without her. I think it's healthy even."

Boy, do I love my best friend. "How did you get so smart, Billy?"

"Lots of therapy," she deadpans, and I know she's not kidding. Lillian is perfect in my eyes, but I respect that she sees herself as a work in progress. She knows her limits and works on expanding them. She makes me want to be better too.

"You're going to be the best aunty to the babies. I don't think you know how lucky I feel to have you as my true sister." Tears pool in both of our eyes as we laugh at how emotional we suddenly got. "I love you, Lillian."

"Love you too, Aspen. Always."

"Always. Now we need to get ready," I say as I pull myself off the chair. I knew the second I sat down that it would be hard to get up, but I did it anyway. Today is the day of the retirement home fundraiser. We already have the gymnasium at the Bluefield Arena decorated, and the town is currently hosting a carnival in the park that we opted to miss because I can't handle the heat or walking right now. It's June. Why am I always so sweaty?

"You're right. Jackson and Simon will not be happy if we're late since this is kind of our thing." Lillian walks into the house and heads for the stairs and I trail behind her.

Once we look like more put together versions of ourselves, we meet Ben out front and head to the dance. Lillian and Ben's parents came into town for the day, so Noah is with them tonight. Maybe Ben will finally let loose for once.

The gymnasium looks even better with the lights dimmed. Couples fill the dance floor as a slow country song plays and I can't help but feel happy that we are able to bring the community together during a tough time and help support the growth of Bluefield. A lot of people had mixed feelings about having any special events happen while women from Bluefield are still missing, but it looks like everyone came out to show their support anyway. Lillian and Ben head off to find Jackson as I make my way toward the cute bartender mixing drinks in the corner.

"What can I get for you?" Simon asks while his back is turned away.

"Your number, please?" I say, dropping my voice slightly.

"Oh boy, I am beyond taken, it's not even funny. Sorry to disappoint," he says just before turning around and making eye contact with me. "You," he whispers, and I just know I'll be in trouble tonight. I can't wait.

"You guys are so cute," a voice cuts in.

Diana plops down in the chair next to me, a sad look on her face. Diana bakes at the café in town and is a true wizard when it comes to scones. I don't know her well beyond her pastry skills.

Simon rounds the bar to greet me with a mostly inappropriate kiss. I'm glad the lights are dimmed because no one can see me blush.

"Yup, I'm dying alone," Diana adds.

"Diana," Simon says, patting her lightly on the shoulder. "You are like twenty-one. You are not dying alone." Leave it to Simon to know the age of the baker at our local café. He doesn't even try; he can't help but know everyone.

"I think I might though," she whines. I notice that her drink cup is empty. Hopefully, Simon is only serving her water from now on. "I have a crush on a guy that won't give me the time of day."

"I know the feeling," Simon mumbles. I give him a scathing look with no real heat behind it. "Who's the guy? Maybe I can't put in a good word."

"You would do that?" she says as her entire face lights up.

"Of course," Simon says. "Just point me in the direction of your dream guy." We all swing around to look out on the dance floor when Diana's arm shoots out as she points to some guy heavily groping a woman on the dance floor. I can't see his face from this angle, but Simon must be able to because he practically shouts, "No!"

"Why?" Diana and I ask at the same time.

"Not Leo. Anyone but Leo." Oh. Simon's arch nemesis. He can't go a day without griping about something Leo has done now. Simon has been begging Sam to cut him loose as a client, but Sam refuses. I think Leo causes him more unnecessary stress than my pregnancy at this point.

"But he's so cute. And nice. And funny. And cute. Did I say that already?" she hiccups. Before she has a chance to continue her rambling, Simon flags one of the women from the marketing department who offered to be a designated driver tonight. She ushers Diana away from the bar and hopefully home.

"She'll figure out she dodged a bullet with him one day," I say. Simon gets back behind the bar as more customers come over.

"You finally agree with me?" he asks in-between making drinks. I'm momentarily distracted by the veins in his forearms as he shakes the mocktail he's making for me. "Kitten?"

"Oh! Well, no. I think your hatred is a bit extreme, but he's already moved on from the woman he was groping to a new one, so I just think he's a player. A sweet girl like Diana would get her heart broken by a guy like Leo."

"I think you're right about that."

"I'm right about everything," I argue. At some point in the last couple of weeks, our hurtful arguing has turned into playful banter. I didn't know it would be something I enjoyed so much, but I do. I blame Simon.

Someone taps me on the shoulder from behind. I turn and the friendly smile on my face quickly falls.

Sidney.

"You haven't even told our parents about your situation yet, have you?" Sidney spews. No greeting, just straight venom. I need to figure out which one of my friends she's following on social media and get her blocked. She has no right to be following my personal life.

"Everyone important to me has been updated about my life," I state. My voice is cooler than I intended, but I need her to understand where we stand. She can't keep showing up here. I've set a boundary, and I want her to respect it. Simon stands behind me, stroking my back without saying a word. He knows I can handle this situation but is ensuring I know he's there if I need him. I love him for that... but I don't actually love him, right?

"Wow, Aspen," Sidney huffs. "You always were cold-hearted." I don't let her words hurt me the way she wants them to. Simon practically growls, but I nudge him with my shoulder so he keeps quiet. I know I'm not cold-hearted. I may put on a happy face when I don't feel bright and sunny like everyone thinks, but I know my heart. And it beats strong for those I love. But they have to deserve it.

"Sidney. Why are you here, again? I thought I made it clear you weren't welcome here. Do I need to get the police involved?" I say as calmly as possible.

"You are so dramatic!" she practically screams. I can feel prying eyes on us, so I pull Sidney by the arm into the hallway. I don't care if everyone in Bluefield knows my sister is having a very childish meltdown. But this is an important event, and I won't let her outshine it.

Sidney rips her arm out of my hold and leans against the wall. She's trying to act unaffected and in control, but I can see right through it. She wants something and for some reason, she thinks I'm the one who's going to give it to her.

"Sidney, I'm only going to ask one more time. What do you want from me?"

She bites her lips, seemingly thinking through her words before blurting out, "I need money!"

That was not what I was expecting.

"What?" I say because it's the only thing I can think of.

"Don't make me repeat myself, please." Sidney at least looks slightly embarrassed. I'm not sure if it's because of her outburst or because of what she just admitted. It's nice to see her acting like she feels at least a little bit of remorse for once.

"Why do you need money?" Simon cuts in. I almost forgot he followed us out here, but I'm thankful for his calm head right now.

"I just need it, okay? Are you going to help me or not?" The moment of embarrassment is gone and now she's back to acting like a spoiled child. I don't even know what to say. She's never asked me for money, so this isn't some patterned behaviour. In all honesty, aside from wanting forgiveness that she doesn't deserve, she hasn't asked me for anything since we were children. This must be killing her ego.

"Why Sidney? I won't ask again," Simon says firmly. His tone is all business, and a silly part of my brain is turned on by it. It's giving daddy, but this is not the time for any of that.

Sidney rolls her eyes, checks her manicure, and fluffs her hair, doing anything but answering Simon's question. When neither of us fills the quiet, she huffs and finally says, "Mom and Dad cut me off and I lost my job. I don't have rent money, and I can't move back home."

"And why is any of that my problem?" I ask. My parents have supported her long after I was cut loose. I'm not mad about it; I've learned how to manage money and work for what I have. I just don't understand how she's got herself in this situation with all the help they've given her.

"You got knocked up by a rich guy. The least you can do is help your sister out."

I can feel Simon's silent chuckle against my back. I'm glad he's finding this funny, and that he's not offended. Considering how much of our relationship is the product of an accident, I'm not worried that he thinks I'm using him for his bank account. I know I've worked just as hard as Simon has to get to this point in his career. We're equals here. Something I never thought I would feel in a relationship.

"No," I say, making sure Sidney hears to finality in my voice. This ends here. I'm not helping and I'm not entertaining her childish antics anymore. Sidney stands in front of me, stunned. I think she really thought I was about to be her next meal ticket. I grab Simon's hand so we can head back into the dance when he stops me.

"You head back inside. I'll walk Sidney out," Simon insists. I don't know why he thinks he needs to be a gentleman, but he can have at it.

I wait for Simon by the bar, but when he joins me, he directs me back toward the dance floor. Before we join the other couples, I ask, "Did you say anything more to Sidney?"

Simon looks to his feet and takes a deep breath before meeting my eyes. "I did. I know you may not like it, but I gave her the contact information for someone I know who's looking for an assistant. It's a bit of a grunt work job, but if she really needs the money, she'll have to work for it. I also told her if I ever see her again, she will be arrested, so for her sake, I hope that's the last of her."

I want to be mad at Simon for this. The Aspen of three

months ago would have started a screaming match with him just for fun. But I'm not going to do that now. I'm too happy with everything else in my life to care that he stepped in. Because *he cares*. And that means more.

"Dance with me," he says while leading me toward the other couples. I guess I don't really have a choice, but Simon can see the excitement on my face. I love dancing.

Lillian and I did ballet for years and I can't help but want to dance out my emotions still. Right now, those emotions are conflicting.

There's fear of the future and all the changes to come.

There's joy for this community and the friendships I've made in Bluefield.

There's pain for the family I was born into but I can't be a part of.

And there's happiness. Blinding happiness I feel when I'm with Simon.

I want to hold on to that emotion and all the other good ones. The ones I can grow into. The ones I can grow with Simon.

So, we dance. And we laugh. And then we go home, and we feel everything we need to feel together.

Chapter 27

Simon

SAM:

> We still good to meet today? It's okay if you're busy

SIMON:

> We're still on. I will always make time for you

I want to spend the morning wrapped up in Aspen in what has become our bed. I never want to leave. That we've reached a point of having a bed that is considered ours is more than I dreamed of when we discovered we would be tied together for life. The last couple of weeks have been nothing but domestic bliss, and I want to soak up every moment of it because something this good can't last forever.

But I have to get out of this bed. Because I made a promise to a kid who looks at me like I'm way smarter than I am, and I don't want to let him down.

I have been trying to meet with Sam once every week or so just to check in.

I leave Aspen in bed to sleep a bit longer and head down to the kitchen, setting up our coffee maker so all she'll have to do is press a button to get her matcha brewing. Then I grab a freezer bag and pack up some premade meals to take with me.

Sam is private about his home life. I know he worked at the General Store last summer and still picks up shifts when they need help from time to time. That isn't very often with the tourism in town so low this year.

From town gossip, I know his parents were never around and his grandma raised him alone. He doesn't talk about her much and I never actually met her, so I want to make sure someone is taking care of him. I would never tell Jackson this, but Sam reminds me of him as a teenager. He is fighting for his place in the world alone. A little bit angry and a lot untrusting. He seems overly friendly at times, but maybe he just doesn't know how to forge real relationships because he didn't have any examples of them growing up.

My parents were there for Jackson as much as they could be. I want to be there for Sam in case he needs that too. Also, I'm a great judge of character, so I don't believe anything Jackson, Lillian and Aspen say about the kid. They're bullies in my eyes.

And if I'm wrong? I'm offering the kid business advice. No one is getting hurt.

Sam agreed to meet him at the cafe in town. When I enter, he's already sitting at a table in the far corner, hunched over, writing in his notebook. I place my order and as I'm heading to the table, I see Diana in the kitchen, looking just as hungover as I thought she would be. Maybe it's my impending fatherhood or just the fact I'll be thirty next year, but I do not plan on feeling like that ever again.

When I sit down across from Sam, he slams his notebook shut and stuffs it into his backpack. He's always writing in there but makes sure no one sees what's on the pages. I'm not going to meddle. Everyone's entitled to their secrets.

Before we're able to get started, Diana comes by and places two scones on the table and Sam does something I've never seen him do. He blushes and looks away. The aggressively outgoing kid in front of me, the one who talks to strangers daily and never knows an awkward encounter, seems almost bashful around our resident pastry mastermind. Interesting. If I didn't know she has a silly crush on Leo, I would tell him to go for it. She's probably a couple of years older than him, but they're both adults, so why not?

Before I can comment, Sam pulls out a binder I know he keeps his records in, and straight into business we go.

After showing Sam how to transfer all his paper receipts into accounting software, I decided that was enough for today. Imputing numbers into a computer for hours is not my ideal Sunday, and I know he can handle this on his own now.

"I didn't see you at the fundraiser yesterday," I say to Sam as we exit the cafe and head towards my car.

"It's not my scene," Sam responds, shrugging.

"A dance with most of the single women in town in attendance isn't your scene?"

"I just have a lot going on, I guess. Plus, I don't think Jackson would want me there. I get the feeling he doesn't like me."

Probably because he kicked Sam off my property and thinks his vibes are off.

"If you ever want to talk about anything, I'm always available," I say, and I mean it.

"I actually did have a question for you," Sam begins. "I was talking to Leo the other day, and he said I should try to expand into outdoor structures. You know, gazebos, pergolas, even decks and sheds. Do you think that's a good idea?"

Fucking Leo.

"Is this something you want to do? You feel like you need to expand your offering?" I ask, trying to keep my voice calm. Sam has had a business up and running for a total of two months and while he's not in the red financially, this is a seasonal business and if he wants to have it going long term, being money smart now is ideal.

"I'm not sure," Sam says, seeming like he hadn't actually put a lot of thought into it. "I don't actually know how to build any of those things, and I don't have the tools to do it, so it would be pretty hard, I guess."

"Maybe just see how this summer goes and then think about expanding in the future. You could always bring on a business partner in the future to tackle small building jobs," I suggest.

Sam shrugs, "Yeah, you're right. I got thinking about how cool it would be to do total backyard transformations, but maybe it's not right for me. There are other things I can do to stand apart from any competition."

"That's the spirit," I say, slapping him on the back lightly. I decide to take a shot at his dating life. "You know, a work-life balance is important for entrepreneurs. You need to make sure you're letting off steam every now and again. You got anyone you're interested in spending time with?"

Sam shuffles his feet, kicking a loose rock into the grass. "Not really. I have some friends from high school, but we've drifted a bit. They're into partying a lot and I'm not. I dated a bit in high school, but it's not what I'm interested in doing right now. You got to prioritize the things that make you happy, right? Well, I'm happy now."

I want to ask more, but I'll let him off the hook this time.

I look at the young man in front of me and try to see where the wariness my friends feel toward Sam stems from.

Yes, his eye contact is intense, but I respect someone who will look you in the eye when you talk.

He tends to linger and keep the conversation going longer than necessary at the end of our meetings. He's probably just lonely. I've never seen him with friends.

He calls Lillian Lilly, but I don't think she has ever corrected him, so that's on her, in my opinion.

"Well, I've got to head out now. Need to run some errands and get home before Aspen gets too hangry," I joke. I try to remind myself that she's eating for three, but sometimes I don't know where all the food goes to. I haven't had to make this much food since I was in high school and Jackson and I learned what bulking was.

As we say our goodbyes and Sam heads toward the General Store as he's still working some hours there between jobs. I'm more confident than ever that I'm right about this. Sam's different, but harmless.

I get into my car but when I look over my shoulder to reverse,

I see the premade meals sitting in my back seat. I know I could just drop them off to Sam now, but they really need to get back into the freezer. Sam's grandma seems to be at home a lot, so I'm sure dropping them off to her would be fine. When I get to the small bungalow around the corner, it doesn't seem like anyone is home. The lights are all off, but the front door is unlocked. I'm going to have to lecture the kid on basic safety precautions, apparently.

I know I shouldn't go inside, but I'm already here and the lack of locks is practically inviting me in. I shuffle inside quietly, even though no one is here to hear me, and stuff the casserole dishes in the freezer. Sam will know I was here uninvited, but I'm not too worried. Just as I'm about to slip back out the door, I hear a moan coming from the back of the house. The voice sounds pained. For a split second, I think about the missing women in town, but let the thought die quickly and slowly approach a back bedroom where the noise came from.

"Hello," I say hesitantly. The moan in response is enough to have me opening the closed bedroom door and stopping immediately at the sight in front of me.

Sam's grandmother is laying in a hospital style bed in the middle of her dimly lit bedroom. She opens her eyes and smiles at me, which is a good sign.

"Would you mind passing me my water glass?" she asks. My feet move quicker than my mouth can as I walk to the night-stand beside the bed and pass her the glass.

"I'm Simon," I say when she finishes her sip. "I'm a friend of Sam's."

"I know who you are, darling. Sam talks about you nonstop.

You are practically that boy's hero. I'm Shelia." I feel my cheeks heat and she gestures for me to sit down in the chair in the corner.

"I don't know about being his hero, but I'm enjoying mentoring him. He's got a good mind for business. I think he's got a bright future."

Sheila rubs over hand on her robe over her heart like she can feel my words. "That makes me so happy. I want to make sure Sam's okay when I'm not around anymore." I'm glad she's addressing the elephant in the room because I have no idea why her room is set up like a hospital. Sam hasn't once mentioned his grandma being sick. "Let me tell you a bit about my grandson's life…"

I sit there with Shelia for over an hour before she gets tired and basically kicks me out. I'm torn between reaching out to Sam to offer my support for his grandmother's condition and keeping my mouth shut. If he doesn't want me to know about his personal life, I can't force it.

By the time I get home, it's just after lunchtime. I picked up a premade sandwich from the deli to tide Aspen over until I have time to make lunch. I park my car in the driveway and head in through the garage when something purple catches my eye through the back window. Aspen hasn't made an indication she wants to be involved in the yard work Sam has been doing around here, but it looks like some purple flowers are waiting to be planted.

I walk around back toward the shed and almost stop in my tracks when I see a vase with artificially dyed purple flowers filling it.

Is the man colour blind? There are flowers that are actually colourful. Why is it necessary to butcher something with natural beauty and make it artificial? Send lavender, or lilacs, not daisies that look like they went to battle with a child finger-painting and lost.

When I installed the security system last month, the deliveries seemed to stop. I assumed John didn't want to be caught on our doorbell camera, but it looks like he's taken it a step further instead. It's one thing to have someone drop them off at the door. It's a whole other thing to be sneaking around behind our house, leaving them somewhere to be found while a very pregnant Aspen is probably asleep inside.

I storm over to the vase and grab the flowers from it before stomping toward the river. If John keeps this up, Bluefield's river is going to be a rainbow by the end of the summer.

I know Aspen doesn't want to get anyone involved, but this must constitute as stalking. Aspen told me she doesn't want to get the police involved, but this guy isn't going away. And it's my job to protect her and our family now.

The John situation is unfortunately out of Dylan's reach of power. It's not for Ben though. Apparently, no one had told him Aspen had a stalker ex-boyfriend and if I thought Ben's big brother wrath was bad after he found out I got Aspen pregnant, it's nothing like what John Dudley is about to have coming for him.

Ben is using his fancy lawyer words on his fancy lawyer paper and sending a cease and desist to John's home address and his work since we want to make sure he gets the message. No one wants their dirty laundry aired for their whole office to see, so this should send a strong message.

He doesn't have to respond, and we may never know his reaction, but as long as the flowers stop, I'll be happy. So will the ecosystem in the river because artificial colouring must be doing some damage. If we start seeing bright blue beavers, we may need to move.

Chapter 28
Aspen

ASPEN:

Simon is the worst

LILLIAN:

No he isn't

ASPEN:

I KNOW

"So I did something..." Simon says, like he thinks I'm not going to immediately be on guard.

We're currently lounging on the back patio. The sun is a bit too hot today for me to feel comfortable at the beach or on the boat. I am always sweating now so fresh air out of the sun is preferred. Life has been good lately, too good, if I'm being honest. How could the one guy who I swore was public enemy number one be slowly creeping into my heart?

Not so slowly, if I'm being honest. The man cooks, cleans,

organizes our lives, plans thoughtful dates, is a good friend, neighbour and colleague and gives me on demand orgasms. Simon Cadwell is perfect, and he's wormed his way into my heart.

He's so annoying.

But this is the moment he ruins everything, I'm sure. This life I dreamed of but never thought I would get is about to crumble before my eyes.

"What did you do, Simon?" My tone is even, emotionless, and I think that scares him more than if I was yelling.

"I got rid of the John problem."

What? John problem? I rack my brain, trying to figure out who John even is. I don't think we have any mutual friends named John. That means he's talking about my ex-boyfriend. The one I told him not to do anything about because he's harmless.

"What did you do?"

He explains to me that Dylan couldn't help, so Jackson suggested they have Ben get involved instead and now my ex probably thinks I'm the crazy one taking legal action against him.

So, Simon didn't contact John, no he had the whole boy gang involved. How did I go from growing up in a household with only a younger sister to having three protectively annoying brother figures and Simon? Simon, my not boyfriend because we've never had that conversation. My live-in lover, I guess. Baby daddy with benefits is the term I'd probably use to piss Simon off. Life partner or something equally soft would be Simon's preference, I bet.

"So let me get this straight. You had Ben threaten a man I

haven't talked to in a year because he's carrying some weird torch for me? You know that's not illegal, right?"

"It wasn't a threat, just a legal suggestion," he defends. "I found flowers from him in our backyard, Aspen. That's trespassing." Well, that's something I didn't know.

"I haven't seen any flowers in weeks. Have you been getting rid of them?" I ask. I'm not annoyed at him for the action, I'm annoyed at the lack of communication. "What else are you keeping from me?"

"Nothing," Simon says quickly. "Absolutely nothing. I didn't tell you because it's something I can deal with, and you can live in blissful ignorance. I was trying to do something good for you."

"Simon," I say, trying to keep my voice as calm as possible. The babies are currently doing flips in my stomach, clearly upset with our argument and if I want to keep my lunch where it belongs, in my stomach, then I need to de-escalate this situation. "No more secrets. I get that you care, but keeping me in the dark to protect me feels more hurtful than helpful. No more secrets."

"Yes ma'am," Simon salutes me, trying to lighten the mood. I hate to say his silliness works on me, but it does.

"Did you know that Julia and Dylan dated?" I ask Simon. If my friends get to peek at the skeletons in my closet, then maybe Simon is up for some friendly gossip.

"They went on one date. I don't think we should call that

dating," Simon responds.

"Irrelevant. Date, dating, whatever. How did you find out?"

"I asked Dylan if anything had ever happened between them? They were both in Bluefield before any of us showed up and there aren't that many single locals hanging around. Plus, they seem like decent friends now."

"And you didn't tell me? We need to share this kind of information with each other!"

"Aspen Arthur, are you a gossip?" he accuses.

"YES. And a proud one, as long as it isn't hurting anyone."

"Oh Kitten, I promise to share this type of information with you from now on." I roll my eyes at the use of his nickname for me while ignoring the flip it makes my stomach do. I'm sure it's because being called kitten is nauseating. It couldn't mean anything else. "Besides," he adds, "you also dated Dylan, so isn't it weird for you to be asking this?"

That makes me sit up from my place between Simon's outstretched legs. I was sitting here first, but when Simon forced his way between me and the lounge chair, I didn't have the energy to move. Simon makes a surprisingly soft back pillow, even with all the muscles.

"I didn't date Dylan," I say.

"Yes, you did. Jackson told me all about it."

"Well, Jackson is a balding liar," I argue. I have no idea where the insult came from. Pregnancy brain. We are always going to blame the pregnancy brain.

"One, Jackson has great hair, and you know it," Simon defends. "And two, you went on a double date, dancing at a bar. I saw evidence on Lillian's social media."

Oh, that night.

After my final breakup with John, I wanted to let loose. So I drove from Toronto to Bluefield, giving Lillian and Jackson almost no warning and ruining their romantic plans. Instead, we went dancing at a bar in Saintrich with Dylan. It was not a date. I'm pretty sure Jackson's exact words when he invited Dylan were, "I could probably handle wrangling Lillian or Aspen, but not both of them. Help a guy out." So, we had fun, and we danced together. I danced with Jackson, I danced with Lillian, and I danced with Dylan. He flirted because he's always a shameless flirt with me, and I flirted back because it was fun. It was not a date.

"It was not a date. It was a friendly group hang out."

"Then why are you two always so flirty together?" Simon asks with an edge to his voice. Ohhhhh, this man is jealous. I love it.

"Dylan is a flirty guy," I defend. "It's innocent, just the way we like to banter with each other."

"Dylan isn't like that with me, with the guys."

"Do you want Dylan to flirt with you?" I ask. "I'm sure he would be flattered, but I'm not sure if you're his type."

"That's not what I meant, and you know it." Yes, but it's fun ruffling his feathers playfully. If I don't, I might accidentally go back to fighting with him every chance I get. Also, I can't believe I have to explain Simon's own relationship with one of his best friends to him. "Simon, when you are with Dylan, what is he like?"

"He's funny, but not all the time. Usually a bit on the quieter side. He's pretty open about what's going on in his life and always down to listen or help out if one of us needs it."

"You know what that sounds like to me? The real Dylan. He and I are friends, but not to the level he is with you, Jackson and Ben. The version I get is the side he likes to show to the public. He's so serious with his job he probably wants to show a more playful side sometimes. You're getting Dylan with his walls down."

"Hmm." Simon thinks this over for a moment. "I guess that's true. Are you very observant, or was this glaringly obvious and I missed it?"

"Neither and both. I guess I can relate a bit. I can play into my chaotic, fun time side more than I want to sometimes. It's easier to show people the version of you they want to see. That way, you can't be upset if they don't like it because it isn't really you. It can get me in trouble sometimes because I tend to forget about having a filter, but more often than not, people like having me around."

This conversation started silly and has taken a very serious turn. Normally, I would make a joke or say something super dramatic to break up the feelings swirling around inside of me, but I don't want to.

I know Simon likes me. He likes my crazy and my chaos. But he also likes my quiet.

So, I let the feelings I just unleashed swarm us in a cocoon of honesty. And in Simon's arms, I feel safe enough to let them be.

Chapter 29
Simon

SIMON:

> Aspen requires your presence

JACKSON:

> Why do I feel like I'm being summoned by the queen

BEN:

> I was thinking more along the lines of jury duty

SIMON:

> Just get over here

I'm not one hundred percent sure what we're all doing here, but Aspen said she had a surprise and asked that I gather all our friends at our house. If I had to guess, I would say this has something to do with her secret project in the baby's nursery.

She managed to change the locks on the door to their bedroom and bathroom, and I conveniently don't have the key to enter.

Lillian, Julia, Jackson, Dylan, Ben, and Noah all sit around our living room, catching up on their weeks until we hear the ringing of a bell coming from the top of the stairs.

"Your presence is requested upstairs," Aspen practically sings.

I roll my eyes at Aspen's theatrics even though I love it when she's over the top. Especially because I know she's acting this way because she wants to be and whatever she's about to show us is important to her. She's putting on a show for herself, not for anyone else's benefit.

Noah squeals with excitement and trips over his own feet, trying to race everyone to Aspen. Ben catches him by the back of his T-shirt, righting him. Noah isn't even the slightest bit phased. Like he just knows his dad will be there to catch him, no matter what.

"Dad reflexes," Ben mumbles to me. "You'll develop them quickly, trust me." And I want to trust him, but part of me still worries. Do I have that fatherly instinct? Will I just know what I'm doing somehow? Or will I fail epically? I've studied every book and article there is out there, but I still worry about being enough for Aspen and our babies. I shake my head, trying to erase my worried thoughts. Aspen needs me present now.

We all gather outside the baby's nursery where Aspen clutches the doorknob, a blinding smile on her face. Where some people might be nervous about unveiling a surprise like this, Aspen looks straight-up giddy. I move through the crowd to stand by her side, holding her hand in mine.

She clears her throat before beginning. "I've gathered you all here because I wanted to thank you for all the support given to both Simon and me as we embark on this surprising new chapter of our lives."

Aspen opens the door and I think everyone gasps. What Aspen has done is magical. All four walls of the nursery, which were previously what Aspen likes to call boring beige, are now covered, floor to ceiling, with a hand-painted mural. Somehow, she has accurately captured a scene straight out of our back-yard. Bushes and trees in all shades of green, a sparkling river winding through the brush, and woodland creatures unaffected by civilization. It looks like it should be the opening scene in a children's movie.

Everyone surrounds Aspen singing her praise, but I stand there speechless. I know Aspen and I both have worries about becoming parents and going from zero to two children. But, with the amount of love Aspen has poured into this hand-craft-ed design, I think we will be alright. Our babies will never for a second feel anything but our undying love for them. We will be enough.

Aspen catches my eye from across the room, clearly noticing that I've lost the ability to form words. All I can do is smile. I have so much to say, but that's a conversation for when we are alone, and I can show her just how much I love this room.

"Aspen, this is great," Ben begins. "And I don't want to rain on your parade..."

"Then don't," I cut in before I can think better of it. Jackson practically shakes beside me, trying to hold in his laughter.

"Calm down, Papa Bear," Ben jokes. "As I was saying. Aspen

this is amazing, but there isn't anything else in this room. I feel like you might need a crib or two?"

Aspen rolls her eyes and walks toward the adjoining bathroom. "Remember my whole speech about how we appreciate your love and support? Yeah, I was just buttering you up." She throws open the door, giving us a view straight into the next bedroom, which is filled with boxes. "You guys are building baby furniture today!"

Now I can't help but laugh. Something about this whole situation is so Aspen. She works hard and is good at what she does, but she's not afraid to tell someone else to do the heavy lifting for her. I love it. I love her.

We spent the next several hours assembling furniture while the women and Noah organize the clothing and toys. Everything moves seamlessly as Jackson puts on his project manager hat and directs Ben, Dylan, and me on what to build and where. Once everything is assembled, Aspen takes over, having us move the cribs, dressing table, and dressers around until everything is perfect.

And it really is perfect.

I've known Aspen is talented. I've seen it firsthand at work. But this? This is magic. Every piece of furniture proves a function and comfort in the space. The room is neutral but warm. It feels like we're tucked inside a cozy forest. You can practically feel Aspen's love oozing off every item she's carefully picked. I feel like I'm always in awe of Aspen, but right now I could bow at her feet.

I want everyone out of our house now so I can get on my knees for this woman.

There's just one little problem, and he's currently tugging on my leg, staring at me with big blue eyes. "Simon, can we go for a walk? Can you pull me in the wagon? Can you go on the boat" I don't know how Ben tells this kid no. His eyes look like a window into his heart and the thought of making him even the slightest bit upset makes me itchy. I hear Ben chuckle from somewhere in the room, clearly reading my internal struggle. We don't have a wagon. I need to order one. Now.

Noah ignores my lack of response and leaves the room, probably to go play with the toys we have in one of the spare rooms. Everyone else files out of the nursery and heads downstairs, leaving Aspen and me alone for a moment.

"You are amazing. Absolutely amazing," I mumble against her forehead before kissing her there. Aspen doesn't blush or act bashful because of my compliment. She stands there confidently, letting me praise her with a smile on her face.

"Thank you," Aspen says, before pulling away. I want her back in my arms, but know this is not the time for that. We head downstairs to say goodbye to our friends and prepare for the rest of the afternoon.

"Good luck," is all Ben says as he heads out the door. While he will be hanging out with Jackson and Lillian tonight, probably heading to the next town over and getting a drink, Aspen and I will be babysitting Noah. I guess it's supposed to be a trial run. I think Noah is at a very different stage in life than our babies will be when they arrive, but I'm not going to turn down the opportunity to let Ben have a night to himself.

I needed the luck Ben offered. After taking a walk without a wagon, taking Noah out on the boat, making dinner, and then setting up the living room for movie night, I'm exhausted. There is no time for a break with a kid this active. I've needed to be engaged and enthusiastic constantly. Considering what a big day it was for Aspen, I'm not surprised that she passed out the second the movie started. She and Noah have a very special relationship. He looks at her like she's a superhero, never questioning if she can do something, just assuming she's good at everything. It makes me fall even harder for her, because that's the truth. I've fallen so hard for Aspen Arthur that I don't know that I could ever live without her now. She's in my mind, my bones, my heart, and the air I breathe. All of this. The life we've built, any success I've had, it all means nothing if I can't fall asleep beside her every night.

"I never asked this before, because I was worried it would start a fight, but now I'm confident I can talk you down if it does." I can tell Aspen is on edge immediately. Her body, which was just soft against me, is now rigid. I continue to draw circles on her back until she melts back into me. "Why weren't you on birth control when we slept together? Not that you should have been. I just assume most women your age are?"

I'm not sure if I worded it properly, but as Aspen nuzzles her face into my neck, I know I haven't completely put my foot in my mouth. After she slept through the entire movie and we got Noah settled into the guest room, we've been lying in bed in comfortable silence.

Something about the events of today has put me in the mood for more serious conversations. There are things I need to know that I've been holding onto for too long. I love silly and outgoing Aspen, but that isn't the real her, at least not all the time. I love her mind and want to understand everything about it. Aspen is a fascinating creature. She's loyal and kind, funny, and smart, ambitious and confident. But to the ones who really know her, she's beyond thoughtful. She makes sure every person in the room feels seen and heard. She listens and really hears what people have to say. Aspen thinks I walk into a room and instantly make friends with everyone, but that's only because I've always found people fascinating. It also makes make my job a hell of a lot easier. Aspen makes friends in every room she enters too because she's magnetic. You want to know her. To earn her smiles, the reals ones, but feed off of her energy. Based on the information I've gathered from Lillian, the guys Aspen was with in the past were parasites. They wanted to take her energy and bottle it up for themselves, live off of it.

I don't want that. I want her energy to expand until she's everywhere. I want all of her dreams to come true and then more. I want her dreaming for things she didn't even know she wanted.

"I wanted to have a baby, with or without a man, so I was starting to prepare for egg retrieval."

"Really?" I ask. Aspen is only twenty-eight. This isn't something many people talk about. I understand bits and pieces because my sister and her partner have contemplated their options for having children.

"I didn't plan this, obviously," Aspen states, sitting up slightly so we can make eye contact. "I wanted children, but I would never try to put you in this situation without your consent. You have to believe that."

"I do," I assure her. "I would never doubt you on that. I just didn't know this was something you were starting to plan for." I hum, feeling a bit smug. "A part of me is very happy I got to you before some sperm donor could."

"You know I wouldn't have had sex with the sperm donor. This isn't some pissing contest. I'm starting to think you have a breeding kink or something."

"Whatever you say, kitten."

She growls at me like she always does when I call her that, but the smile on her face shows that she likes her nickname more than she lets on.

"Super sperm," I mumble under my breath. I am convinced I have super sperm.

"Any other questions?" Aspen asks. *So many.* I want to know everything.

"Why do you hate me?" It's been plaguing me lately. Now that Aspen and I are in a better place, a great place, a part of me is so scared to mess this up. I did something to start our feud. I met Aspen at a party once, and everything was good. Then I don't see her again for years. Suddenly she is everywhere and hates me. If I don't know I did wrong in the first place, how do I avoid doing it again?

This life that Aspen and I are building together is everything to me. Everything. And I want to protect our peace the best I can. So even if this may be an uncomfortable conversation, it's going to happen, and it's going to happen now. Hopefully.

"Does it really matter now?" She asks. "We're good. I don't want to bring up the past. Can't we move on?" I would love to move on, but I need to know. I wish I were the type to let things go; I'm a problem solver.

"Please tell me. We won't fight about it, I promise." Aspen rolls her eyes, but I know I've won this one.

"Fine," she huffs out. "But if this does end in a fight, just know you started it."

I gesture to the space between us. "Please proceed." That gets me another eye roll.

"So, we were at that party at Jackson's house. The only party I ever went to there. Lillian wouldn't come with me because it wasn't her scene." That makes me chuckle. Lillian at one of our high school parties would be a sight to be seen. She would probably break out in hives with the number of people we crammed into Jackson's house when his dad wasn't home. "So some girls from the dance team I was socially friends with were going and I went with them. Within minutes, I got separated from them, so I decided to dance and mingle on my own when I bumped into you."

This part I remember vividly. Aspen turned around a corner quickly and split her bright red drink all over my white t-shirt. I honestly didn't really care; my mom still did my laundry, and I was too distracted by Aspen's pretty eyes to pay much attention to the mess. She kept apologizing, and I milked it for a little just to keep her attention. There were many eyes on Aspen at that party. She's a brunette bombshell with a blinding smile, captivating eyes, and a fun personality. I was determined to keep her attention for as long as I could. We talked for what felt like hours and five minutes at the same time. When my shirt started to harden to my body, I stepped upstairs to get changed. When I came back down, Aspen was gone, and I then didn't see her again until last year. She ignored every friend request I sent and never came to another party I attended. If it wasn't for Lillian and Jackson, there's a very real chance I would have never seen Aspen again.

"I ruined your shirt, we talked and then you made up an excuse to leave me so you could go hook up with someone else," Aspen says, completely catching me off guard. I know for a fact that didn't happen.

"What are you talking about? You think I left you for someone else? I went to get changed and then you were gone."

Aspen makes a rumbling noise in her throat, sitting straighter, preparing for the fight we said we weren't going to have.

"Simon, do not lie to me. I saw you with her."

"Again, what are you talking about?" I ask.

"My friends were leaving, so I went to find you to see if you wanted me to stay or not." I wanted her to stay. SO badly. "I went upstairs to where I heard voices. The door to the bedroom was slightly open, so I peeked in when I heard your voice. You were standing there, shirtless, with a girl in your arms. I may have been younger and less experienced than you, but I knew where it was leading. I got the hell out of there. I'm pretty sure you went to prom with her later that year. You were being a sleaze, so I left and that's that." It certainly isn't. All this time Aspen has hated me, and she has no idea what she saw.

"Aspen," I say in the calmest voice I can muster right now.

I'm trying not to laugh at this big misunderstanding because I know it will only make her more upset with me, but it is almost comical how wrong she read that situation. "You saw me hugging Jessica, who yes, I went to prom with, but not because we were ever—and I mean ever—together in the way you think. Jessica was my sister's high school girlfriend." The annoyed look on Aspen's face immediately drops to a shocked one. "I went upstairs to change when I found Jessica up there crying. My sister was supposed to come home that weekend but ended up staying at university. Jessica had a bit too much to drink and got weepy. I was shirtless because you spilt on me, and I didn't want that to transfer to her shirt when I consoled her. And yes, Jessica and I went to prom together, but that was because she hadn't come out to anyone at school yet and asked if I would go with her so she still got the prom experience." Jessica was one of my good friends, so I was more than happy to go to prom with her. We had tons of fun and sent photos to my sister all night so she would be jealous. I'm a little brother. I have to piss off my sister at least once a month.

"Oh," is all Aspen says.

"Yeah," I say as I pull her towards me. Aspen hides her face in the crack of my neck and for a moment I think she's crying because her shoulders start to shake. Then I feel a vibration against my skin and realize Aspen is laughing.

"My poor hormone infused teenage brain went straight to the worst-case scenario. I was such a nut. I am such a nut."

"You're not a nut," I say as I stroke her back. "It probably looked pretty bad. I just wish you would have given me another chance."

Aspen drops a light kiss on my lips and then presses her forehead to mine. "I think it happened how it needed to. Jackson and Lillian needed to find their way to each other at the right time. And I think we did too."

I can agree with that. Aspen needed to hate me so we could have a truce on New Year's Eve. Without all that, we wouldn't be weeks away from being a family of four. Or five if my surprise tomorrow goes over well.

"Speaking of my sister, Claire is coming to visit tomorrow."

"She is? I'm so excited to meet her," Aspen squeals. Claire has been travelling all around deep in wedding season, so she and Aspen haven't met in person yet. I know they text quite a bit, being in a group chat with my mom, but I asked Claire to keep this from her as there is more to this visit than Aspen knows.

Chapter 30

Aspen

LILLIAN:

> Make sure you get your beauty sleep tonight!

ASPEN:

> WHY

ASPEN:

> What do you know that I don't know???

When I wake on Sunday morning, it's to a surprise. Although not how I had hoped I would be, with Simon between my legs, but instead with my best friend's blonde curls practically choking me. Not what I was expecting, but a nice surprise. We haven't had a slumber party in a while. I don't know if this counts as one since she wasn't here when I fell asleep, but I'm going to make an exception since she is flat out on Simon's side of the bed.

"Billy," I whisper, brushing her curls out of her face. She looks so peaceful like this, without her anxiety ruling her reactions. Therapy has made a big difference in her daily life, and having the concrete support of Jackson, of course, her anxiety isn't as bad as it once was, but I still wish I could take all of my best friend's burdens away. "Billy, wake up."

She grumbles something under her breath before her eyes shoot open. "I fell asleep?"

"I assume so, since you are in my bed and I had to wake you," I laugh out loud.

"Whoops. I came upstairs to wake you..." She glances at the clock on my nightstand, eyes widening. "An hour ago. Not great Lillian. Anyway, this bed is so comfy, I need this mattress in my life. Well, time to get up. We have a big day ahead." She pops out from under the covers, fully dressed in a floral sundress and heads downstairs. "Julia will be up soon to help you with your hair and makeup."

She's gone from the room before I can ask what the hell she's talking about.

Julia appears moments later, makeup case in her arms, and ushers me to the bathroom, where she then does a full "natural" glam on my face and loose waves in my hair. No matter how many times I asked what we were getting ready for, she was tight-lipped. Sitting on my bed was a pretty cream dress that is tight all over, really showing off my large belly. I love surprises, so I try not to pry for details and go with the flow. When I get downstairs, Lillian shoves a cinnamon bun in my face and ushers me to Jackson's truck, where we drive back to her place.

In the back of my mind, I know this has something to do with Claire's surprise trip to see us and I am correct when we get to Lillian's and see her waiting for us on the beach.

Claire runs into my waiting arms the second I'm in the sand and engulfs me in a tight hug.

"You are gorgeous," she says when she pulls away. "How the hell did you end up with a goof like Simon?" I knew I liked Claire from our text messages, but I have a feeling picking on Simon is going to be our new common interest.

"I'm so happy you're here. But why are you here? Like on the beach. I assumed we would be having lunch together or something."

"Maternity photoshoot," Claire says, her fingers wiggling to imitate jazz hands. "If you're okay with that, obviously. I would love to capture your glowing beauty."

I'm not going to tell her that this was a theory I had on the drive over and I've already been mentally thinking of possess I want to do, but I am more than ready. "Let's do this!"

An hour later, I am a bit too sweaty to be photographed and more than ready to invite myself into Lillian's air-conditioned cottage. I would even settle for an air-conditioned vehicle. Claire has been fiddling with her camera for five minutes now, while Lillian and Julia make pointless conversation. I am holding my tongue because they put in a lot of work to pull off this surprise, but I need food and to be off my feet now.

"Okay, just a couple more shots," Claire says, directing me toward the water once more. "Why don't you sit on your heels at the edge of the water, so the lake is to the side of you?" I follow her instructions, grateful that the water has cooled the sand I'm

sitting on. "Excellent. Now look down at your belly and rub it."
I do as I'm told and hear the rapid fire of her camera clicking as
she snaps the shots.

I mentally prepare myself to ask if we can end the session
soon when a small furry blob jumps onto my belly and a little
pink tongue attacks my face. "Oh my god!" I yelp as the puppy
continues to remove most of the makeup from my face. "Where
did you come from?"

A shadow falls over us and then Simon is kneeling in front of
me, trying to wrangle the golden puppy off of me. "Surprise,"
he says warily.

"Simon! Did you get me a dog??" I love him already, but why
am I being gifted a dog?

"If you love it, then I did. If you don't, then he's Claire's."

"No, he isn't!" I hear Claire yell from a few feet away as she
continues to capture this moment.

"I mean, we are about to have two babies. Is a puppy a smart
idea?"

"I think we should embrace the chaos, don't you?"

This is absolutely crazy and also so something I would do. I
love that Simon thought of this. We will probably be kicking
ourselves when we are sleep-deprived and cleaning accidents
off the floor in a couple of weeks, but how could I turn down
either of the puppy dog looks I am getting from both the golden
furball and Simon?

"I love him. Thank you, Simon." With the puppy perched on
Simon's knee, licking my belly, Simon pulls me into a slightly
indecent kiss. Claire gags as we hear the click of her camera, but
I can also hear Lillian giggling and Julia whispering, "Swoon."

Simon pulls away and says, "One more surprise for today." And that is how I find myself at my surprise baby shower thirty minutes later.

"Aspen, this is my wife, Willow," Claire says as a redheaded beauty pulls me into a warm hug.

"You're a tree too," I say without thinking. Thankfully she laughs and puts her arm around Claire's waist.

Everyone that I would want is here. Simon's mother, Claire, Willow, Lillian, her mother, Julia, Mrs. Langley, some of the girls from work, and half the women that live in Bluefield. Even Dr. Azarian, or Faith, as she insisted I call her, is here. I'm not sure if it's normal for doctors to attend their patients' events, but she's new to Bluefield and this will give her a good opportunity to meet everyone.

I feel completely showered in love today.

We're all ignoring the police cruiser parked out front of our house as we snack in the backyard. Jackson, Simon, Dylan, Ben and Noah are all inside the house, leaving us to have our girls' afternoon, but if I had to guess, Dylan has a patrol stationed out front to make a statement. If the town is having a problem with women going missing, having half of them located in one place makes for an easy hunting ground for whoever the creep is behind the disappearances. I've tried to keep this thought in the back of my mind and enjoy the day, but it is the unfortunate reality we are all living in.

Lillian pulls me from my doom spiral when she approaches with the cutest puppy there ever was in her arms. Bart is his name. When Noah got here and heard his father call the puppy a little fart, he heard Bart and Ben didn't correct him. I don't have the heart to change it. Ben is going to owe me for the rest of the dog's life for that one.

I snatch my baby out of her hands and prop him on top of my belly. Who knew being the size of a transport truck would be so convenient?

"I'm going to take him inside so we can open gifts," Lillian says, trying to take him back. I know I should let him walk, but I don't want to miss any of the puppy snuggles. Just wait until Simon realizes he's losing his spot in bed to this little guy.

Simon has really outdone himself. This shower is everything I could have dreamed of, but why did no one tell me that opening presents in front of a large group of people is so awkward? I've been to a couple of bridal showers, and I never noticed how uncomfortable the bride must have been. I'm overjoyed that so many people took the time to buy me these thoughtful gifts, but schooling my reactions in real time is a chore. To be honest, I'm just trying not to cry. It's overwhelming.

Every time I've had to say, "Thank you for the...thank you.," because I have no idea what this baby item is for and it's quickly bringing my mood down. I don't want anyone to notice, but I'm starting to feel very unprepared and like a total failure of an expectant mother. There is so much I'm supposed to know but baby brain doesn't let me retain all of it. How do mothers do it?

I search the crowd for something, I'm not sure what, but the second my eyes land on Simon, I know it's him I need. He must see the urgency in my eyes because he walks away from his dad mid-conversation and jogs toward me.

He leans over me, hiding me from the rest of the party attendees, and whispers against my neck. "How are you doing, kitten?"

I don't have the brain capacity to articulate all the feelings running through me right now. I grab his neck and pull him closer to me, breathing in the calming scent that he seems to always have.

"Join me?" I manage to squeak out. It sounds like a question, but really, it's a plead. I need to feel like I'm not alone in this. I know I'm not alone in this, but I need the reassurance right now.

Instead of grabbing a spare chair and sitting next to me, Simon pulls me out of my chair, plops himself down, and settles me in his lap. He rests his head on my shoulder and squeezes my hips once telling me to proceed.

Lillian hands me the next gift in the pile. The card says it's from Simon's parents. I cast a soft smile in their direction and then pull the box out of the gift bag. I immediately think it looks like a small coffee maker. I'm sure it's labelled, but the panic starts to set in, and I can't make the letters form words.

I feel sweat collect on the back of my neck just as Simon's soft voice hits my ear. "It's a bottle warmer for milk. It can be used for breast milk or formula. I think this model also sterilizes bottles." I instantly feel my shoulders fall and my death grip on the bottle ease.

We continue to open presents this way. The second I hesitate, Simon is in my ear, explaining the gift and its purpose. When everything is unwrapped, I thank everyone for their generosity and sneak inside, pulling Simon with me. As I commit to hiding from our guests, the laundry room seems like as good of a place as any to have this conversation.

The second the door is closed behind us, I practically launch myself into Simon's arms. "Are you okay?" he immediately asks. He takes a couple of steps until he's able to place me onto the top of the washing machine but continues to hold me.

"I'm okay. But like, how? How did you know all that? Why don't I know any of that?"

Simon chuckles, but it doesn't sound patronizing like I once thought it did. No, Simon's laugh is comforting. If he has that easy smile on his face, I know everything is going to be okay. "Your job during this pregnancy is to grow our children. Which you've been doing a fabulous job of. My job is everything else."

"I'm not sure that's really how this all works," I huff out, pouting slightly.

"I've read a lot of baby books," Simon admits. "Probably every book ever written, to be honest. There's a stack hidden inside my desk." Part of me loves that he's been doing research. The other part of me hates that Simon is better at something than I am. In this case, I'll let the mature side win for once.

"Could you share them with me?"

"You can have anything you want, Aspen. Everything you want." After everything that happened today, this is the moment that holding off tears is the hardest. I let them fall, knowing Simon will catch every single one of them.

Chapter 31

Aspen

ASPEN:

> Thank you all, for everything!

LILLIAN:

> LOVE YOU

JULIA:

> xoxoxoxox

CLAIRE:

> Welcome to the family!

B y the time the party winds down, I am beyond exhausted. If I could take multiple naps a day, I would at this point in my pregnancy.

Simon's family took care of all the cleaning up so I could put my feet up on the couch. Swollen ankles? My new best friend, sorry Lillian.

Simon joins me on the couch, asking for a recap of my entire day, while Bart snoozes on his dog bed by the fireplace. Simon bought every dog accessory there is so needless to say, Bart is a very happy, but spoiled, puppy.

"So it was a good day?" he asks.

"So, so good," I say, kissing his jaw. I may be tired, but not enough to keep my hands off of Simon.

"Oh yeah," he says, gently pushing me back until I'm flat against the couch and he looms over me. This position is a bit awkward with my belly between us; and Simon's long arms are locked straight on either side of my head. If he gets tired, he can reposition us, I guess. "What was your favourite part?"

"All of it," I say as he trails kisses down my neck. "The photoshoot, Bart, all our friends and family being here, you right now."

"Oh, I made the list, did I?" he says between kisses. He pushes the strap of my dress off my shoulder to continue his path of kisses. "What about me made it so great?"

This man loves it when I stroke his ego. I'd like to be stroking something else, but my abs muscles are nonexistent, so there's no way I'm able to sit up and reach.

"You setting everything up, surprising me, getting us a Bart, giving me an even bigger chosen family than I already had. Just you being you. You are good. To me. For me. Always."

"Aspen," he croaks into my neck. I hear the emotions in his voice. This would be the perfect time to tell him how I feel about him. We've both been all in for a while now, but I want him to know exactly how I feel. I want him to know I love him.

"Simon, I..." I start just as Simon's phone begins to ring from the coffee table. Normally, I know he would ignore it, but it's Dylan calling. He wouldn't call this late at night unless it was important.

Simon pulls himself off the couch with more grace than I ever could and grabs his phone.

"Hey Dylan, what's up?" I can hear Dylan's voice coming through the phone rapidly but can't make out what he's saying.

"No, no one is here anymore." I gesture for Simon to put it on speaker. "I'm putting you on speaker. Aspen is here with me."

"Hi Dylan, what's going on?"

"Hi Aspen, I hate to call on such a special day for you, but do you know when Diana left your place?" I try to think but there were a lot of people there and I wasn't conscious of the time.

"Um, it was probably a bit earlier than the majority of the crowd. She mentioned wanting to get some baking in tonight to prep for the week." Diana was at the party for a bit today, but couldn't stay long. "It would have been after we cut the cake, but not by long if I had to guess. I honestly can't be sure. What's going on?"

I already have a feeling, but I need to ask.

"Nothing is for sure. But Diana was supposed to call her brother tonight and never did. The last people to see her were you guys at the party today. I have someone heading over to the cafe now, but I wanted to check in in case there was somewhere else we should be looking."

"She said she was heading to the cafe. I know that with one hundred percent certainty," I say confidently, even as my stomach fills with knots. Diana is as sweet as can be. I hope nothing bad has happened. "Let us know if, no, when you find her."

"Thanks for your help." Before we can say anything else, Dylan hangs up. I guess he's got a job to do.

"Woah," Simon breathes out. I am at a loss for words. The missing women have been close to us in the sense that they live in Bluefield, but I didn't know any of them personally. If Diana is missing after leaving our house, I don't think I'll forgive myself. I didn't even think about the fact that she was leaving alone. I've seen her walking around town before. She probably walked to the cafe or back home all alone. This whole situation has me sick with worry.

"Can we go up to bed?" I ask Simon. I just want to curl up in bed with Simon's arms wrapped around me and pretend this world isn't such an ugly place sometimes.

Once we have both completed our nighttime routine and Bart is comfy in his crate—Simon immediately put his foot down on Bart being in bed with us—Simon pulls me into his arms so I can lay my head on his bare chest. I lazily brush my fingers through his soft hair. I hope our kids get Simon's hair. It has more of a wave, almost a curl to it. I think a little boy and girl with matching chocolate curls would be a dream.

"Are you growing your hair out?" I ask. It's gotten longer over the summer and Simon hasn't cut it once. I'm used to seeing him with a clean-cut year-round. His shaggy waves don't fit the uptight businessman look I used to hate, but now secretly love.

"Yeah, I guess. I don't know. Do you like it?"

"I do like it." I love running my fingers through it and giving it a nice tug when he's between my legs. "Do you like it?"

"I think so. It's silly but, I got this idea in my head that I want to be a cool dad who's always outside with the kids having fun. For some reason, growing my hair out a bit seemed to fit that image."

"That is a bit silly," I agree. "But I think it looks good. I mean, you always look good, but this suits you."

"Thank you. It's nice getting a compliment that you didn't have to ask for," he jokes. I smack the back of his head lightly as he kisses the top of my head.

I feel my eyes getting heavier and just as I'm about to let sleep take me, Simon's phone dings with a message.

"False alarm, Diana is safe," it reads.

But how safe are any of us in this town?

Simon drops his briefcase where his desk should be. It clatters to the ground with a loud thud. I hope there wasn't anything too valuable in there. Simon left early this morning to get some work done with a client and I got to work doing something entirely different. After all the surprises Simon had for me yesterday, I have one for him today. Although he may not like this one.

Simon looks at the floor, where my yoga mat now lies, up to me and then back to the floor.

"Um, Aspen? Where's my desk?" Simon asks in a voice that is too calm for the situation. My nerves spike in my belly. Either that or the babies don't like his tone either.

"It's in the garage," I say quietly. I'm not sure how he missed it on his way inside. He clearly wasn't looking for it in there.

"And why is my desk in the garage?"

"It smells bad in the garage, and I wanted to do some yoga. I needed the space." It's half the truth. There are fans in the garage, and I could open the doors and windows, but I don't like the feeling of being watched and Sam is here today cutting the grass. The kid already stares at me more than is polite by society's standards, so I don't want to give him any extra excitement while he's operating machinery.

I haven't mentioned to Simon the way Sam's constant lingering gaze makes me feel. After our initial conversation with Jackson and Lillian about him, I have kept all opinions to myself. Simon and Sam seem to have some weird bond, like brothers, or something. They're always joking, talking about sports, and Simon gives him personal and professional advice. Sam seems beyond happy when Simon's attention is on him, so I mostly want to stay out of it. Sam will be heading back to school in a couple of weeks and then I won't have to worry that he's peeking in the windows at me.

"Did you lift it on your own? Aspen, that desk is solid oak. How the hell did you get it out of the room?"

Oh, this is the part of my plan that I love, but he will hate. "Jackson and Dylan moved it for me!"

"You called the guys to move my desk? They willingly helped you move my working space into the same area we sweat in daily. Why would they do that?"

When he says things like that, he just screams annoying little brother who never got a taste of his own medicine. Claire told me about her underwear floating in the lake, her ruined makeup, and the prank calls she suffered growing up because of Simon and Jackson.

Did Lillian and I piss off Ben? All the time. Did he return the favour? Always. I mean, I have a dog named Bart because of him.

"Those assholes," he mumbles under his breath. I can't help but chuckle. Jackson and Dylan were all too happy to help me mess with Simon. At least they assumed that was my motive. Dylan was whistling happily, and Jackson had a stupid smile on his face as they grunted the desk out of the house. "Why couldn't my desk stay inside? The living room? My old bedroom?" Simon hasn't slept in his room since our first date, so that would have worked in theory, but I needed the desk out of the house.

"I'm nesting," I lie. I mean, I have been nesting. I painted a mural in the nursery, a cute nature scene with the Bluefield River winding through the woodland creatures. The cribs are prepped, closet full. I've even started turning one of the bedrooms into a playroom. I know they won't be using it for a while, but Bart now has most of his toys in it, so it'll get used either way.

"Should I be alarmed that your version of nesting is removing my belongings from the house?" Simon looks beyond confused, a little amused, but mostly annoyed. I don't blame him. We both work from home as much as possible. I even have some of my team come to the house when I'm too tired to drive to the office. I just can't tell him the real reason the desk needs to move.

I can't look at it.

I can't look at it without thinking dirty thoughts.

It's become one of Simon's favourite places to strip me down and now I can't work in the office room without getting hot and bothered. The mirror? It's in the garage too.

No more hanky panky in the office. My productivity needs to be up before I end up on maternity leave and my dirty thoughts are my number one de-motivator right now.

"Can I move it back into the house, please?" he asks.

"I don't think that's a good idea," I say with fake sorrow. "You don't want to mess with my nesting. Hormones and all that could make me do crazy things. Your suits could be next." That has Simon standing up straighter.

"You touch my suits, and we will have a real problem, Aspen. They have nothing to do with babies. Leave them alone."

"But what if the babies don't like suits? Scary men wear them." I keep my face neutral and my tone even so he thinks I'm being serious.

"Are you okay, Aspen? Do you need to get some fresh air?" he says while approaching me like I'm a wild animal who might run away if spooked. I can't help the smile that slips through my façade. Simon thinks I'm losing it. "You're joking," he says, relaxing as he pulls me into his arms. "Never a dull moment with you."

Chapter 32
Simon

JACKSON:

Poker night, attendance is mandatory

SIMON:

You got it boss

BEN:

I want to make a comment about you respecting me because I'm Lillian's brother, but I've got nothing

DYLAN:

See you soon

It's the first poker night we have had in months. Since I discovered fatherhood was upon me and Dylan has been beyond busy at work, it wasn't a priority for any of us.

None of our lives seem to be slowing down, so we decided

to make it a priority. After Aspen gave me some insight into my friendship with Dylan—smart woman—I've been trying to make sure I reach out to him practically daily just to check in. He's been in the garage gym often, which to me means things aren't going well and he needs a physical outlet.

I've decided to not hold Dylan and Jackson's part in Aspen's scheme against them. I caught her blushing as she walked past my desk this morning on her way to see Lillian and Julia, and it told me everything I needed to know. Seems I'll just have to get more creative and make sure Aspen can't look at any of our furniture in the house without having dirty thoughts. Challenge accepted.

Jackson's basement is all set up for us. There's a table, chairs, and a beer fridge. That's all we need. The space is completely unfinished for now, concrete floors and walls. Some insulation and in-floor plumbing, but it certainly puts the cave in man cave. He said he'll get around to it eventually, but they don't need the space yet. Yet, as in, there are only two people living in the house. For now.

I think Jackson officially has baby fever, or baby rabies, as Dylan has decided to call it.

"So you and Lillian won't be far behind then?" Dylan asks as we position ourselves around the card table. Ben is set up on a computer across from me on a video call so he can join in.

"We're just practising for now," Jackson says and then winces as Ben groans. "I'm sorry, I'll shut up now," he insists, but still shoots a wink in my direction. "We've talked about it a lot. Lil has it in her head that she and Aspen need to have kids around the same age, so you may have pushed up our timeline, Simon."

"I'm not going to apologise for that. If it weren't for the babies, it may have taken a miracle for Aspen and I to get where we are."

"I don't know about that," Ben cuts in. "I think you'd have ended up together eventually."

"Really?" I ask. I didn't think anyone thought Aspen and I would call a truce, let alone be in a committed relationship. This time last year, she was shooting daggers at me across the room.

"Yeah, I thought they were more likely to kill each other than sleep together," Dylan adds.

"Oh for sure," he says confidently. "Maybe it's because I've known Aspen practically my whole life, but you got under her skin so quickly, there was no way this wouldn't be how you two ended up. Aspen dated guys she had no future with for some reason. I'm not going to try to understand how any girl's brain works, especially not Aspen's, but there was a switch this year. She wasn't ready for someone to challenge her, but also treat her like an equal before. This all had perfect timing."

"I can see that," Jackson says.

"I'm not going to put too much thought into it. We're here and we're happy. That's all I can ask for. I just need Jackson to catch up to me, apparently," I say.

"Yeah, yeah, yeah. Don't add any pressure on me. I didn't have a great dad for a role model. I need more time to get myself ready."

"Oh, you'll never be ready," Ben cuts in, laughing. "Never. No one is."

Dylan laughs but says, "Ben, you're going to scare them. Go easy."

"I'm telling the truth," he defends. "It's hard, everyday being a father is hard and nothing could have prepared me for it. It's also the best thing that ever happened to me and I wouldn't change anything in my life if it meant I didn't end up doing it with Noah. Sorry for getting all deep on you guys, but it's true. Don't wait because you're scared. That feeling will probably be with you well into your children's adulthood."

"I, for one, appreciate your wisdom, Ben. You are the only dad I know that isn't the same age as my dad so if you see me calling you at three in the morning a couple of months from now, please answer your phone because I will probably be desperate for your advice."

"You got it. What about you Dylan, will we see babies in your future?"

"I mean eventually," Dylan winces. "Starting a family, hell, dating even hasn't been a huge priority lately."

"You've got lots of time. I'm sure the girls would be happy to set you up with someone," Jackson offers.

"Oh no, I don't want them anywhere near my dating life. My sister calls me weekly, asking for updates. I don't need anyone else involved. When it happens, it happens. I should probably put some effort in when all this clears up. If all this clears up." Dylan looks away, clearly frustrated with the lack of progress they've had with the missing women cases.

"Oh! Before I forget, I heard from Dudley's lawyer," Ben says. Dylan rubs his hands together in anticipation. Since he wasn't able to help with this, I know he wants the guy to back off.

"I hope this is good," Jackson mumbles around the lip of his beer bottle. I can't wait to hear this guy crying about not getting the girl. Sorry, loser, she's mine now.

My hope immediately dissolves as Ben says, "It's not, not really."

"What do you mean?" Dylan asks before I have a chance to.

"His lawyer sent a letter back to me saying his client hasn't reached out to Aspen in any way, verbally or in the form of gifts, since they split up last year. He said if my office continued to send unjustified notices to his office, he would file a defamation suit against Aspen. So basically, he's not the one sending flowers." If it's not John, then who?

"Does Aspen have anyone else who would be sending them to her?" Dylan asks, going straight into constable mode. She hasn't mentioned anyone else. I don't think it's her sister or her parents. That isn't how they communicate. I guess it could be a different ex-boyfriend, but wouldn't they leave a card or say something so she knew it was them making an effort?

"I think she was certain it was Dudley."

"Maybe I'll stop by tomorrow and see if I can ask her some questions to try to spike her memory of a reason for the flowers. If it's not a random ex-boyfriend, this could be more serious..." Dylan trails off.

"Do you think she has a stalker or something?" Jackson asks.

"Don't want to jump to conclusions," Dylan says, while pointing in my direction. It's then I notice I've already risen from my chair, one foot directed toward the door. Toward my path back to Aspen. I slowly sink back down and let him continue. "Given everything that has been happening in Bluefield, and the fact that the flower deliveries were in Toronto and now Bluefield, I think we should take this seriously. Whoever it is knows not only that she moved, but has her home address here. Her name is nowhere on any property documents. I know town gossip is wild and people will give away personal information easily, but they're becoming more cautious. If someone was snooping around and trying to find her, I would have heard about it on our tip line by now. I want to take this seriously."

Three missing women in the span of three months is not a good statistic for the town. We all want Bluefield to be back to its shining glory, welcoming people to the town so they can fall in love with it too. We all want it to be a safe place to live. I want it to be a safe place to grow my family. This night was supposed to be about spending time with each other and having fun, especially for Dylan. Instead, we've brought up his lack of dating, lack of time, and unsuccessful work matters. We need to fix this now.

Jackson must be thinking the same thing. "That's fair," Jackson says while giving me a squeeze on the shoulder. "We'll deal with all that tomorrow. Tonight, we play. Should I deal?" Jackson asks as he shuffles the cards.

"Let's do it," I say just as a beep comes through Dylan's phone. He's not on call tonight so this must be an emergency and judging by the way his entire body stiffens with the tension that slowly drained out over the last hour, it must be bad.

"I'm out," Dylan says, giving no further information. We let him go as a silence falls over the room.

"Are you sure you guys should stay in Bluefield? I don't feel like it's a safe place anymore," Ben says through the computer, and I have to agree with him. The idea of leaving town isn't one I want to entertain, yet it had been in the back of my mind for weeks.

It would be easy to run and hide. Jackson would let both Aspen and me work remotely if we left. Hell, he would probably let us out of our contracts all together. It's not that it's an unsafe work environment, it's that Bluefield has become an unsafe town.

Chapter 33

Aspen

JULIA:

Again??

LILLIAN:

I'm scared

ASPEN:

I don't even know what to feel

Another woman was reported missing today. Janine Sparrow is only thirty years old, new to town, single, has two young children and didn't show up to pick them up from summer camp today.

According to town gossip, when police went to her house, they found her coffee cup sitting on the counter, cold but marked with her lipstick and her cell phone and keys dropped on the floor. This is the first time one of these women's houses has given any indication that a crime has occurred. There were drag marks in the fresh mulch of her garden beds, but the trail disappeared in the fresh-cut grass.

There is no way we can pretend there isn't a seriously dangerous person lurking in Bluefield.

It's hard to decide how much paranoia is justified at this point. All the victims have been single women, no older than fifty, no younger than I am. None of them have been especially vulnerable, all healthy and established in their lives. And yet, one day they are going about their days, and the next, their faces are all over the news and another search party is being formed.

Jackson has offered to let everyone put a pause on any current projects and Mane Construction so they can leave town if they feel unsafe. One of my interns packed up her desk and practically ran out of town.

The thought has crossed my mind to do the same.

There's just one problem.

I don't think I can run away from the one place I've ever felt at home. Bluefield, my friends, this house, and Simon, they are my home. And after everything I've done to get to this point in my life, all of my hard work and struggles, I don't want to give that up.

Dylan has given our friends, and everyone else in town, strict instructions to stay safe.

Lock your doors, always. This isn't something a lot of people in a town this size are used to doing.

Don't go out at night alone, travel in groups when possible.

Don't answer the door for strangers.

Get a security system installed if you can.

Simon and Jackson have spent all day installing doorbell

cameras all over town for free. When Simon left the house this morning, he was torn between wanting to stay home with me, wanting me to come with him, and wanting to help the people of Bluefield. I assured him I would be behind our locked door with the security system armed working from home all day until he returned.

Between the crime in Bluefield and us nearing my due date, Simon has been in full-on protector mode.

He's going to be such a good daddy.

What I assume is baby girl, based on my last ultrasound, gives me a good kick like she's reading my thoughts. Every time I think something nice about Simon, she lets me know she agrees. She may have a future as a soccer player or kickboxer, but I don't doubt she will also be a daddy's girl.

Baby boy is much more chill. Aside from the pressure he puts on my bladder almost constantly, he's more quiet about getting attention. I'm not sure where that comes from, as Simon and I have never been accused of hiding from the spotlight.

Although I will say, I've felt at peace being at home lately. Keeping my head down and keeping to myself. My lack of energy might have something to do with it. Or it's just the growth within I've felt over the last couple of months. I haven't felt like I have to prove myself to anyone lately, or that I've needed to impress someone I barely care about. I've even stopped obsessing about all the rules I've made for myself. Partly because once it's in writing, it seems like I'm more likely to break it, and partly because I'm letting life happen without forcing it.

I've just finished up my dinner dishes when my phone rings. The screen lights up with a picture of Lillian kissing my swollen belly.

Before I have a chance to even say hello, Lillian practically screams, "Have you talked to Julia today?"

"I texted her this morning about my bulk order of your books, and she said it should be coming next week." Supporting my bestie's career as a children's book author and my other bestie at her bookstore by buying every book Lillian has ever published felt like the move when Simon built floor-to-ceiling bookshelves in the nursery.

"What time was that at?"

I pull my phone away from my ear to check my text thread.

"Just a little bit after noon. Why? What's happening?" I ask. Lillian sounds more than frantic, and a feeling of dread seeps through my body.

"Apparently Julia put up the lunch sign on the door of the bookshop. You know the one that says back in thirty minutes? Only she never came back. Diana at the cafe noticed when she was closing today and called Dylan, who is obviously very busy, so he texted Jackson to check on her. He's on the other side of town, so I've been trying to get a hold of her, but her phone is either dead or turned off. I want to go to her place to check if she's there before we have the whole town searching for her, but I don't want to go alone." Before Lillian has even finished her sentence, I'm already in the mudroom, grabbing my shoes and keys.

"I'll come pick you up and we can check on her. Be there in five."

"Thank you," Lillian breathes out. "Jackson specifically told me not to do this, but we can't just sit around."

"I agree," I say as I unarm the alarm for the door leading to the garage and reset it as I leave. "I'll see you soon."

I close the door and lock it from the garage and head towards the side door. Since my ugly flowers are typically delivered to the front door, I've started to avoid using it.

I unlock my car, causing the lights to flash and illuminate our side yard, including the gardening shed I've never been in. There's a reason I've been so impressed with the landscaping at this house. My thumb is only green with indoor plants.

A movement from inside the shed catches my eye and before I know what I'm doing, I'm doing an ugly crossing between a jog and a waddle toward it.

My headlights dim just as I reach the door. I pause for a moment, my hand hovering above the latch. This is probably not the best time to go creeping into dark buildings. The sun is still in the sky, making its way over the lake, but with all the trees on the property, it seems a lot closer to nightfall than it is. I've already taken the time to see if there's something or someone where they shouldn't be, and I know Lillian is waiting for me, so I need to get this over with so we can look for Julia. I open the door quickly, hoping that taking the rip-it-off-like-a-Band-Aid approach will secure a good outcome. I pull my phone out of my back pocket to use it as a flashlight, something I should have thought of sooner when something, or more accurately someone grabs my arm and pushes me to the hard ground, my phone smashing as it falls with me.

I grunt as I hit the wooden planks. I'm pretty sure I have about fifteen splinters in my hands and butt instantly. I instinctively grab onto my stomach to shield my babies from any pain. The fall wasn't too hard, but any sudden movement at this point feels like it could bring on labour.

When I look up, Sam is standing above me, holding a baseball bat over his head.

Sam, who hits on me at the General Store. Sam, who makes awkward conversation when he sees you in town. Sam, who cuts our lawn every week. Sam, who Simon is mentoring. Sam, who looks like he's about to kill me.

I brace for impact, clutching my stomach and closing my eyes, but it never comes.

I slowly open one eye and then the other. Sam is still standing over me, but he's dropped the bat to his side and has his head hung, eyes downcast.

"Ssssam," I stammer out. "What are you doing in my shed?"

Sam raises his eyes the slightest bit to me and instantly falls to his knees in front of me.

"Something bad happened," he whispers.

I slowly climb to my knees, so that I'm able to stand if needed, trying not to make any sudden movements.

"What happened, Sam?" I ask, although I'm unsure if I want the answer. I'm alone in my shed, no one knows where I am, and I'm with someone who seems to be having some sort of mental breakdown.

I'm about to become a statistic.

I don't know all the finer details of the missing women's case, but one detail is now glaringly obvious, especially in Janine's case. Her grass was freshly cut. So fresh that it was assumed the lawn was cut after she disappeared.

And who is a new lawn care business? The person sobbing in

front of me.

Is guilt causing this emotion from him?

I watch a lot of true crime and sometimes the killers aren't able to feel that emotion. This could all be an act.

"Sam," I say a lot more firmly. "What did you do?"

"I didn't do anything. At least I didn't mean to. But I think I saw something I wasn't supposed to," Sam says. His body is shaking and I can see the tears sticking to his long eyelashes. He puts his hands over his mouth to muffle his cries. Sam no longer looks like a dangerous man, but a scared boy.

I will be the first to say that Sam has given me the creeps since the first-time Lillian told me about him last summer. He always seems to be lurking around town, holds eye contact a bit too long, and is weirdly friendly to everyone. Maybe I'm cynical, but in my mind, nineteen-year-old boys are douchey and cocky assholes. Sam is too nice.

And even with all the wary feelings I have felt towards him in the past and the judgments I have made about him in my head, seeing him crumpled in the corner of our gardening shed, all I want to do is pull him into my arms and comfort him.

Maybe it's my motherly instincts kicking in, or the fact that I know Simon likes the kid and has spent a decent amount of time with him this summer, but I feel like I should figure out how to help him.

"What did you see, Sam?" I reach for my phone, hoping to call anyone to come help me. I mostly want Simon. He would know exactly how to calm Sam down and get information out of him. I also want him here because I haven't seen him all day. I'm scared and needy, and I just plain miss him. My phone screen is cracked beyond repair. I can see bits of the ultrasound image that is my background, but I'm pretty sure there are whole chunks missing. There is no way I can call anyone on this.

I'm pretty sure I read once that there's a way to make an emergency call by pressing some of the buttons but I can't get my brain to dig that information out, because the panic has begun to settle in, it's getting worse.

"Sam!" I say again since he still hasn't answered. "I need you to tell me what you saw!"

"I was at Mrs. Sparrow's house this afternoon cutting her grass. She's a new client, so I wanted to go above and beyond. She had mentioned wanting to plant flowers around the patio stones under her fire pit. She thought they would stop the weeds from growing there. It's a smart idea, really." He pauses to compose himself between sniffles. I grab his hand to comfort him and me. He looks shocked for only a second before he gives my hand a squeeze and continues. "I put the patio stones down just last week so everything should have been level, but it wasn't. I tried to fix the couple that seemed really off, but I knew to do it right, I would have to start over. Simon told me to pretend every task is like an item on my resume. If I cut corners, I may as well have misspelt my name."

I can practically hear Simon's voice saying that to Sam. I glance at my phone again, hoping there will be a message from him, but knowing there won't.

"So I removed all the stones and wanted to dig into the dirt a bit to see if there was a tree root or something that would cause the stones to unlevel themselves. I got down a couple of feet when I saw a hand. Like a human hand. I ran. I didn't know what to do, so I ran, and I swear a car was following me for a bit, so I hid in the woods and then snuck in here." Sam is practically hyperventilating now. The poor kid is beyond traumatized.

"Breathe, Sam. Everything is going to be okay," I say, even though I'm not sure if that's true. Whoever is behind the missing woman has a reason to want Sam to keep quiet.

"Why are you hiding in our shed? Why not go to the police?" I ask.

"I dropped my phone somewhere when I was running and I was scared the police wouldn't believe me. If they searched my house, they might not think I'm innocent." My grip on Sam's hand loosens slightly, which he picks up on. He holds me tighter. "It's not bad, I promise; it just might look bad."

"What is it, Sam?" I ask in the firmest voice I can. I need to get the story out of him and then go get help.

"I'm the one who's been sending you flowers!" he blurts out with his eyes closed. *What?*

Sam opens his eyes slowly and peers up at my dumbfounded face. "You've been sending me flowers?"

"Did you like them?" he asks hopefully.

"Sam. Why were you sending my flowers?" I try to pull my hand out of his grip. He holds it tight before letting go.

"Please, please hear me out before you freak out," he asks. I gesture for him to continue. "So this is going to sound a bit crazy, but if it didn't work, I wouldn't have done it. Last year, right before I first met you, my grandma got sick. She has cancer." My heart hurts for him, but I need to know what that has to do with me. "She has a really nice flower garden at our house, and she loves bright colours, so I planned to fill her hospital room with flowers. The doctors wouldn't allow it; it wasn't sterile enough, I guess. Then I heard you complaining to Lillian about your ex-boyfriend, and I thought maybe you wouldn't mind the flowers. I needed to do something with them. I snuck a peek at your licence in your wallet when you were paying at the General Store and got a friend of mine who lives in Toronto to help with the delivery. The day he dropped them at your door, Grandma got a good test result. So I kept getting flowers delivered to you and she stayed alive."

He grabs both of my hands in his before he continues. "You have to understand, Aspen. My parents took off when I was a baby. My grandma is all I have so if sending you flowers somehow helps her get better, I wasn't going to stop. I don't know that it's helping much anymore because her recent tests haven't been that great, but I didn't want you to be upset if the flowers suddenly stopped. I know it was really, really weird of me, but I'm desperate for her to be okay."

That is a lot to process.

Sam has been sending my flowers as some sort of superstitious good karma deed to keep his grandmother alive. Although that is a wild correlation he's making, he hasn't done anything illegal really, so I guess I'm okay with it?

"If the police came to my house, they would find my flower lab. Not a great look," he finishes.

"Sam, that is all a lot and a bit weird, but I am not upset by the flowers, so I think we should head inside and call the police."

"Yeah, you're probably right. I hope Simon isn't mad at me for being in here with you. That guy is obsessed with you."

"Yeah, he kind of is, isn't he?" Amid all this chaos, I can't help but smile at the thought of Simon's reaction to his prodigy Sam being behind the flowers instead of my ex-boyfriend.

Sam stands and then reaches for my hand to help me up. We both step towards the shed door when it goes flying open and a large shadow looms over us.

Chapter 34
Aspen

"Leo, what are you doing here?" I ask, though I'm pretty sure I know the answer and it isn't good for me or Sam. Sam stands in front of me and shuffles us back until I'm pressed against the back wall of the shed, Sam standing in front of me, blocking my view.

Leo chuckles under his breath menacingly, causing a chill to run up my spine. We're currently in the middle of a heat wave, but you wouldn't know it with how the temperature has seemed to drop in here. "I needed to make sure my little accomplice kept his mouth shut," he rumbles.

I've always thought Leo was a conventionally attractive guy. The fact that he knows it is a bit of a turnoff, but looking at his face now, all I see is an ugly, evil man.

"I had nothing to do with whatever you did to that person," Sam responds. I can tell he's trying to be brave, but his voice cracks at the end, giving away his fear.

"That's not how I see it. If I was to point the police in the direction of some missing women's bodies, do you know what they would find, Sam?" Sam shakes his head. "They would find them buried under some elaborately placed landscaping. The new pond at the Miller's, the flowerbed at the Smith's, and of course the patio at Janine Sparrow's, but you already know about that one, don't you? I had to go clean that one up myself before coming back for you here. And you've even brought me a present." Leo leans over Sam's body to look at me. "Hi, Aspen. I'm so glad you could join us."

Normally, if a man tried to leer over me like Leo is to intimidate me, I would be swinging my fist in seconds. Unfortunately, not only is my centre of gravity so far off kilter I'm sure I would fall if I tried, but I have three other beings I need to be conscious of. If my brain is formulating everything that has happened and everything that Leo just said correctly, then he is a very dangerous man.

At least three missing women, and three locations a body could be found.

Leo is a killer. The Killer.

Those poor women.

I've watched enough crime dramas to know that the killer only admits to their crimes to people they don't plan on letting live. Leo is currently leveraging naming Sam as his accomplice so he may have a chance at getting out of here alive. Me, on the other hand, he has no reason to spare. My only hope is that I can keep us alive long enough for help to come. Surely Lillian is looking for me at this point. I'm at least thirty minutes late to pick her up. Given the disappearance happening in Bluefield, she's probably sounded the alarms by now and help should be on its way.

I hope.

I need to keep Leo talking.

"Why did you do it? Why them?" I ask. Sam gives me a

wide-eyed, confused look. I'm sure he doesn't want to know what's going on in Leo's disgusting brain.

"Well, you see, Aspen, women love me. I know you've been making eyes at me all summer. The situation you've got yourself in doesn't really do it for me though." He points at my stomach, and I instinctively cover it with my hands. "After it's been dealt with, I'm sure we could have had fun." I hate that he's speaking about me in the past tense already. To him, my fate is sealed. "I'm a lot of man though. It takes a special kind of woman to handle me, and unfortunately, I haven't found the right one yet." Leo strokes a hand down his face and scratches at the scruff on his jaw like he's reminiscing a cherished memory. I don't know if I want to cry or vomit at the sight of him.

"So what, they aren't Mrs. Right so you kill them?" I ask, to keep him talking.

"If only it were that simple, Aspen. If only." He pauses a moment, before his voice rises with every word until he is practically yelling in our faces. "No. These women don't know how to submit properly. If they are in my life, I am the only one. They're always complaining about their friends, their ex-husbands, their kids. If they could just give up on all these useless people and focus on me, everything would be perfect. But they never do. I would make them happy, me and only me." Spit hits my cheek, but I don't move to wipe it.

Leo shakes his head and then takes a step back. In a completely calm voice, he says, "I save them from a lifetime of unhappiness. It's the humane thing to do."

That is so deeply disturbing. I'm not sure if my body is numb as a form of preservation, but I don't see how still I am standing until I feel Sam vibrating beside me. I grab his hand and hold it with mine against my belly. I try to give him as reassuring of a look as possible.

We have to make it out of this, there is no other option in my mind.

"Is this how you've always dated?" I ask. I really don't want the answer. If I don't make it out of here after learning about more women's death I will be haunting Dylan until he uncovers them all.

"No, not always," Leo says casually. "I used to let them go on with their simple unhappy lives, but I wanted to make a difference in the world. The first time I helped one of these women end her sad cycle of life, I felt at peace. Like I finally found my purpose. My zen. It also helped that I'm able to travel a lot with my high income. I can spread my humanitarian work to other areas. The annoying authorities only became an issue here. Maybe I'll have to deal with Constable Peters before I leave town. My family will probably be upset with me for leaving my uncle's company to dissolve, but what's a guy gonna do? I'm trying to find love and change the world. They should want that for me."

The level of delusion happening in this man's brain is something to be studied. When we get out of here and tell the world what he did, a docuseries will be produced to tell the world his story. I would rather he dies; the women's families get some closure and we never receive an ounce of fame from all of this.

I don't think Sam and I can overtake Leo on strength alone. I'm not very agile right now and Sam looks like he's about to pass out. My only option is my broken phone. I have it gripped under Sam and my hands, out of sight. I don't know what combination of buttons needs to be pressed or held but if I try all of them, something has got to work. I press the lock button multiple times until I see the screen light up against my shirt. Swiping my thumb around until the screen goes black again, I hope help is on the way.

Suddenly Leo takes a couple of steps away from us, standing in front of the closed shed door. "As much fun as this all has been, I need to get going. Bluefield is getting a bit stale for me. I need a bigger pond to swim in. Normally, I like to feel the life leaving the lives I'm bettering, but I think it will be more fun to have Sammy here clean up my mess."

Before I have a chance to fully register his words, I see a glint of metal and a gun trained straight at me. I try to scream but it's muffled by Sam's chest as we both fall to the floor.

Everything goes black.

Chapter 35
Simon

Jackson and I have been installing doorbell cameras all day. It's not hard work necessarily, but we have a long list of Bluefield residents to get through and it's started to get dark. I would love to call it a day, head home, wrap myself around Aspen and not move until morning, but there are a lot of scared people out there and I would rather finish up our list tonight so that these people will sleep a bit easier.

When we finish up at our final house both Jackson and I pull out our phones like the lovesick puppies we are, to see if our girls have texted us. That's not completely true, we aren't entirely sure where Julia has been all day so I hope to have a message from Lillian or Aspen saying it's all a false alarm and she's fine.

Instead of an all-clear message, I have more than a dozen missed calls from Lillian and by the looks of it so does Jackson. I see him dial her number just as a police cruiser pulls up. Dylan rolls down the window as Jackson and I jog toward the SUV.

When Dylan is in uniform, he's always straight to business.

"Have you talked to Aspen in the last hour?" Everything in my body feels wrong the second the words are out of his mouth.

"What happened?" I ask as I dial her number. I know she's not going to answer her phone. I feel in my bones that something isn't right and I'm correct when I reach her voicemail.

"Aspen, call me back as soon as you get this. Please," I practically bark into my phone. I'm sure I'm going to get an earful from her when she listens to it, but if she's yelling at me, then she's alive and well, so I don't really care.

"Lillian called me while we were out with the dogs and said she and Aspen had plans to go check on Julia. Aspen was supposed to pick her up but never did and now she isn't answering her phone. I sent a constable to your place to check on her. He said her car is in the driveway but she isn't answering the door. I was on my way over there as backup when I saw you two. Follow me."

Dylan pulls away quickly breaking the speed limit while forgoing his lights and sirens. I'm sure he's trying to avoid having everyone in the town following us and getting in the way.

As soon as we get into Jackson's truck a call from Lillian comes through over the Bluetooth. He answers and the truck is filled with the sounds of Lillian's broken words as she cries.

"Are you with Simon? Does he know where Aspen is? No one's seen Julia in hours! We need to find them!"

"Shhh," Jackson coos. "We're on our way to see Aspen now. Dylan is in front of us and there's already an officer there. It's going to be okay."

While his voice sounds calm and soothing, Jackson's hands grip the wheel so hard his knuckles are white and I can feel the truck gaining on Dylan as Jackson presses harder on the accelerator.

Lillian continues to cry and mumble unintelligible words across the phone as Jackson tries to reassure her. I wish I could help, but I can't force any words out of my mouth.

Aspen needs to be okay. The babies need to be okay.

My entire world and purpose is wrapped up in Aspen, without her I won't be able to go on.

I can't think like this.

Aspen is okay.

She has to be.

Dylan meets us out front after the house is cleared. As they approach, it is glaringly obvious that Aspen isn't with them, so she must not have been in the house. My knees buckle under me and Jackson grabs my arm before I faceplant. "I got you," he says as he lowers me until we're on our knees.

Dylan crouches in front of my face. "She wasn't inside, but there was no sign of a struggle. The alarm was set and all the doors were locked. Aspen left the house by her own free will."

I nod because it feels like I've swallowed my tongue. Aspen isn't in the house but her car is here. I know she's been trying to stay active through her pregnancy but there's no way she would even think to walk all the way to Jackson and Lillian's, it's at least five kilometres from here.

The river is all I can think of.

If something has gone wrong here, the house backs onto the river.

When I bought this place, the river out back immediately sold me. Now the thought of Aspen being somewhere near a moving body of water at night seems idiotic. She might have heard something and went to check and fallen in. I know she's been hoping to get a photo of the family of beavers whose damn we saw last week. Maybe she thought catching them after dark would be easier.

I'm sure the thoughts in my head are beyond illogical, but I can't just stand here. Aspen is out there somewhere.

I get to my feet, Jackson trying to support me the whole way up. I walk, jog, run and then sprint until I'm at the water's edge. I can hear the others following behind me shouting, but I can't stop. I look around and see nothing. Absolutely nothing.

Some delusional part of me thought for sure I would find Aspen sitting on the dock giggling at the beavers. But she isn't here. Wherever she is I just hope she knows how much I care for her. How much I love her. Because I do love her, more than I've loved anything my entire life.

I'm not going to sit here and say I don't know how or when it happened, because I do know. I know the exact moment I was done for.

It was the moment she gave me a chance. I'm not talking about this summer, I'm talking about New Year's Eve in the Shaw's cottage. The second Aspen agreed to a truce I was a goner.

My stomach lurches and empties into the river.

Sorry Mother Nature.

Jackson and Dylan are talking over each other trying to talk to me I think but my ears are ringing. Some place deep inside of me swear I can hear Aspen's voice. I try to focus on it. Is she trying to talk to me? Trying to tell me where she is? Am I finally losing it?

Except I think I do hear her. She's crying and there's the sound of muffled voices coming from the other side of the property. Dylan and Jackson must hear it at the same time I do because they both finally shut up and look in the direction the voices are coming from.

"Stay," Dylan barks at us then takes off running towards our gardening shed.

I respect Dylan, and I appreciate that he is very good at his job. That's why I give him a ten-second start before I chase after him.

We're about halfway there when a shot rings out. Dylan draws his weapon and sprints towards the shed. I'm a bit unsteady on my feet as I try to keep up but he pulls ahead. I can see him whip the shed door open, enter and then two more shots ring out.

Jackson practically drags me to the shed entrance where Aspen lies in the middle of the floor in a puddle of blood.

Chapter 36

Simon

The tears I've been holding in all day finally fall as they lower the casket to the ground. Lillian sniffles beside me and I see Jackson hand her a tissue before he reaches behind me and hands me one as well.

I swore I wouldn't cry today. I thought I could be the strong one today, but I can't hold it together any longer. The service was beautiful. Exactly what a woman like that deserves. She sacrificed so much to care for those she loved and she will be remembered by all of us.

Especially the young man beside me.

Sam has been a mess all week; I don't blame him. He's been fighting an uphill battle since birth and I wish I could lessen this burden for him. But I'm not who he needs right now. No.

Who he needs is the woman beside him.

But the woman beside him, who just so happens to be the love of my life, is all but holding him up now. Both physically and emotionally.

In the wake of Sam's grandmother losing her battle with cancer, Aspen has stepped up to be anything and everything he needs.

I'm not sure if we will ever know all that happened in the shed before Dylan shot Leo, because aside from the statement they both made to the police, neither of them want to talk about it. I do know that Sam jumped in front of the gun and took a bullet for Aspen. He saved her life. He saved our children's lives. He protected the most important thing in this world to me, and for that, I owe him everything.

So, if he needs to borrow Aspen's shoulder to cry on, move into our guest bedroom permanently and basically join our family, it's done. Sam gets whatever he wants.

Thankfully, the bullet intended for Aspen hit Sam in the shoulder, missing all important arteries and organs. He spent some time in the hospital recovering, where he was able to spend time with his grandma during her final days. Since Aspen didn't want Sam out of her sight and Lillian, Jackson and I didn't want Aspen out of our sight, we all were able to get to know Sam and his grandmother on a deeper level.

None of us have seen Julia since the night of the shooting, and I think that's causing an unsettled feeling within our group of friends.

Julia is safe, she always was, she just wasn't in Bluefield. Julia had to leave town suddenly for a family emergency that is taking a while to resolve. She hasn't said much to us aside from sending her well wishes, but I'm sure once she's back in town, the girls will be all over her with questions.

After the service is over, everyone heads back to their homes to decompress. Sam excuses himself to the garage, wanting to sweat out his internal turmoil while working on his physical therapy. Aspen and I head up to our bedroom to change into comfier clothes, I think we will all be lounging around the house today.

My mind has been going a mile a minute since the night everything went so wrong, and so right. Bluefield welcomed him into the community, many welcomed him into their homes, trusted him. And he was vile to his core. A killer had been living amongst us.

Thankfully, he no longer walks this earth.

Bluefield has made national news as they connect Leo to a string of missing persons cases across the country. I've tried not to get too caught up in the reports for my own sanity. I've got enough troubling thoughts and things I need to work through.

What could we have done differently to protect those we love? Was there anything? Signs we missed? I know we're all swirling through the same mental gymnastics.

One thought, that is anything but troubling, that is always at the forefront, is how in love with Aspen I am. When I was searching for her, it's all I wanted to tell her and it's been on the tip of my tongue ever since. I didn't say it at the hospital, or the days following, because I wanted it to be a moment for us. Not something said with desperation or pain. I wanted it to be a moment filled with joy and understanding that this is it. This is us. And I'm in this forever.

But is there ever a perfect moment? Had things gone differently, I may have never had the chance to tell Aspen how I feel and I can't risk that happening again.

"Aspen," I say quietly, as she pulls one of my sweaters over her head. She looks up at me with a silly smile on her face as her hair stands in every direction from the static. I am so in love with her. I take a step forward until we're as close as her round belly will allow. "I love you."

A million emotions run across her face. Confusion, shock, joy, happiness. And then the tears fall and the best emotion shines through, love.

"I love you too," Aspen whispers as she throws her arms around my neck.

"Thank you for building this life with me. I wouldn't want any of this without you," I say against her lips.

"I love you," she says against my lips before our kiss picks up intensity. "Now show me how much you love me... daddy."

Heaven. Aspen is my version of heaven.

Chapter 37

Aspen

I look across the yard at the guys when I hear one of them grunt. What a sight it is. Ben has Noah on his shoulders as he pretends to hammer in a nail, Jackson and Simon are assembling what looks like the frame for the swings and Dylan just joined them, pulling off his uniform shirt so he's only wearing a white undershirt. And of course, they're all wearing tool belts.

"This is better than dilf porn," I mumble. That one probably should have stayed an inside thought.

"Aspen!" Lillian whisper hisses at me as she smacks my legs resting on her lap. I guess one of those men is her brother so my comment is a bit uncomfortable for her.

"We were all thinking it," I defend.

"No, we weren't," she argues back.

"I was," Julia pipes in, knocking her beer against my virgin Pina-colada. "This is hot."

Sam comes out the patio doors, dropping off a new drink for Lillian before joining the men as they build a treehouse. It's not attached to a tree, so maybe it's a playhouse. It's mostly way too big, but apparently, Jackson and Simon have been planning it since Simon bought the place. Lillian said she found miniature 3D models hidden in Jackson's home office last week.

Honestly, I'm fine with whatever they want to do out here. Now that the old shed is gone, and Simon had it replaced with a shed version of our house. It actually looks like a shrunk replica. Simon can do whatever he wants out here, as long as he lets Sam continue to perfect his landscaping.

He was all but set on quitting the whole thing, dropping out of school and working at the General Store for the rest of his life.

Simon talked him down from that ledge.

Instead, Sam transferred to a college that is just over an hour from Bluefield and is taking as many courses online as he can so he can be close when the babies come. In the course of the last month, Sam has wormed his weird self into all of our hearts, and our home. He is now claiming the unofficially big brother title for our babies, and Simon said he would be Sam's big brother in return.

I'm not even going to try to wrap my head around where I fit into that situation or what my title would be. All I know is that Sam saved my life, he's family now.

You would think that Simon is fully engrossed in the building project the men are working on, but I know he's not. I told him this morning that I was feeling extra uncomfortable and he's been sneaking glances at me all day. I am trying so hard not to snap at him.

I look like a whale. A very pregnant, sweaty, uncomfortable whale.

I would prefer that no one look at me right now.

But there's Simon, casually leaning against a tree, drinking his water and pretending to listen to whatever Ben is saying. His eyes, however, are staring into my soul.

He's quirks his eyebrow. Are you okay?

I roll my eyes but give him a soft smile. I'm fine...thanks for caring.

The fact that we can communicate silently makes me want to both throw-up and squeal with joy. My life is not what I expected it to be when the year started, but I couldn't be happier. I could do without feeling like I'm going to pee my pants constantly though.

Or actually peeing my pants apparently. I wish I could say this was the first time this has happened, but it isn't. There just isn't enough space for the liquids to remain in my bladder for more than a couple of minutes before they get physically kicked out of my body by baby boy.

I stand and quickly excuse myself from our conversation. Julia and Lillian don't bat an eye at my sudden exit, they've heard all about my bladder struggles. I hardly have the powder room door closed when it's pushed back open as Simon joins me in the small space.

"Everything okay?" he asks, his hands behind his back hiding something.

I look to the wet spot on my dress and back to him, then begin to wiggle out of my underwear. These things are big enough to put on a flagpole and not the least bit sexy, but they are absorbent, made for situations exactly like this one.

Simon produces a fresh pair of underwear and a dress from behind his back. He must have grabbed them from the laundry room on his way in. I don't know how this man is ever going to want to see me naked after all the perfectly natural, but unsexy things I have put him through.

Simon helps me change before pulling me into his arms. "It will all be worth it. They'll be here soon." I'm officially thirty-five weeks today so technically, the twins could come at any time.

"Is it bad that I'm excited and scared?" I ask. He drops a kiss on my forehead as we start to sway side to side. If Simon wasn't so tall, I don't think he would be able to hold me like this. Somehow, even as a whale, I feel safe in his arms.

"I think it would be more concerning if you weren't feeling that way," he answers. "I'm scared too. I'm excited too. We're in this together. We'll figure it out as we go and we have so much help along the way. Jackson told me the Shaws are going to be staying at their cottage for the fall, just in case. And you know my parents are already making sure Sam's grandma's house is ready for them. If it really takes a village, then we have one. All of Bluefield is probably going to be there to support us. We'll be okay."

I don't know how this man does it, but everything he just said was exactly what I needed to hear. I know all of this. I've reminded myself of all the support we have multiple times. But Simon's strong, confident voice washes my fears away, even if just temporarily. I know he has a similarly supportive speech ready for tonight in bed when my brain will start to doom spiral again.

"Come on." He laces his fingers through mine and pulls me out of the bathroom, depositing my soiled clothing in the laundry room on our way before leading me outside. "The sooner we get this done, the sooner I have you alone," he whispers against my neck, sending goosebumps all over my body.

I went from wetting my pants to spiralling to horny in under five minutes. I think that's a new record for me. Simon saunters away, chuckling under his breath as I rejoin the girls.

DILF porn for sure.

ㅁㅁㅁ

Just as planned, our beautiful babies arrive into the world via C-section in Saintritch, Ontario. Simon says I am a rock star, but I am eternally thankful for the hospital staff who made the whole process seem seamless.

Calla Lillian Cadwell, was first out, a full head of brown curls and lungs of steel. Her brother, Clay Jackson Cadwell, is already showing us he will be the calm to her chaos, scarily similar to me and Simon already. We love them both so much; my heart has never felt this full. We decided early on that their middle names would be in honour of their godparents. Without Lillian and Jackson, Simon and I wouldn't have made it into the happy bubble we have today.

We kept this a secret until after my delivery so when I was returned to my room and stable enough to have visitors, a weeping Lillian and teary-eyed Jackson were waiting for us.

"I just want to squish their little faces. How are they this edible?" Lillian asks as she gently rocks Clay side to side. "Can we have one of these?" She looks towards Jackson who is holding Calla.

"Umm," he shutters out before schooling his expression. "Maybe if you stop threatening to eat these ones, we can talk about it?" Lillian squeals and gives me a devilish look. I'm sure a ring and babies are in her near future. Simon pats Jackson on the shoulder and takes Calla into his arms.

Simon has never looked better in his life. The jeans that are perfectly faded, the Henley pushed up to his elbows, his wavy chocolate hair curling behind his ears, and the adorable bundle of pink in his arm. *Can I have five more, please?* If he has the super sperm he thinks he does, then we might be in trouble because I don't think I could say no to more of these little bundles. I'm sure when I'm sleep deprived and over stimulated in about a week my opinion will change. But for now, I'm living in bliss.

More family and friends make their rounds through the hospital during the week I'm there. Although the twins are healthy, their weight is just a smidge low, so it was recommended we keep them here. I am not complaining about that; I can't even sit up without wanting to cry. If Simon tries to watch me go to the bathroom one more time, I will scream.

After our week stay, we finally are able to go home.

Home to Bluefield.

Where we made this house our home. Where I grew our children. Where we added Bart into our chaos. Where we figured ourselves out. Where we fell in love.

I love our house. I love Bluefield. I love my family. And I especially love the man next to me. The one holding my hand as we get the babies to sleep. The one I want holding my hand forever.

The End.

Epilogue
Simon

A spen told me she has a surprise for me today. I'm a bit worried about it, because I also have a surprise for her. And I had planned on doing it today.

I've had a diamond ring hidden in my desk drawer for months now. The second Aspen showed me she was open to more, to giving us a try, I made an appointment with the jeweler my father uses. It may have been a bit premature, but I'm in on Aspen Arthur. I've always been in on Aspen Arthur.

And I want to make her Aspen Cadwell as soon as possible.

Having a newborn baby is not for the weak. Having two of them at once? I'm a fraction of a human being right now. I don't know how Aspen does it. I swear she's pumping all hours of the day and yet we're still supplementing with formula. One or both of the babies are always crying, and I don't know the last time I slept more than four hours in a row.

Until last night that is. It may have taken us two months to get here, but we both slept for six hours. At the same time. In the same bed. I got to touch Aspen in a way that was more than a comforting hug or light kiss for the first time since the twins were born.

It was life changing, I'm sure.

So of course, I'm riding that post-making-love-to-the-woman-I-love high and I want to put it to good use. I've got as many pink roses as I could fit in my car. Sam offered to dye them bright colours. I declined. He's currently setting up the surprise for me. November is cold by the lake; the sun is shining, but the wind has a bite to it. Thankfully, Aspen has an entire closet of warm coats waiting to be used.

Claire had already planned to be in town today. Since my parents officially bought Sam's grandmother's house, we've had a rotating door of family in town helping us. Claire is in charge of hiding and capturing the moment. I didn't let Lillian or Julia in on our plan; they are great but neither of them have a poker face. Aspen would know in seconds. Instead, Ben has them watching Noah at Lillian's place, and Dylan offered to watch the twins from inside our house. Jackson is loitering at his own house, waiting for a signal to bring everyone over here, while Ben keeps the parents away and distracted until the deed is done. It would be so typical of my parents to show up at our house and make us late to our own engagement.

Aspen is up in our bedroom finishing up her hair when I bring her white wool coat to her.

"Let's go for a drive," I say as I hand her the coat.

"How long will this drive be? We have plans this afternoon." The plans being her surprise for me.

"I have a surprise for you too," I say.

"Can we do my surprise first? It's important." And I'm sure she thinks it is, but last time she had a surprise for me it was a two-litre jug of maple syrup. We do eat a lot of pancakes, so I was happy with it, but asking her to marry me trumps food

314

toppings.

"It won't take long," I offer. "We can be home in an hour if you need to."

"What about the twins? Are they coming?"

"Dylan is going to watch them."

"No," she yells. "I mean, no that's okay, Lillian said she would. We should drop them off at her place." Maybe I should have involved Lillian after all. Cleary Aspen's surprise is not food related if Calla and Clay can't come with us.

"Why don't I ask Dylan to drop them off there. We need to head out now."

Aspen huffs out a breath but puts on the offered coat and follows me to my car. I don't even bother pretending I'm not driving in circles for ten minutes. Aspen is used to my surprises by now, so even if she suspects something, she keeps it to herself because she knows I won't give anything away.

I park in our driveway, but instead of heading for the house, I direct Aspen to the backyard. As soon as the river comes into view, I hear Aspen let out a whimper, and I honestly don't blame her. Sam has done an excellent job. Dozens of pink roses and petals are dusted on the shore, making a path leading to our new dock. At the end of the dock is an arch, also made of roses. Candles line the path as we make our way to the dock. When we reach the end Aspen's face is lined with tears, but her smile tells me she's happy about what I'm about to do.

"Aspen, kitten." Aspen blushes like she always does when I call her that. "Our path here may not have been conventional. We got pregnant first, then decided to live together before we eventually fell in love, although I think I've been in love with you since New Year's Eve. I've never met someone who pushes me to be better, encourages me to let loose, and loves me as unconditionally as you. You are my best friend and love of my life, and I want this forever."

Tears are falling from both of our eyes as I drop to one knee and pull a ring box out of my pocket.

"Aspen Arthur, will you marry me?"

"Yes," she screams as she drops to her knees to meet me for a passionate kiss.

I'm sure Claire is somewhere near snapping pictures of this moment but all I see is Aspen. All I ever want to see is Aspen. When we finally break from the kiss, I slide the gold band with an oval diamond on Aspen's finger.

"I love you," I say against her lips.

"I love you too," she says between kisses.

"Now, what's my surprise?" I ask jokingly. "You think you can top this?"

Aspen laughs before she says, "Simon Cadwell, I have an appointment for us at the courthouse. You're not the only one who planned on making this a forever thing."

I am beyond surprised, but I shouldn't be. A life with Aspen is full of the unexpected.

More by Heather

Want more Simon and Aspen? There's a bonus epilogue available on my website.

Haven't read Lillian and Jackson's love story yet? INKY WATER is available now.

Curious about Bluefield's resident baker, Diana? Her Valentine's novella, KNEADING LOVE, is coming in February 2025.

Can't wait to get back to Bluefield? Julia's story is coming in March 2025.

THE BLUEFIELD BEACH SERIES
Inky Water - Lillian & Jackson
Staged River - Aspen & Simon

Content Warnings

The content warnings for *Staged River:* discussion of toxic childhood environment and parental relationships, pregnancy, violence, mentions of cancer and death (off page) and explicit sexual content.

Acknowledgements

Writing acknowledgments always feels surreal. It's the true finish line of a novel.

First I would like to thank my husband. Thank you for reading other romance books so that you could tell me whether this book was good enough to publish. I would have done it regardless, but I appreciate your support and encouragement. Having you come to me saying, "I think Aspen would like this song" is surreal. Thank you for loving these characters as much as I do.

To my mother: Thank you for supporting me in every life decision. You are always the first person to read my books, even when they aren't finished.

To my Street Team: You guys are awesome. Thank you for always hyping me up and sharing your excitement with me.

To my Editor, Tayler: Thank you for your support throughout this entire process. I can confidently say that this book would have been a bit of a hot mess without you. I'm so glad we are on this journey together.

To my ARC Readers: Thank you for taking the time to read *Staged River* and for your support and kind words. Seeing you all love Aspen and Simon as much as I do is something I will treasure always.

To the members of LPP: You guys are rock stars. Having a community are fellow Canadian Indie authors is something I didn't know I needed, and now I couldn't live without it.

To the person reading this book: Thank you. Thank you for being apart of my author story and I hope you will join me again in Bluefield, very soon.

About The Author

Heather is a Canadian author who loves romance, with a side of suspense. Every good love story needs a bit of drama, right? After years of working in the financial sector, she decided to ditch Excel for Word and share her stories with the world. When she's not writing, or dreaming up stories, you can find her cuddled up with a book with her pets nearby, spending time with friends, or outdoors with family.

To stay up to date on Heather's upcoming projects, connect with her on social media @h.greywrites

www.heathergreywrites.com